THE CELL BLOCK PRESENTS...

A.O.B.

Published by: The Cell Block™

The Cell Block
P.O. Box 1025
Rancho Cordova, CA 95741

Website: thecellblock.net
Facebook/thecellblockofficial
Instagram: @mikeenemigo
Corrlinks: info@thecellblock.net

Cover Design: Mike Enemigo

Send comments, reviews, interview and business
inquiries to: info@thecellblock.net

PROLOGUE

Rosa's whole body tensed as she banged two fingers in and out of her pussy according to Manny's instruction. She was right at the verge of reaching her peak for the second time as he growled into the phone, driving her over the edge into another climax.

The bass in his voice sent imaginary vibrations throughout her entire body in a way that was more than she could handle. She lost all control of herself and completely surrendered to the commands coming through the loudspeaker of her cell phone. Her hips humped hungrily against her hand as she came so hard a shiver was squeezed out from the strain of her pelvic muscles.

Riding the rhythm of her own touch, she moaned. "Ooooh, shit. I'm cummin' again!" Then she shot out a generous squirt.

When the last wave of her inner euphoria had finally passed, she caught her breath and marveled at how this mysterious man could so effectively seduce her using nothing more than his words. He often talked her through the full spectrum of sexually satisfying herself, and he did it with an intensity that left her feeling as if it was his hands instead of hers that coaxed the explosions from between her legs.

They'd met one day online when Manny decided to randomly reach out to her and introduce himself. After a few days of sending messages back and forth, they exchanged phone numbers so they could talk directly. But he was in California while she was in Texas, and neither one of them were doing well financially, so meeting in person wasn't an option at the time.

However, the vibe between them was a strong one. Their talks were long, deep, and personal, with a lot of details they'd never normally share. They genuinely liked what they saw in the pics they exchanged, and Rosa seriously enjoyed the sound of the words Manny spoke, even though he left her lost when he'd drop hints about doing what she had to do in order to get where she needed to be. And her confusion seemed to always cause him to say no more.

Since the long-distance situation was all they had to work with, they made the most of it. But day-to-day life will always prove to be a distraction to his kind of arrangement, so in spite of how memorable their phone calls never failed to be, the frequency still faded over time, until they eventually went their separate ways.

And yet, an impression was made upon their future that neither of them would have ever imagined possible. The energy of their mutual attraction tied the threads of their existence together, so that at some point, their paths were bound to cross...

CHAPTER 1

JOINING FORCES

"There is a difference between wishing for a thing and being ready to receive it."
– Napoleon Hill

Two years later...

Maaan, this shit is crazy, Manny thought to himself as he drove down the street in his black Super Sport Impala on 22-inch rims with 12-inch speakers bangin' away in the trunk. *Here I am in Stockton on some square shit wit' a bitch I damn near went broke to get away from, and now, as soon as she say she got some weed, I come runnin' back to smoke wit' the bitch.*

He laughed at himself as he drove down Charter Way, being too real to excuse his own compromise even as he made the move. He planned to be in constant disapproval of his actions the whole time he blew blunts with the girl.

The square lifestyle just wasn't a good fit for him, even though he was endlessly plagued with being able to like the girls he met. But when dramatic episodes of jealousy and a possessive mentality started to crop up in his relationships, his only instinct was to leave.

I could love a bitch if love was all I was lookin' for, he thought to himself as he stopped at a red light.

But any further thought was cut short when his eyes suddenly caught sight of something that scrambled his senses. After a spilt second of initial shock, he was able to actually register what he was seeing. Walking toward him on the sidewalk was one of the most impressively built Mexican girls he'd ever seen. She was "thick" in the physically attractive sense of the word. Her hips hinted at what Manny was sure would be a very wide and round butt. There was no doubt that she could stop traffic if she tried with the almost see-through black leggings she was wearing.

While he sat through the changing of traffic lights captivated by her image, he got a better look at her face as she came close enough for him to make out more details. That's when he understood why his attention was so stuck in her direction.

"That's my bitch!" he said out loud to himself in recognition.

All at once, his thoughts raced to recall her name as it raced through memories of the pics in his cell phone that she used to send, and the details about herself that she used to share. *She did say she used to live in California and had a son who lived with her dad, along with other family in or around the Stockton area.*

Trying to think of what to say to her, he was also faced with the challenge of getting her attention from behind his dark tinted windows. On top of the dark tint, he was in the far-left lane away from the sidewalk, stuck in traffic with a row of cars between him and the girl whose name he'd forgotten, as she walked on by without knowing he was even there.

Life itself seemed to jump into fast-forward as Manny's options both multiplied and ran out at the same time. So as soon as the traffic light turned green, he made an extremely illegal U-turn against on-coming traffic. This caused a symphony of horns to shriek in protest at how close Manny came to crashing into other drivers.

The girl noticed his wild move and expected it to be a prelude to some sort of harassment, so she quickly followed a particular protocol by aiming her attention elsewhere, and making her way into a nearby corner store to avoid being caught by this madman who was beeping his horn and aggressively edging his car into the lane next to the curb where she was walking.

Manny's thoughts were all over the place as he excitedly tried to avoid the multi-car pile-up his movements threatened to cause. Being from the Bay Area, he had a certain kind of exposure that rang a specific bell in his mind when he saw how the girl reacted to the way he was trying to get close to her. But he couldn't land on any conclusions because he was still preoccupied with trying his best to remember as much as he could in hopes of making a successful introduction. Something clicked in him when he recognized the face that made him want to freeze this moment before it passed him by.

Everything about this moment revolved around the big-booty Latina girl his eyes were on at the time, so like a man who'd never heard of traffic laws, he pulled up next to her as she tried to get into the store. When she disappeared inside, he hit his hazard lights and hopped out right there in front of the store.

"'Ey, lil mama!" he yelled urgently to be heard over the sounds of his music and the wail of horns beeping behind him.

She went inside the doorway of the store and peeked out a semi-safe position where she could hear with a reduced risk of being harmed. Seeing she was listening, Manny continued to call her out. "I bet you think I'm just another nigga you need to be runnin' from, but I know you! Look at my face for real. We used to chop it up on the phone back when you was in Texas a couple years ago! You don't remember me?

"Yo' mama name is Linda, just like my mama. We was trippin' on that. And you got a son named Tookie, right?" he said in a rush of relevant information.

Her expression was somewhere between surprised curiosity and suspicious confusion as she fought the impulse to ask who he was, but the accuracy of the facts he fired at her proved he was indeed someone who knew her.

Knowing he had her attention, Manny started talking as if his life depended on every word he spoke. "Yeah, you know just any-ol'-body ain't gonna pop up on point like that, huh? I can't remember yo' name, but we was rockin' and rollin' kinda tough for a minute. I'm not tryna come at you crazy, but we 'posed to be together, girl! Whatever you doin' out here need to be includin' me! I'ma yank up in this parkin' lot so the police don't get me for stoppin' traffic, but don't bounce on me! You should come check me out!"

He tossed a few more facts at her about herself and then jumped back behind the wheel to pull out of traffic. There was no time to make sure she was coming, but his mind was back to thinking again.

If she brings that ass around this corner to see what I'm talkin' 'bout, I got me one for sure! he thought as he slid his big Impala into an empty parking space. He wanted to be visible, so he only pulled in halfway in hopes of her peeking into the parking lot and seeing him easily.

But nobody came around the corner of the building at all.... At least, not at first.

A wave of willpower went out from him to cover the space between them and hold her in place. Slowly, her hesitation went away and she approached him cautiously.

Very carefully, Manny said, "I ain't tryna play you. We met online, and you was far away. Now you close, and I'm tryna bring that shit back. If you out here doin' what it look like you might be doin', then you know what I mean when I say you should choose. And if what we was on ain't no fake shit, then you know we really ain't got no choice anyway, right? We gotta make somethin' happen."

While the words were falling from his mouth, understanding became recollection, and a look of recognition came over her features. She took the last few steps up to where Manny stood, and without word or warning, hugged him like a long-lost friend.

They stood in that embrace for a while as the cars drove by. No one in the world would ever believe they'd just been witness to what destiny could do, but the drivers of those cars were in proximity to more of a miracle than any of them could ever imagine.

Then she broke the spell: "My name is Rosa. And you shouldn't jump out on a bitch like that unless you want her to think you out here kidnappin' hoes!"

They made their way back into the car and Manny took Rosa to her motel room not far away.

After inviting him inside, she was quick to point out which of the two beds it was OK to sit on. He took note of this but made no comment.

Her immediate plan was to roll a few blunts and smoke their way into whatever happened next, so she retrieved a large bag of Northern California buds she had stashed in the dresser drawer. Laying a few Swisher Sweets cigarillos out and breaking some of the skunky smelling marijuana down, she saw Manny must've had the same plan when he picked up the blunts to prepare them for rolling.

Their harmony seemed natural with a very noticeable level of comfort between them – like old lovers who needed no extra effort to find familiarity.

Rosa didn't say much, but her mind was going a mile a minute. She now remembered very well exactly who Manny was, as well as where he fit into her past. It all came flooding back as she replayed the episodes of him turning her on over the telephone back when that was all they had. Now she had somehow been blessed with the opportunity of having him for real, and she'd be damned if she didn't try him out.

"Well... I don't know how the hell we ended up here after all this time, but you may not want me when you know for sure what I'm out there doin'. I'm tryna get my baby some school clothes, bein' about my money. That's why I don't want you on that other bed, because it's the work bed," she said in an effort to be straightforward before her instincts told her to lie.

When she glanced at him to check his reaction, she was met with a strange smirk on his face. Being somewhat self-conscious about what she'd just shared, her natural response to his expression was one of embarrassment.

"Oh... You think that's funny, huh?" she mumbled in a self-defeated tone.

"Naw, what's funny is the fact that you thought I didn't already know. As soon as you told me which bed to sit on, it was obvious. I wasn't born yesterday."

"So, you're OK fuckin' with a ho?"

"As long as you ain't tryna make me a trick!"

She smiled at his matter-of-fact way of speaking. "No, no, never that. But how is this supposed to work, though? You wasn't talkin' no pimp shit on the phone."

"No, I wasn't. And you wasn't a ho back then, either, right?"

"That's true. So now you gonna just snap your fingers and become a pimp?"

The smile went away and he looked at her very seriously. "I'm from the Bay, bitch. I know how to be whatever you need me to be. Since you happen to be a ho, I guess I need to be a P. Ain't nothin' I can't handle."

Rosa got anxious when hearing the bite in his tone. "I'm just sayin'... I ain't thinkin' you stupid or nothin'. Just trying to keep shit real."

"Well, luckily I'm a real nigga then, because real niggas do real things, right? So, it's whatever as long as you know it ain't no sucka shit."

They sat quietly for a little while as Manny twisted up the first blunt and lit it. After he hit it and passed it back to her, she noticed the strange half-smile back on his lips again.

When he saw she was paying attention, he slowly spilled a little speech he'd thought up.

"Look, Rosa. You ain't gotta be able to always guess what I'ma do next. That keeps you honest. But you do need to know that I won't ever change up on you unless you try to play me. So just make sure you gonna be in it all the way if you decide to fuck with me.

"As long as I'm around, consider yourself spoken for in every way. This includes everything that comes with you or from you. As far as I'm concerned, it's all for me – unless you say no. If that's the case, I'll be on my way."

Rosa had to think about that, but she didn't think for too long. She reached her decision, passed Manny the blunt, and quietly got up to go to the bathroom without saying anything.

When the sounds of the shower came from behind the closed door, Manny began to roll up another blunt. He'd made his move, and he wasn't going to say anything else until she did something to let him know what his next words should be. About halfway through smoking the blunt, he heard the water shut off, followed by the sounds of Rosa moving around in the bathroom.

Now for the next move...

He knew that the general rule in this kind of situation should be to get the purse first and ass last, but he also knew from watching his uncles that the rules were based more on principles than procedures.

Just as he came to a conclusion about what he might do, Rosa came into the room. She wore nothing except the smell of her body spray as she walked over to where he sat. And when she stopped to stand naked in front of him, it was clear that she was offering him her greatest gift.

Manny had no doubts that Rosa's body must be her most prized possession, and there was absolutely no question about why this was the case. She had round, firm, medium-sized breasts, and a soft, smooth stomach that sloped down between gorgeously-rounded hips, into a shaved pussy nestled neatly at the place where her luscious thighs met.

Without a moment of hesitation, he snatched her by the arm and flung her down onto the bed. The excitement that showed on her face was the only reaction she had time to experience before he followed up his move by flipping her onto her belly.

He kissed his way up from her lower back around to her sides. The whole time he did this, he expertly worked one finger, then two inside of her from behind. This type of teasing continued until her pussy was soaking wet.

When Rosa had grabbed the weed from the dresser drawer, Manny had spotted an obscene amount of condoms in there as well, so he had grabbed one for just this kind of possibility.

After removing his pants quickly with his free hand, he rolled the condom into place, removed the fingers of his occupied hand, and replaced them with his long, hard dick.

He grabbed her by the hips and drove himself into her. She met him thrust for thrust with a greedy arch of her back that raised her ass to receive him. A moan escaped her mouth.

It seemed only to encourage him and he fucked her even harder, pumping his dick into her until she was ready to cum.

She could tell from his hoarse breathing that he was getting close to orgasm himself. He used his slim, powerfully chiseled body to beat his way into her from the back. Then, suddenly, her whole world spun and she came with a shudder that rippled through her whole frame. This triggered Manny into exploding seconds later, releasing a brief groan.

"That shit was... Wow!" she said after a moment.

When Manny's breathing relaxed, he braced his body above her with their faces now close together. "Yeah, bitch, but don't you go thinkin' I just fell for no pussy-poppin' technique. I'm gonna pimp for you, and you gonna ho for me. So get yo' lil sexy ass up and give me whatever money you got in here so I can feel good about the rest of what I'm about to do to you," he said against her cheek.

Her obedience was immediate, spurred into action by the anticipation of getting more of him. She returned to the bed with what he demanded, and he delivered what she desired until the next day. The only interruption they tolerated were smoke breaks.

CHAPTER 2
LOCKIN' IT IN
"I got a good heart... But this heart can get ugly..."
— DMX

Over the next week, Manny came by every day to smoke and talk with Rosa, but he never stayed long or got comfortable. He would text her a lot, and sometimes she would see his car from a distance, moving around in the area near her motel while she was working.

At first, he offered no instruction at all; just gave her a puzzled expression whenever she answered his questions about how her days were going. Then, one day, he went to her room early in the morning with two cups of coffee from the gas station, both loaded with so much flavored cream and sugar, they tasted like hot milkshakes.

Rosa was already awake, but far from expecting him so early. She was surprised to hear him pull up in front of her room, but like always, excited when she heard the music bangin' from his car.

She was still wearing boy shorts and a wife-beater when she opened the door to let him in. He quickly handed her a cup of the super sweet coffee and went into his next move as she sipped it.

"Don't know what you up to, cutie, but it's time to change your plans. Pack up whatever you can't leave or throw away, and let's take this show to the next level!" he said enthusiastically before spinning back out to his car.

Rosa was left with no chance to respond. All she could do was collect her belongings. She didn't have much, just a few outfits and cosmetics. Her whole little world was barely enough to fill up a pillowcase. But rather than be sad about her reality, she was thrilled to think about how much her life was about to change, and she smiled when she looked around the now empty motel room as she imagined what was yet to come.

The honk of Manny's horn brought her back to focus. She hurried outside to put her things into the back seat and climb into the car with him. They rode off into the rising sun as they set out on the rest of their adventure...

$$$$$

Seeing that things were about get much more serious, Rosa wanted to close all the doors of expectation that may exist in the minds of the people from her past. This consisted mainly of her son's father. Before Manny had come along, there remained a bit of uncertainty about what to do with herself. And out of the desire to be with her son, she played with the idea of reconnecting with his dad.

The problem was that that experience had already taught her how bad of an idea this could be. He liked to blame the lack of respect he had in his social circle on her, so when his friends tried to hit on her behind his back, he found it easier to beat her up rather than fight any of them.

Now that Manny was in her life, she didn't want to cross herself up between the two men. And she couldn't just disappear, because she had her son, so some kind of understanding had to be reached.

She tried to get away with letting her son's father know what was going on from the safe distance of a phone call, but before the call was disconnected, her son got on the phone and asked her to come see him. The issue of his school clothes still stood, so there was a practical reason to grant his request. However, she knew not to trust Tookie's father since he was known to satisfy her ego at his expense. And since she had just cut him off, it was fair to say his ego was not in the best position.

Her only option was to ask Manny to take her to give Tookie his school clothes before they got into what would probably be keeping her busy for months at a time. And he surprised her with an additional suggestion to go with the granting of her wishes.

The plan became to make a fun day out of the whole ordeal by picking Tookie up and taking him to Chuck-E. Cheese the following Sunday. But on their way out of the studio Manny had moved Rosa into, she decided to voice her concern regarding what they might be walking into.

"Hey, I don't want you to have no drama because of my leftover bullshit. But if you got somethin' you can bring with you, it might be a good idea just in case this fool try and put on a show for his homies. He be tryna act like he hard."

Manny responded by going back inside and coming back out while tucking a stainless-steel revolver into his waistband. Rosa felt safer, but she was till feeling a bit of nervous energy.

13

As they drove out to Modesto on the 99 freeway from Stockton, Manny was unusually quiet. Then, as they neared the exit to their destination, he suddenly started to speak a sequence of instructions to her.

"OK, so it's either gonna be cool or it ain't. If it's cool, you need to leave it at that. But if it ain't, it's gonna go down as soon as we get there, or when we come back. Either way, I'm sure he'll come at you when you're away from me, because when niggas see this car, they figure I'm about somethin'.

"I want you to keep shit short and sweet, but if he get outta line, just get yo' ass back to me. It'll be my business when he bring it my way, you hear me?"

Rosa nodded her head and kept her growing fears to herself. Manny turned his music up even louder, kockin' the bass belligerently as they continued on their way.

When they pulled up to the little house where Tookie was waiting with his grandmother, Rosa's face lit up with joy at the sight of him playing outside.

Seeing his mom get out of the Impala, his face lit up in a mirror image of her smile as he ran to hop up into her arms. The only difference in their facial features was the darker tone of Tookie's skin, resulting from the African heritage of his father.

Manny smiled privately to himself as he watched the two of them come together in obvious love and happiness. He knew how the game of life could sometimes play out, so he passed no judgement on Rosa. But a decision was made on the spot to make sure she could always do whatever this little boy who looked so much like her might ever want or need from her.

While these thoughts were going through Manny's mind, he couldn't help but notice the vibe of the whole situation had changed as apprehension replaced the happiness that was on the face of the scene he was watching. Both mother and child steered their attention to a dark blue Oldsmobile Delta 88 from the 80's. The box-shaped car pulled up to the curb wearing a shabby, faded paint job, with only two of the four hubcaps in place on its rims.

Inside the car were two gangbanger-type guys looking extra hard and thugged out. One was dark skinned with a stocking cap on his head, and the other one was a lighter shade of brown with scruffy cornrow braids going to the back. The lighter one, who was the passenger, hopped out aggressively, looking like he had something on his mind. The driver remained near his car when he got out to eyeball Manny's Impala with envy.

Sizing up the situation made it clear that "scruffy braids" was the bummed-out baby daddy, and as soon as this distinction was made, the object of Manny's attention slowed his stride when he noticed Manny's car parked on the curb in front of his mama's house.

Recognizing that he was becoming a part of the agenda, Manny eased the .357 magnum into his lap to provide easier access. Then he let his window down in order to be visible. This last move brought a more animated response to his unexpected presence.

"What up, nigga!" the baby daddy said when he saw Manny eyeing him.

But Manny said nothing. He just raised his chin in the universal "what's up" gesture recognized by all hood folks. Manny stayed in the car, out of the way, as Rosa made whatever small talk necessary with the guy before they went into the house to get Tookie ready. But within five minutes, she suddenly popped right back out of the house with her hair slightly messed up, speed walking her way straight toward Manny's car. Scruffy braids was right on her heels, trying to grab her, and once the whole situation registered as reality, the guy began screaming in rage.

"Oh, you think yo' nigga gon' save you? This fool can't fade me out here!" he roared recklessly at her retreating form.

While all this was going on, Manny slid out of his car smoothly like nothing was wrong. But the cannon in his hand sent a more serious message. He looked briefly at the homeboy who seemed unsure of what role he wanted to play in the drama that was unfolding, then he addressed Rosa with authority. "Get yo' ass in the car! Let me find out this muthafucka tryna put his hands on somebody!"

Rosa quickly obeyed and said, "No, I'm good. Soon as he started up, I did like you said."

Manny looked over at his opponent and was glad to see he had enough sense to at least not run up too quickly. This gave him time to bring attention to the gun he held casually at his side. At the sight of it, the baby daddy stopped and shut the fuck up.

"What you tryna do, my nigga? This bitch fuckin' wit Manny Fresh now. So take yo' place in history and let that shit go," Manny said coldly. "I got this Bulldog ready to bark if you niggas wanna trip, though…" he added.

This brought a whole new attitude when a voice was finally found in response to the clear and present danger. "Oh, OK. You got that. We ain't gotta do all that at my mama house," the baby daddy said in a much more respectful tone.

Manny took a half step in his direction and said menacingly, "Yeah, nigga. You better remember where you at, before you make me air this muthafucka out!" Then he stood there for a few seconds with his mug on mean to make sure he was understood before backing up and getting into his car. He sat the gun in his lap, started the Impala, took his time turning up the bass, then pulled off so slowly that nobody could ever say he ran away. The entire time, his eyes were locked onto his target with a look that dared the man to do anything further. The only thing he got back was a neutral expression of defeat to go along with the posture of a whipped dog.

At a snail's pace, the Impala crept off into the rest of whatever would be coming next...

$$$$$

The thing about the haters of this world that makes them hard to deal with is that they're part of a team that grows faster than the players they hate on. So when his street research brought word of Rosa being in Stockton, the baby daddy decided Manny was due for a surprise visit.

His name was Rashad, and a week after being put in his place, we was still salty about how things went down that day in front of his mother's house. He wanted to even the score, but he was extremely unprepared to act on the idea. With no car, no gun, and very little experience beyond a few fist fights, his chances were slim when it came to successfully handling his business in the streets.

All Rashad had to help his ambition was the hate in his heart. But there was enough of that to move a mountain if even a little bit of luck or sensible thinking should happen to find its way into the mix.

His plan began with calling around to find a gun, which was not as easy as he expected it to be. He didn't really know anyone who made those kinds of moves, and the average thugs he did know were all more into the image than any real action.

With gunplay being such unfamiliar territory, Rashad wasn't working with many options in his search. The few people he knew who did have something didn't have the means to replace what they had, so they weren't giving it up. The best he could do was secure a promise or two of keeping him in mind if something turned up.

Rashad carried on into the following weeks, unsuccessful in his goal of doing some "gangster shit." But he wouldn't give up or forget, and negative energy is extremely powerful, so the concentration of hate set the stage for harmful events to happen in times yet to come.

CHAPTER 3

GETTIN' STARTED

"I move for the money, it's never no kind of pressure."

– Kevin Gates

Manny showed Rosa a street called Wilson Way, in another part of Stockton, where she could work at a steadier pace. Wilson Way was a full-blown track, where all kinds of girls hustled to find success in the world's oldest profession. Most of the traffic in this area represented potential customers who regularly came in search of forbidden pleasures, and the flow was usually healthy enough to provide much better results than the area Rosa had started off in.

One cold night while working, Rosa noticed Manny at a stop light about a block from where she was walking. "I see U, Daddy," she texted him. "Just got done with another one."

"Where you at?" he replied while turning the corner.

"Don't go 2 far. I'm right behind U."

"OK, boss. I'll pull over," he shot back as he pulled into the nearest parking lot.

Manny looked for a spot where he could blend in while still being able to see the entire intersection behind him. Then he backed into the space so he could spot her before she spotted him.

As he rolled a blunt, he thought to himself, *If she deserves a break, I'll smoke with her. But if she ain't breakin' bread, I'ma light this shit up right as I kick her ass right back out this car.*

His aim wasn't to be mean, but he wanted to always be meaningful with everything he decided to do. Lost in his thoughts of how to maximize his pursuits, Rosa caught him by surprise when she tapped urgently on the passenger window to be let into the car.

He hit the power locks to let her in while fixing his face with an unreadable expression. "Bitch, next time call my phone or something before you go on to beatin' on the damn windows!" he growled at her as he finished twisting up the blunt.

Slamming the door shut and slightly out of breath, Rosa had to struggle to hide her smile. "Don't knock my head off for bein' sloppy, Daddy! I had this broke-ass nigga on my bumper and I ain't want him to see where I'm dippin' off to. Gotta stay in pocket, right?"

Now it was Manny's turn to hide his own smile. To do this, he lit the blunt prematurely and said, "Well, we gonna still have a problem if gettin' chased around is stoppin' you from catchin' all this money out here."

Rosa reached into her bra and removed a little knot of cash. Then, while she handed it to him she said, "I'll trade what I'm holdin' for what you're holdin', papa. This should be about three-fifty, and throughout the day I gave you about four more."

Manny took the money and put it in his pocket without saying anything about it. He'd heard from his uncles that it was best not to count what a hooker gave you in front of her. That way, if it was a nice amount, she wouldn't slow down on you instead of going to get more after seeing you were satisfied.

In Manny's mind, he appreciated that Rosa seemed to be coming correct so far. It took some thought on his part before he was able to come to the conclusion to bring her to live with him in his studio, so to see it was paying off made him happy he'd made the right decision.

Of course, he didn't share any of this with her as he looked at her sitting in the gray leather seat next to him. The only thing he allowed himself to say was, "Looks like you tryna get it right. That's what's up. But let's get a little more before we bounce."

Rosa hit the weed he'd given her a couple more times and passed it back to him, then prepared to make her exit. "Yes, sir, Mr. Deep Thinker. Call me when you ready," she said as she made a major show of looking around before hopping out of the car.

Manny watched her make her way back into the flow of traffic and congratulated himself again on his decision to bring her home...

$$\$\$\$\$\$$

Much later that night, Rosa was asleep, naked, with only a small portion of her body covered by a bedsheet. As usual, Manny laid awake before smoking himself into oblivion to get the rest he needed.

Rosa stirred as he inhaled the smoke loudly, maybe from the noise or maybe from the smell. When she came into consciousness enough, she slipped her hand into his lap. When she found her target, her head followed with her eyes never opening.

Manny inhaled the potent weed smoke as Rosa sucked his sex until the sauce of his satisfaction suddenly shot into her mouth. She swallowed and slurped him with soft strokes until her lips slipped away and she dozed back off to sleep.

$$$$$

As time went on, Manny shared more of the things he knew regarding the hustle Rosa was into. For the most part, this consisted of better places to get money, as well as a more professional approach to reaching profitability. He also showed her how and why they should manage those results wisely in order to avoid the aimless approach most people took.

Together, they spent most of their moments focused on growth and development, while she thrived on playing her part in their forward-moving pursuits.

"I got some news for U, Daddy!" she texted him one day after talking to some of the other girls on the track.

"I hope this news come wit' some money!" he shot back after a short while.

"UR gonna like it! And yes, I got money! Duh! LOL!"

"OK. Meet me @ the room ASAP. Waiting on U."

Rosa hurried around the block to the cheap motel she worked out of and found Manny parked in the gleaming black Super Sport. As usual, he was backed into the parking space so he could see everything. The beat of his music was turned down low, but bass still vibrated the car.

Rosa skipped her way to the driver's side window and made a hand motion for him to roll it down. He looked at her blankly for a moment before doing what was asked of him.

"Yes, dear?" he said innocently as if he'd not been expecting her.

"Daddy, you want me to get in with you, or we goin' into the room?" she asked sweetly as she leaned over into his window.

"You should pro'ly get yo' ass in this car before you bring every trick in the area right up to the windshield with all that ass you got on display!" he whispered loudly like he was sharing some kind of secret.

With a big smile, she walked her way around to the front of the car, but once she was in the passenger seat, she knew to be about business. Her smile was gone, but her playful tone was still present as she began to debrief.

"OK, Mr. Superstar, this might qualify for a trip to the car wash. You got the whole track buzzin' about 'Manny Fresh,' so people gonna be in our business here," she said proudly.

Driving to the car wash was a slick little move she noticed Manny used whenever he needed to do anything that took any time. This way, they never looked suspicious or drew too much extra attention being parked for too long.

Respecting her vibe, he threw the car into drive and made his way into the direction of the car wash. That was the only response he felt she needed so far.

Rosa placed her money into the center console and turned up the music so she could feel the bass throbbing through her body. Manny's sound system was an object of her obsession as she was a serious lover of music. She rocked her body to the beat of something slow he was listening to, and he allowed this for the time it took for her to rest and relax her feet.

After they'd driven a few blocks, Rosa turned down the music and began to give up the information. "OK, Daddy. So, there's a ho I speak to here and there named CoCo. She fucks wit' a lil hot boy named Miami, or whatever, but he ain't on your level. Anyway, the bitch told me the other day about a lil town called Salinas, where the Mexican tricks will have a bitch banked up by midnight...

"I know you always say that everything that glitter ain't gold, but I've been hearin' this from more than one girl. So, I'm thinkin' you might wanna know about it, right?"

Manny listened close as he drove them into the car wash. It sounded good, but it wasn't new to him. "Yeah, I heard about that spot a few years back. From the pineapple to the Big Apple, there ain't a track gettin' money that I don't know about. So, if it's still poppin' out there, it may be worth takin' a look."

But Rosa wasn't done with her sales pitch. "Well, you know I can't let these hoes think we don't know what's up, so I been sayin' we planned to go anyway. They believe whatever I say because I fucks with Mr. Manny Fresh, and you got the cutest car on the track, so we must be doin' big thangs over this way.

"Now, CoCo tryna see if her and her folks can ride wit' us whenever we go. Her dude keep some Js on his feet, but he ain't got no car. They still young and –"

Manny cut her off immediately. "Bitch, you better not be bookin' no rides for no underage bitches in my car!"

"No, no, she grown, just young – like nineteen or twenty. She got a big sister and mama out here who gets down, too. A whole family of renegades that ain't worth yo' time. But CoCo cool when it's just me and her, though. At least cool enough to show us where she gettin' that money at."

24

Manny looked at her and saw the rest of what looked so good to her even though she was side-steppin' the details. She was interested in a place that paid more for doin' less. But he didn't hold it against her, because he knew that whatever benefitted her would also benefit him. So as long as CoCo wasn't some kind of underage runaway, it could be worthwhile to pick her brain on a trip or two.

"Well... you might just be onto somethin' since the lil bitch been out there recently. Next time you see her, give her my number so her folks and me can link up. I'll take it from there."

Beaming with pride, Rosa sat back in the big leather seat, pleased with herself. "I'll do that for sure, Daddy! So can we do lunch at the burrito truck before I go back to work?" she asked in a playful baby voice, hoping her humor would side-step any bad reactions.

Manny recognized the move, but let it pass. "Yeah, I guess you got that comin' since you got ya mind on ways to get more money," he said with a touch of sarcasm. It was enough to let her know that she wasn't getting over on him, so she wouldn't go too far into feeling herself. He knew that a lot of women in this life didn't think too highly of themselves when you looked beyond the surface, because subconsciously they see what they do as going against what the world considers to be acceptable. So, his job, as a pimp figure in a ho's life, was to keep her from letting overconfidence cause a habitual self-destruct. Because if they ever see too much good in themselves, they'll usually screw it up somehow, earning the punishment they've been programmed to expect.

"That's why panderin' and ho handlin' calls for proper management!" his uncle used to say back when he taught

Manny the Game. "The bitch will have you fucked up wit' self-destruct if you can't keep her off that path of bein' in her own way! If you gonna properly pursue a pimp profession, you gotta give up the goodness in small doses, mane! Don't overdose the bitch, and don't ever act wit'out thinkin' first! That's for a sucka and a square, not pimps and players!"

Manny never forgot those lessons, which made up the majority of his childhood. But it didn't take a lot of thought to know that everybody had to eat. *Guess I can't starve her if I wanna keep bein' able to charge her*, he thought to himself as he made his way to the burrito truck.

$$$$$

A couple of days later, Manny got a call from an unfamiliar number on his cell phone. Not recognizing it, he sent it to voicemail instead of answering. Then, out of curiosity, he sent a text message to the number. "Who is this?"

"Miami," was the reply.

Manny called the number and got an immediate answer. "Hello?"

"S'up, mane! I ain't know ya number, so I had to be careful. But I see our hoes been ho-cializing, huh?" said Manny.

"Yeah, mane," Miami replied. "My lil work told me you tryna put a move together. I been hearin' a lot about you on the blade and ya girl be in pocket, so I know –"

Manny cut him off immediately: "Hey, man, that's my bitch! Don't be callin' that ho my girl. Fuck around and make her forget she's a prostitute!"

They both laughed at that since most pimps tend to get extra pimp-conscious when in proximity of each other.

"OK, bro, you got that. I'm jus sayin', though. I see yo' shit is on point, so when I hear Manny Fresh is tryna holla at me, I'm tryna see what's up," Maimi said.

"Yeah, man, I can dig it. I'm 'bout to grab some trees right quick before I slide through, so if you snatch up a Swisher or two, we can link up and put somethin' in the air."

They agreed to meet at the McDonald's next to the motel their girls worked out of and disconnected the call. Twenty minutes later, they were together ordering snacks from the menu on the wall.

Manny had done his homework on Miami and knew he was dealing with a young man who was known for being on the wild side, so he didn't want to be seen with him. He also knew he'd have to control the situation if he wanted to be sure he wasn't associated with the things Miami was known for.

Noticing that Miami was calling CoCo to come get a chocolate sundae he'd ordered for her, Manny texted Rosa with instructions to stay on the job if they were together. Her reply informed him that she had a date due to arrive shortly so she'd be busy anyway.

"Hey, bruh, my bitch 'bout to be on a money move, so would it be cool if I send her snack back with yo' folks?" Manny asked Miami when he saw CoCo hurry herself into the direction they were sitting.

"That's all good, big bro. I got you," Miami replied as he went to meet CoCo at the door. When he did this, Manny made himself look busy on his phone.

Manny had seen CoCo in the area doin' her thing. She'd even been in some of the groups of girls he made a habit of pulling up on and screaming slick sayings to just to see them scatter. That's how he got his name to be so well-known in such short time.

CoCo was a cute little Puerto Rican girl with a thick shape and shoulder-length curls of dark brown hair that had blonde streaks. She always wore shirts that showed off her large breasts, and that day she wore a pink tube top with a pair of tiny white shorts.

As CoCo walked up with Miami, Manny ignored her intentionally before sliding Rosa's snack across the table and excusing himself to go to the bathroom. After checking his appearance in the mirror, he made his exit, heading straight out to his car. From there he sent Miami a text: "Handle ya biz. I'm in my whip when U done."

A few minutes later. Miami came outside, still talking with CoCo. After sending her on her way, he got into the car and settled into the passenger seat. That's when Manny decided to check some details.

"Man, I sure do hope that ho is eighteen or older. Shit get ugly for a pimp when them white folks get to sayin' a nigga got a young bitch out here," he said casually as he broke down a fat bud to smoke.

Miami looked at him as if he'd just said the sky was falling. "Oh, fa sho, big bruh! I been wit' the bitch over a year. She all good."

Manny let it go at that. "Well, last I heard, checkin' ain't cheatin', right? Pimpin' ain't wit' the kiddie porn, ya dig? Now, if you break down one of those Swishers I hope you got, we can blow one."

Once the slight tension relaxed a bit, Manny continued his probe. "So is lil mama ya first piece of work, or have you been rockin' like a P for a while already?"

A somewhat sheepish look came over Miami's face as he answered. "Naw, I ain't even gon' lie. I was on some D-boy shit before I came across ol' girl. But she been at it for years wit' her mom and sister. I got me a thoroughbred, mane!"

Manny heard the misplaced pride in Miami's voice and took himself a good look at his passenger as he handed him the weed on a folded piece of paper. The young man had the look of a thuggish crack dealer in baggey jeans and a hooded sweatshirt that would never make anyone consider him to be a pimp. The conduct that went along with that kind of look could prove very undesirable for Manny's agenda, so he tried to establish some guidelines.

"OK, check me out, bruh. Ain't nobody tryna play you close, but I'm here to pimp hoes, and that's it. Me and my bitch ain't 'bout to be on none of that hot shit.

"I see you kinda feelin' ya-self with ya lil work, and that's what's up. But at the same time, you don't wanna make a big show outta havin' a ho nowadays. This shit is illegal, for one. And for two, you don't wanna scare the tricks away. We play the background and let the hoes have the spotlight. That's why we call 'em our stars, feel me?"

Miami nodded in understanding, so Manny went on with his speech.

"I ain't out to run ya program, but if you gonna rock wit' me, I need you to catch on to how I roll. Don't be packin' no pistols or holdin' no dope while you in my car. If you dirty, please go get clean. And if ya clean, then please blaze that shit up."

The speech was digested with an obvious discomfort, but the man who spoke was respected so his words were recognized as real.

"I'm cool, mane! It's A-O-B now wit' me! I respect game when I see it and I'd rather fuck wit' a real P than have everything I know come from a ho," Miami said before sparking the blunt.

Manny started the car, and in a puff of smoke, they slid off into traffic...

CHAPTER 4

WHEN A REAL DOG BITES

"Fuck all that verbal gangsta shit, you gotta show 'n prove it."

—

Mozzy

Once they got off the exit in Stockton, Rashad had the homie drive him around the town in hopes of spotting Manny's big-body Impala. In his lap rested an old 20-guage pump-action shotgun loaded with six rounds of buckshot. He'd managed to bully a youngster out of the weapon after he'd heard of the kid crew coming up on it in a burglary. Now he felt equipped to get back at Manny, and he had been finding a way to Stockton on his hunt as often as he could. But, he had no place to match the poison of mindless hate in his heart.

"Man, I thought you said you knew where to find this nigga at," Rashad's homie said. "We can't just be ridin' 'round dirty for no reason!" he added as they turned onto Pershing Ave. off March Lane.

"This muthafucka been runnin' from me since he heard I'm after his punk ass," Rashad lied in his best imitation of a tough guy.

The truth was that Manny had never given him a second thought, and the only thing known about how to find him was an image of his car and the name of the mean little city they were now driving around in. But as Rashad privately admitted these truths to himself in the aftermath of the lie he'd just told his buddy, another truth revealed itself to him. it was now also true that a black Impala Super Sport from the '90s was parked invitingly at the 7-Eleven they were passing.

"Man, we just talked up on that nigga! There go his car right there! Pull this muthafucka over and I'ma run up on him," Rashad ordered his homie.

$$$$$

When Manny stepped out of the store, he glanced around at his surroundings before moving toward his car. There was no real reason for this other than the following of general hood commandments – "Thou shall always stay on your toes." That's when he got a peek of Rosa's babby daddy trying to creep up on him.

Instead of climbing into his car, he laughed to himself and walked across the street to an even smaller side-street where he'd just dropped Miami off. This would take him out the sight of a camera or bystander that may otherwise have a view of what he was about to do. Once he got a short distance down the block, he quickly gripped his pistol from his waistband and held it down at his side.

$$$$$

Rashad was thrown off by the maneuver and paused his approach. He was filled with confusion on how to proceed. Had he been seen? Should he follow on foot, or get back in the car? Would it be best to wait for his target to get back to his vehicle?

All questions were cut short when the decision was made for him as his homie pulled up next to where he was crouched beside a parked car, so he hopped in and they hurried down the side street in hot pursuit of their prey.

$$$$$

Manny was glad to see the car coming down the street behind him. He'd figured his "hunter" wot not want to come alone on foot. Now that they'd taken the bait, he would see if he could set a proper trap.

Halfway down the block, Manny came up to a row of parked vehicles, and this was exactly what he needed. There was a truck parked behind a van, both large and old, and it was in line with a few cars, all one after the other.

Manny ducked behind the van before the slowly approaching car was able to pull up next to him. Now out of sight, he crawled up to the front of the parked car at the head of the line. If these guys were as inexperienced as he thought they were, he was about to have the advantage of surprising them...

$$$$$

"Come on, nigga! Get up on him! Don't let this fool get away from us! Damn it... he just ducked off behind that green van. Stop right here so I can bounce out," Rashad demanded in rapid-fire excitement as the car slowed to a stop.

Rashad hopped out in a rush to catch his target, hunched over with the shotgun ready in his hands. Trying to appear unafraid, he dipped recklessly behind the truck with his mind set on sneaking up to the van, but as soon as his foot touched the curb, all kinds of hell broke loose.

BANG!

A deafening shot suddenly rang out, causing a chunk of concrete to explode from the sidewalk right near where he was standing. The cowardly part of his heart took over immediately to make him retreat. He withdrew back towards the car he'd just vacated, but his homie was already reversing in an attempt to get out of harm's way. Out of pure panic, Rashad let off a useless shot at the general area of the van before he scrambled after the car that jerked to a halt a few feet away.

Manny stepped out from behind a car almost 25 feet above the point where they thought he was and sent more gunfire at Rashad. The shot missed, but managed to punch a huge hole into the hood of his homie's car. Nearly being hit caused Rashad to flinch with his finger on the trigger sending yet another useless explosion into the ground. Then his survival instinct kicked into gear, so he chambered another round and shot wildly in Manny's direction.

After one more blast from the shotgun, Rashad hopped into the car with his homie. they tried to quickly whip into a U-turn, but the narrow backstreet proved unforgiving of such a mistake. As they struggled with the limited space, Manny went into full attack mode, sending shot after shot into them until they finally sped off in the direction they come from. The end result was two busted windows on the passenger side, and multiple holes throughout the body of the car....

$$$$$

Rashad now knew he had bitten off more than he could chew. His heart was racing as he saw steam spewing from the front of the car where Manny had shot through the radiator. It was a miracle that he found no holes in himself when he checked for injuries before looking around, but his feeling of being blessed faded fast when he glanced at his homie.

The bullets that miraculously missed him had hit his boy two out of three times. Blood poured from his neck as fast as the steam poured from the radiator. He was alive enough to drive, but only barely so. The jagged holes in the side of his face where his jaw had been ripped open in the onslaught brought the gravity of their situation into full focus.

When their eyes met, the fear that flooded the compartment forced words out of the equation. Both men were terrified and praying their own prayers privately but one was sure to meet his maker a lot sooner than expected.

Swerving to a stop on the side of the freeway left Rashad glad that he'd ditched the shotgun a few miles back. His homie was unresponsive when Highway Patrol finally got to the scene, and the only living witness quickly drew the investigation to a dead end. He couldn't speak about what Manny had done without incriminating himself, so after vaguely answering a few questions with a lot of lies to the cops, his friends, and his homie's family, he considered himself lucky to be both alive and free.

After that, Rosa never had any issues seeing her son because Rashad avoided her and let his mother deal with whatever was needed...

CHAPTER 5

DROPPIN' JEWELS

*"I'm on a mission, baby, ain't yo' everyday Joe.
I need a go-getter, not yo' everday ho."*

— Pimpin' Tre.

After a few days with no issues, Manny found himself in Salinas dropping knowledge on Miami as they sipped a couple of beers in a taco shop.

"Check game, my nigga. It's so easy to get money out here that it could spoil a good bitch. Because good hoes is good thinkers, so they'll feel like it's cool to relax. So a pimp gotta be on the lookout for moves the bitch might make tryna find a hole in your commitment to the cause. It's in her nature! So, you mark my words. . . one of these hoes is gonna pull some punk shit before she come all the way correct. I can almost smell it!" Manny said as he surveyed the scene.

Since they'd met, they shared each other's company for the most part of each day. Feeling each other out and comparing notes about the Game they were in; Miami had grown to really respect the information he received from the unique perspective of Manny Fresh. This consisted mostly of instructions about the oldest profession, and details that mattered most to the men who chose to profit from it.

"My bitch is A-1, big bruh. She know I'm tryna pull us a car outta these next few trips, so I got her focused on a goal like how you was talkin' 'bout the other day," Miami said as Manny sipped his beer.

As always, he sounded extremely proud with anything that had to do with CoCo. But Manny was still working with leftover viciousness from the fumbled attack on his life earlier that week, so he wasn't letting a lot of things slide in his presence.

With an evil grin suddenly upon his face, he said, "Baby bro, you swear yo' bitch is oh so flawless. But on some solid shit, though, you must either be blind, or doin' yo' best to fool me. No disrespect, mane, but I watch niggas like you to remind myself of what *not* to do. So stop serving me that sauce about how perfect that ho is.

"If that was the whole story, you'd already be on yo' feet in a major way off that bitch after all the time you've had her. Yo' Ism startin' to sound like some sucka-for-love-type shit, mane!"

Miami tightened up a bit at that and tried to interrupt, but Manny waved him off and continued his attack.

"Look, bruh. I like my bitch, too. But we don't let these hoes get a pass on our pimpin' for any reason. Because it's people out there who wouldn't touch these kinds of women with a ten-foot pole, so a ho actually owe you for fuckin' wit' her regardless of what she do.

"You ain't 'posed to have to babysit a bitch, interacting with the ho a million times a day like you can't stand to be apart. What part of the Game is that? If you want a real P to believe that almighty shit you keep spittin' about that bitch, you gotta start livin' above average off that bitch. Let the proof be the truth! Flip some cars, stack some racks, and bump some big shit off that ho's hustle."

He looked Miami dead in the eye with an exhausted expression on his face as he spoke. It was obvious to see that he was tired of all the empty boasting with no evidence of success to show for the claims being made.

Miami knew Manny's words were true, but he was still right on the edge of being offended by the rough way he'd just been spoken to. He didn't quite know how to take what he heard, and the man who'd just spoken the words wasn't always so easy to figure out.

At this time, it felt pointless to defend his actions, so he let the tension of the moment pass without feeding into it further. "Yeah, I feel you, man," was all he said.

But Manny still wasn't quite ready to let up.

"I'm just bein' real, bruh. It take a lot more to be a good bitch than dressin' up and goin' out. A lot of these hoes be out here playin' for attention instead of really gettin' paid.

"Muthafuckas let these backwards-ass bitches get away with weed money and the next day's rent for a motel, then get all high and mighty like that's really pimpin'. Got a whole herd of lazy hoes not knowin' how they 'posed to hustle. Givin' bitches props instead of lettin' 'em know how wack that shit really is.

"If I do it, I'ma do it for real, bruh. Ain't no punk bitch commin' outta my camp. We gotta hold these hoes to some higher standards instead of fuckin' up the Game on some punk shit!"

Manny downed his beer after that and left Miami at the bar to digest the speech while he made his way out to the Impala. Miami sat still for a moment, reflecting on what was said for a minute. Then he downed his own beer before he followed Manny out to the car.

Climbing into the interior as the blunt was being sparked, he acknowledged the truth. "You right on that note, my nigga. No bullshit, though... muthafuckas really be in the way with this shit. I'ma start smashin' hard on my bitch from now on."

Manny slowly shook his head to that and said, "Nah, bruh... don't go blow ya bitch on actin' all brand new. She ain't the enemy. Y'all gotta be on the same team at all times. Make your adjustments understandable to her. Don't get mad, just get pimpin' on that ho.

"What you do is this. You make up some punk rock bitch you heard about who you know don't compare to her at all. Then you tell her how the imaginary ghost bitch is doin' the most by doin' what real hoes is 'posed to do. That's when you pop on yo' bitch about steppin' her shit up to keep these lesser hoes from outdoing her. If yo' bitch is a good one, her pride will make her go harder. Simple as that."

Miami passed the blunt and nodded in agreement.

"Yeah, P, that's some smooth shit," Miami said. "You got me playin' back this whole time I been havin' this bitch, and all the shit I been seein' go down with her moms and sister. It's almost like you tellin' me how them ratchet-ass hoes got like that.

"Damn, big bruh! I wouldn't even have known it if you ain't speak on it right now," he said in awe.

"The average nigga won't ever know it, mane! But a pimp ain't the average nigga, though. Not even almost. We got a job to do, and that's to make sense outta this shit so it can make dolla's," Manny said before he hit the weed a couple of times before continuing. "That's why I don't talk to niggas on that track in Stockton. Because they ain't operating how I gets down. The ho stroll in Oakland looks like a car show every day, bruh! So imagine how I feel on Wilson Way drivin' around in the only fixed-up car on the whole damn track!

"Like niggas don't keep the same standards on they pimpin', mane! That's playin' wit' the Game, to me. Burnin' out a bunch of good bitches just to barely survive."

He passed the blunt and the discussion continued on until the sun went down. And as the day turned into night, Manny's prediction became a reality without either man expecting that it would prove to be true so soon...

CHAPTER 6

CHECKIN' A TRAP

"Will she sell her lips, her hips, and her fingetips?"

– Pimpin' Ken

As the night went on, Manny stayed out of Rosa's way so she could work. There was so much traffic going in and out of the Motel 6 where they'd opened her hustle was going at a very healthy pace. So when they were out of touch for a few hours, he paid is no mind, thinking she must be showing off by catching as many dates as possible. And when a light rain started to fall, he just sat back in his car, trying not to draw any attention that might spook the customers.

He considered what she had to go through normally to get her money and concluded that she deserved the more comfortable arrangement that only required her to look out of her window and call the next client to her room. So he smoked his blunts and hung out with Miami, whose situation seemed to be doing noticeably well that day.

When things started slowing down, the younger man got restless to get back to CoCo, so Manny sent Rosa a text to check her status. "Hey there! What U lookin' like?"

But he got no answer.

No big deal. She was probably busy, so he waited about twenty minutes and reached out again.

Hmmmm, he thought to himself after receiving no answer. *She must have 'em lined up waiting for her*.

No suprise to him, so he gave it more time.

This went on for over an hour before Manny began to get worried. The room was rented while he was present, so he was able to get an extra key from the lady at the check-in counter, but he still knocked before letting himself in the room.

No answer...

Now he was getting even more concerned. Uncertain of what might await him, his mind raced through images of all the horror stories he'd heard about how wrong things could go for a girl in this particular profession.

He slid the card-key through the slot and opened the door carefully. The sight of what he saw was the last thing he ever expected to see. It caught him so much by surprise, he couldn't even control his reaction.

He laughed out loud.

Rosa laid there in the bed, as peaceful as can be, snoring lightly under the covers. *She musta worked herself to sleep and passed out on me*, he thought to himself. This was understandable because he knew she'd been on a very demanding schedule. So he didn't bother her at first, figuring that she must've put her money into the dresser drawer and crashed from exhaustion.

But the drawer only held a phonebook and a Bible...

Oh well... That's a smart move with all the different dudes in and out of the room, he thought to himself. You don't want ya' cash just layin' around waitin' for a thief. She hid it like she 'posed to.

"Wake up, pretty girl," he said gently as he shook her shoulder. "I hate to wake you up, but I can't find the money. Where you hide it at?" he asked while she slowly shook off her sleep with an aura of confusion.

"Mmmm... What time is it?" she asked nervously.

"It's almost one in the morning. You musta dozed off before you called me when it finally slowed down for you. That's cool, though. I just couldn't find the dough, so go on and set it out and you can get back to yo' rest," Manny said without yet grasping how wrong this all was.

But he started to suspect something was wrong when Rosa sat there on the bed, quiet for a moment. Her eyes avoided his, and the whole vibe in the room grew heavy with the unspoken answer to his question.

Then she said, "Awww, man. I musta fell asleep without knowin' it. Damn! I ain't got nothin' yet. That weed we smoked earlier was –"

That was as far was she got before she was cut off from the "POW!" sounding off in her brain from the smack delivered to her cheek so fast that she never saw it coming. As she rolled off the bed, Manny kicked her in the butt before she made it down to the floor. When she looked up from her short fall, she encountered an entirely different man from the one who had so sweetly stirred her up out of her sleep.

Manny stood over her and began to take off his belt. Rosa saw the fury in his eyes.

"You punk-ass bitch!" he growled. "Been layin' yo' ass up in here doin' nothin' while every other ho in the buildin' been workin' like a champ all this time! Got me out there in the rain lookin' stupid while these raggedy bitches run circles around yo' broke-down ass. Bitch! You in here 'sleep on the job while I'm out there puttin' our program on a pedestal like it's superior, while the whole time you ain't got a dollar?"

The rapid-fire explosions of the pops from the belt had her moving faster than she'd ever moved before as he continued his tantrum.

"I swear to God in Heaven, ho, if you don't get yo' funky ass up out of here to replace the money you missed, I'ma beat all the skin off yo' body with this belt!" he said viciously as he smacked her again with the belt to emphasize his point.

Rosa tried her best to apologize, but Manny didn't hear a single word of her stuttering attempts to calm the situation. He never paused once to let her speak.

"I don't give a fuck what you gotta do, or where you gotta go, ho! You can catch the death of pneumonia while you out there gettin' that shit right. But I better not see or hear from you without you having exactly what you told me a bitch 'posed to get out here!

"You ain't gotta fuck wit' me, bitch! But if you do, it ain't gonna be by trickin' me into faraway places so you can take a nap on my pimpin', I promise you that!

He chased her out of the door before she could even grab a coat, and it was all she could do to avoid the belt he was swinging like a wild man.

Through her initial shock, a part of her felt betrayed at the thought of how he'd just treated her. But some of what he said also brought to mind a few facts she couldn't help but see clearly.

$$$$$

After the moment of madness he'd just manifested, Manny felt like a fire had burned through his system and left only ashes behind where his emotion used to be. He almost experienced a guilty conscience when he saw Rosa's coat laying over the back of the chair, but remorse never managed to outweigh the heavy hurt of unexpected disappointment.

Rather than replaying the negativity, he sat down and rolled himself a thick blunt, smoked it down to nothing, then climbed under the covers into the space Rosa had so recently vacated. "Now we trade places, but not positions," he mumbled to himself before finally falling asleep.

As consciousness slipped away, he remembered the saying about loving something and letting it go so it could come back to you if it was really yours...

$$$$$

On the other side of the same situation, Rosa cried until her eyes were dry before deciding to leave Manny for good.

"Here I am out here in the rain, freezing my ass off with no coat!" she said angrily to herself. "He know the motels stop rolling early out here. Now I ain't got no room to work out of either! Fuck him! I'm not about to be dealin' with this kind of shit!"

But her lack of immediate distraction made it impossible to lie to herself about the bigger picture, so when the cold settled in on her senses, she had to imagine how Manny must have felt out there waiting for her while she had him thinking she was handling her business. That made her face head-on the truth of how he must've felt to hear she wasn't busy at all, but sleeping while he'd been trusting her to play her part. This opened the door for embarrassment to enter her heart as she imagined how she must've been looking right then in comparison to the other girls working that same motel that day.

"Even a half-assed ho with a piss-poor pimp is lookin' better than us right now," she admitted to herself. And in spite of the fact that she fought it for at least a half hour, her conscience forced her to face the fact that the mistake was hers more than it was his, because he wouldn't have come out here had she not asked him to. Therefore, as angry as she was, the truth was undeniable about how untrustworthy she must've appeared to be in his eyes.

She knew that, since they'd met, he'd made many changes in his life to move her into it. He had her back when she needed it, and he even made room at his little studio for her instead of keeping her in a motel like so many of the other girls who worked the track from day to day.

It was easy to hate what Manny had just done, but she also had to love just about everything else he did up to that point. The good outweighed the bad, and when she considered what brought about the situation, she was holding against him, she had to wonder... Should she blame him? *Could* she blame him?

The more she allowed her mind to honestly look at it, the more she realized that she was seeing what Manny always said about a mad move being a bad move. And it was her anger and shame that had her ready to shift blame and turn her back on him, instead of just getting to what brought them here in the first place.

This reality came to her attention while she walked her way through the darkness of the late night. When she looked up, she noticed she was coming upon a bar that catered to the Mexican migrant population that seemed to make up the majority of the people in Salinas. The good things about this is how this same population provided the best clients a girl in her line of business could ever hope for.

She then realized upon further reflection that of all the women sure to be at the bar, she was probably the only prostitute available at the moment. And her need for cash gave way to a thought that sent her prowling into the parking lot.

That's when she noticed a single male figure bent over behind his truck throwing up. She hooked him under the pretense of helping him into his truck before she transformed into his drunken dream come true once they were inside the vehicle.

She could've robbed him on the spot with no problem, but instead decided to send him back into the bar to bring his friends out to the truck so they could "date" her, too. With this, she turned one customer into a whole line-up of cash for her to work through.

Out of the cold and dry from the rain, she finished each client off in record time. She was like a dangerous animal that quickly attacked every man who dared to come within reach. There was no time wasted once a trick was in her presence, and she dominated each encounter to achieve her goals as soon as possible – a grab of a hand to run against her pussy so they'd be ready when she rolled the condom into place, or an arm around the next guy as soon as he was close enough so she could grind herself up against him. If they pulled her closer, she responded with even more aggressive pressure, turning them on with her private show as she led them into their engagement.

She laid on her back with her legs wide open to meet one man and got on her knees with her ass in the air to meet the next. Each one got a different introduction to the ecstasy he experienced. As soon as the door was shut behind a client, he was hers. She ripped shirts open and pants down to get her work started. She was a beast. A seemingly end of dicks throbbed under her touch, one after the other. Some she sucked savagely as if she was starving for the taste, while others she jerked off when she saw they were far enough gone that she could get away with it.

The foreplay was bypassed completely. She got straight to the point each and every time. A switch had flipped in her mind, and she became a trick-pleasing monster.

"Come on! Come on! Fuck me, baby!" she screamed into the ear of the truck's owner as she rushed him through his second round to pay for using his vehicle as her personal place of business. And he was going for all it was worth with an awareness he didn't possess during his first intoxicated attempt, but this was more accessible than a motel on such short notice, so Rosa gladly entertained it.

It was as if the bar never closed, because the parking lot never emptied out for long after the lights were out and the doors were locked.

Once she ran through the group, she took a few repeat customers to a nearby motel and relieved them of whatever cash they had left in their pockets. She remained busy with this until sunrise, earning a little over six hundred dollars from her efforts. Then she gave her last client a sad story that cost him an extra hundred dollars toward a nonexistent car that was in an imaginary shop. And the lie led to the calling of his cousin who was a mechanic with a shop full of employees that were also potential customers.

By six o'clock that morning, she had the cousin in the motel room "dating" her, and by seven o'clock the cousin was taking her back to his shop to meet a few interested employees. When eight-thirty rolled around, she was in a taxicab back to her little workstation of a motel room to catch the rest of her morning rush. After a few walks back and forth to the gas station, she had a healthy amount of traffic coming her way.

CHAPTER 7

MUTUAL RESPECT

"Girl, you perfect, you always worth it. . . And you deserve it, the way you work it, 'cause girl you earned it..."

– The Weeknd

Rosa felt like a zombie as the morning came to an end, but at least her embarrassment was gone. Her shame still remained, but that would disappear as soon as her efforts were acknowledged, so when checkout time came around, she was back at the Motel 6, waiting for Manny to come outside. Reluctant to knock on the door, she sat on the curb next to his car. When he finally came out of the room, she was right there with two cups of the coffee she knew he liked with all the flavored cream and loads of sugar.

Hers was half gone and his was cold, but she gave it to him anyway as a peace offering.

"You might need to warm this up, sir," she said to him. "Thank God for microwaves, right? And I got your damn money, too. Next time I'm wrong like that, I hope you'll at least try to tell me to go fix it. A bitch might just listen."

Manny had a hard time hiding his relief. He'd figured if he hadn't heard from her by when the front desk called for checkout time, he wouldn't be hearing from her at all. So he smiled at her little presentation and he allowed his mind to be curious about what she had managed to bring him.

Pride had kept them both from speaking after they parted ways the night before, so neither of them knew what to expect when and if they met again. But there was no question about the fact that she'd just earned a better response than the last one he delivered, so Manny met the situation with the improved attitude he knew she deserved.

"Step into the room then, sleeping beauty," he said to her. "Put that money in my hand and roll us up a blunt while I go pay the rent. Can you manage that without fallin' asleep on me?"

"Oh, you got jokes now, huh? Yeah, I can handle it if the weed is where I can find it," she said with a hint of a smile as she produced a roll of cash and handed it over.

Manny went to go pay the rent. As soon as he was out of her sight, he paused near the ice machine to count what she'd given him. After all the bills had been totaled up, he'd added a little over twelve-hundred dollars. He counted again in disbelief, just to make sure he got it right, and sure enough, it was twelve-hundred dollars.

When he made it to the lobby, Miami was on his way out from paying up on his room.

"What up wit' it, P?" Miami said. "Top of the mornin' to ya, mane. Got my shit paid up and I'm ready to rock. Bitch hit me wit' a nine-piece last night."

Manny smile at the news without sharing any of his own yet.

"Let me go get mine out the way, bruh. I did all right last night; pretty fair for a square," he said vaguely.

Miami screwed his face up in disagreement with the evasive statement. "Maaan, save that cap for some sucka! We both know fa sho you ain't no square, my nigga."

Manny didn't answer, though. Instead, he just went into the lobby to pay his room and recharge the card-key, leaving Miami hanging outside to wonder how their situations compared to one another.

$$$$$

When Manny got back to the motel room, he was met with the sight of two blunts on the nightstand where a cigarette lighter laid next to them. As he closed the door behind himself, Rosa looked him in the eyes from where she sat at the edge of the bed giving some much-needed attention to the blisters on her feet.

After a brief pause to acknowledge her presence, Manny walked past her to the bathroom to fill the tub full of bathwater for Rosa. As the tub filled with soapy bubbles, he came back out to casually snatch one of the blunts. He lit it, hit it, and passed it to her so he could sip on his super-sweet coffee.

As Rosa puffed away, Manny looked her in the eyes again, through the smoke, without saying a single word. She met his gaze with confidence this time, with a hint of a smile upon her lips.

An invisible energy enveloped the room with a magnetic field that pulled a part of them together. It was the melting down of misunderstandings between them and the making up of mutual respect.

Manny had shown Rosa that he wasn't playing, but in her own way, Rosa had responded with the same level of demonstration. And without too many words, they still both knew that neither one of them really wanted to be without the other.

Being proud of what she knew she'd proved, Rosa still also knew that, without his push, she would've never crossed that milestone within herself to discover what she could do if she had to.

Her body was aching, her feet were sore, and her mind still flinched at the memory of his momentary madness, but a perverted sense of appreciation still shined through by the way she could say that she felt right then and there.

Head spinning from exhaustion, tears threatened to spill at any moment. She broke the silence to distract herself from the overflow of emotion.

"I'll be good, Daddy. But you need to decide if you want me to take a nap and recharge my battery, or drink some five-hour energy shots for however much longer you need me to stay awake, because all I know is that bubble bath is calling my name right now," she said before limping carefully into the bathroom.

$$$$$

Soaking in the bathwater seemed to soothe Rosa's body, but it didn't do a lot for a particular stain that refused to leave her soul. A stain that Manny's actions unexpectedly brought to the surface of her mind, with memories of other times that she'd been snatched from her sleep to serve a sexual purpose.

When Rosa was just eleven years old, her brother snuck into her bedroom one night. She woke up to the pain of him piercing her. He had his hand over her mouth to muffle her cries. There was nothing she could do to stop him since he was much bigger than she was. And there were no words her child mind could ever conceive that would ever convince anyone that he had done this to her, so she didn't tell.

That only served to encourage him to come a few days later. This time he threatened her to ensure her silence. And after that, his nighttime visits became a regular thing. But what increased Rosa's shame the most was the surprising fact that she came to enjoy herself around the third or fourth time around.

The thrill of the secret, the tingle of the midnight touches, and all-day anticipation... It was all a new chapter in her life that her impressionable young mind understood as fun and exciting instead of the rape it was.

By the time she was thirteen, she was her older brother's sex slave, and they did "it" every chance they got. He would even bring his friends over to take turns on her, and this lasted until her high school years.

When Rosa shared her secret with a friend who asked her about the rumors going around about her, she was shocked to realize just how shameful her acts were. This is when she finally understood how foul her brother was for what he'd been doing. And that was the day when a piece of her came to connect love, hate, and sex with each other as different parts of the same emotional experience.

Every episode beyond that point was forceful. She was either taken against her will, or blackmailed with threats to tell their parents. And she could never ignore her body's reaction each and every time the deed was done. Her pussy still got wet, her nipples still got hard, her mouth still watered, and her asshole was still hungry for the penetration of a dick.

She was a freak to the fullest, and how this came to be did nothing to diminish the fact that it was undeniably true. So whenever her services were demanded, she lost herself in the delivery... Because life itself had taught her to be that way.

$$$$$

On the other side of the door, Manny was a world away, slowly smoking the rest of the blunt and searching his mind to find a feeling he could identify. When he decided to take this journey, he also decided that he wasn't going to screw it up. He'd been raised up watching his uncle Johnny practice this profession his entire life, so there wasn't much about it that was new to him.

The only thing he could reach as a readable conclusion to this whole situation was that the proof is the truth. And with that thought, he sipped his cold, sweet coffee on his way out of the door to begin his day.

While he sat in his driver's seat warming up, he sent Rosa a text to say what his mouth would never allow him to speak out loud: "U did good! Get that nap. I'll wake U up later, K soldier?"

After a short while, her response came back.

"Yes, sir!"

CHAPTER 8

SHOW AND TELL

"Act as if, and you shall become."
– Delancey Street Foundation

The next few days went by successfully for Manny and Rosa. Their names created a highly-respected buzz throughout the area for some reason, and it wasn't until he was sitting again one day with Miami at the same taco shop they came to in the beginning of the Salinas trip that he understood just what the reason happened to be.

On this day, Miami seemed to be looking at Manny through new eyes, in a way that caught the younger man staring at his mentor on numerous occasions. He was working some kind of puzzle out in his mind as he listened to the words that were starting to finally fall into place for him.

After a little while of this, Manny casually asked as they ate enchiladas, "What the fuck got you all googly eyed over there, bruh? You been sneakin' peeks at a nigga like you got somethin' on ya mind,"

Miami laughed a little bit to lighten the mood then shared his observation.

"Big bruh, you is a cold piece of work for real. Not too long ago you sat right here in this joint talkin' shit 'bout how a ho 'posed to get down. So I listened to you and got on top of my game, 'cause I honestly thought you was braggin' on ya bitch real slick like. But I couldn't hate 'cause everybody know yo' work be rockin' for real, so I respect it.

"Now, don't get mad at ya bitch, P. She don't be exposin' ya bidness or nothin', but I can tell from what she did tell my folks that all this time you coulda been shuttin' muthafuckas down 'round here."

Manny's smirk was the only hint that he had any idea of what Miami was talkin' about, so Miami knew he had to spell it out if he wanted to get the subject onto the table for discussion.

"Man, yo' bitch told mine what happened that first night out here and how she came out of it lookin' like a champ because of how you was too much of a boss to accept some punk shit. But you ain't tell nobody a damn thing.

"I know I woulda been lettin' all these niggas know what it was with me and my bitch on some shit how we just did some impossible shit wit ' my pimpin'. But you just kick back and walk it like you talk it. That's some solid shit right there, bruh."

Now smiling openly around a mouth full of Mexican food, Manny managed to mumble, "Well, when it's what it's supposed to be, a real P don't gotta say much, mane! Other people gonna do it for him."

$$$$$

At a pawn shop one day, Manny spotted something special laying alone among all the rest of the trinkets in the display case. It was a single sterling silver chain necklace made by Tiffany & Co.

The way it stood out was like he wasn't meant to see anything else in the whole store. He imagined it all polished up, hanging heavy around Rosa's neck. And the image replaced all intentions he had of finding something for himself at a bargain price.

$$$$$

When the few days went by, a time came when Rosa was due for a trip to the mall with a few dollars to buy herself some things. With her leftover money, she bought a cheap, ugly little chain. She thought Manny would be impressed with it because it had a little rhinestone encrusted pistol dangling from it. But when he saw it, he laughed out loud, hurting her feelings.

"Well. . . I thought it was cute when I saw it. Ain't like I know all about jewelry, so... whatever," she said sadly.

"I'm sayin', though. If you had jewelry on ya' mind, why you ain't say somethin' to me?"

"For all you know, I could surprise you with proof I'm on the same page," he said mysteriously.

Rosa admitted she was not used to being able to just say what she wanted with any real expectation of getting it. And that's when Manny decided to teach her a lesson about being in a better position than she was used to.

"See, bitch, that's how I know that you would do better if you knew better. And that's why hoes fuck with pimps. Because we bring progress into yo' prostitution experience and hit you with the kind of guidance you won't get on your own. It ain't like hoes is stupid, but just like most people, y'all will usually repeat what you know. But pimpin' is good for helping you grow through that," he said creatively, working his way up to the point he wanted to make.

Rosa's eyes took on a look of uncertainty as he spoke. She knew that sometimes he said things in a way that made him look as good as possible. To her it was just a cute macho-type thing that he didn't know she was aware of, so she didn't mind it much. But this time, he had that weird look in his eye that never failed to put her on alert that there was more to his words than just what she was hearing.

"Yeah, yeah, yeah," she said playfully, suspecting that he was putting on a show. "So, what exactly is it that I don't know then?"

At the same moment, Manny reached into his pocket and said, "Nah, you ain't ready to know yet. Because if I give it to you all at once, you only gonna hold on to bits and pieces. So let me just give you a piece for right now since I can show you better than I can tell you."

With a curious smile plastered across her face, Rosa said, "I wish you'd stop draggin' it out and come on wit' it already! Why you playin' wit' me Daddy?"

"Because I gotta make sure I got yo' full attention before I hit you with some shit you might just miss the meaning of."

With that, he pulled out of his pocket the silly looking pawn shop bag, all crinkled up like trash. Rosa went silent at the sight of the unimpressive package that he handed her, but when she opened it up to pull out the brightly-polished links of the thick necklace with its oval shaped Tiffany tag twinkling in the center, she melted with surprise.

"Awwww..." was all she could say in the low voice that came from her heart as her hand began to shake.

Something sentimental made it a struggle to keep her emotions in check as she stared at what was in her hand. She looked up at him and smiled at the pride she saw in his eyes before he opened his mouth and said, "Bitch, you better put that on right this minute! Here, let me see it. I got you." He reached for the chain and draped it around Rosa's neck.

She felt the weight of it, cold and comfortable right where it belonged. "I feel like I won the Olympics or something and this is my medal," she said seriously.

"Nah, never that. The Olympics call the silver medal for second place. But when I compare the rest of these hoes to how you run yo' race...you come in first as far as I can see.

When Rosa showed her necklace to CoCo later on that day, Miami pulled Manny to the side and jokingly accused him of having gimmicks to promote his pimpin'.

In Manny 's mind, it wasn't much, but at that moment he knew the necklace meant a lot to Rosa. And the all-around reaction it received was enough to boost the effect it had on her in a way he was sure she'd remember. So he counted it as a slam dunk, and with that mission accomplished, the day passed on into a growing list of good memories.

$$$$$

Days became weeks and weeks became months for the crew of cash collectors in Salinas. But money can often cause the downfall of even greatest of friendships when all parties involved find they're not on the same page. Miami made Manny mad at him about a misunderstood money move they made, so when Manny took things to a very dangerous level, they went their separate ways with one of them having to learn a very expensive lesson about keeping his word.

The underlying truth was that half of getting what is wanted consists of knowing what must be given up in order to get it. Manny had outgrown the things that fell short of financial increase, and this included the friends who could not keep up with his level of intensity.

Manny took things as they came, never complained, and refused to ask himself if he was right or wrong. This drew him to other places in pursuit of his profession, and for the most part, all the moving around served to help him keep his situation highly focused. But it is human nature to be social, so friendship of some kind is almost unavoidable. Especially in the face of the loneliness that can leave its mark upon the life anyone who seriously plays in the game of prostitution. Therefore, it was not a strange occurrence when Rosa made somewhat of a friend. Sweetie was her name, and she was an older hooker who worked for an old, established pimp named Saucey Mike.

Sweetie was an attractive Black woman in her forties that managed to maintain her youthful figure and face. With chocolate skin, dark eyes, and a mouth made of full lips that always looked like she was about to blow a kiss, she looked at least fifteen years younger than she really was. And at first glance, no one would ever think that thirty years had gone by since that day she'd first been "turned out" by Saucey Mike.

"Bitch, I can see you down for yo' peoples, and I respect that," Sweetie said to Rosa as they smoked a cigarette while crossing the street one night on Harbor Boulevard in Anaheim, California.

"Yeah, I can't see myself with nobody else, Sweets! He work a bitch like a slave sometimes, but he make it worthwhile and I like what he do with the money," Rosa replied to the pretty little veteran bitch.

Sweetie grew quiet for a moment after that. Then, when she finally spoke again, there was a bit of a chilly quality to her words.

"Baby girl, let me tell you something you should never forget. In this game, love can get real expensive on a bitch. And I ain't ever seen no real pimp that ever gave a ho a credit account on what he's gonna charge her. So enjoy it while you can, but don't slip up and expect him to give you any more than he thinks you paid for," Sweety said seriously.

Rosa took this in with the respect it was due. But when it came to Manny, she thought she knew better, so she spoke up in his defense.

"I hear you on that one," Rosa said. "But my folks fucks with me for real, though. He'll check a bitch for sure, but even then, he got a method to his madness."

"Oh, I bet he does have a method. No doubts about that, bitch! Just please believe that, no matter how many dreams he can make come true for you, this still ain't no Fantasy Island.

"All I'm sayin' is that the game we play is based on how much we pay, not on if the love is real or fake," Sweety said as she lifted her shirt up to her breastbone to show Rosa a large ugly scar that went down the center of her belly.

"I got this when some jealous fools from my folks' old hood decided to shoot up our car with us inside it. The doctors had to cut me open to make sure my guts was still workin' and had no holes in them anywhere."

Next, Sweetie hesitantly rolled up her sleeve to show the dark lines and tiny puncture scars going up and down the inside of her left arm. Rosa would've had a hard time noticing them unless they were pointed out.

Sweetie continued where she'd left off. "For a couple of years along the way of loving my man, we fell into fuckin' with that heroin kinda tough. I was tryna be down like I thought a good bitch 'posed to be.

"He almost died of an overdose one day and I was too far gone into a nod to help him. Luckily, we had another bitch at the time who could call the ambulance for his ass. They brought him back, but ol' girl left after that, and we never fucked wit' that shit again."

Sweetie rolled her sleeve down and said, "I got other scars and even more stories, baby girl, but I'm sure you get the idea. When I say it's expensive and we pay, I ain't only talkin' 'bout money. Whoever act like they real is gonna have to experience some real shit. What's real is usually raw, and that don't always taste too good.

"I stayed with Mike this long because I put in too much work to give up on it. But please believe, if I had it my way, I would've at least made sure the good outweighed the bad so I had more than scars and stories to show for all that I've put into this shit."

Sweetie looked Rosa in the face for a moment, made a decision, then said sincerely, "My nigga told me to bring you home. But I wouldn't wish my situation on you. I ain't gonna talk bad on his name, but I ain't 'bout to offer you no bad deal, either. So just make sure that fuckin' wit' ya folks can give you something good to say about whatever price you pay by the time you make it to be my age, baby girl."

With that said, the two girls carried on with the rest of the night's work, leaving Rosa much more enlightened than she was when the night began...

CHAPTER 9

IN THE TRENCHES

"That's how it goes, I'm a pimp and it shows, stayin' on my toes."

– Mac Dre

Being so close to Disneyland was Manny's cue to put it into Rosa's mind that her son Tookie needed to benefit from their frequent trips to Anaheim. And not long after her talk with Sweetie, a mini-vacation was planned out. It was another slam dunk for Manny Fresh in his ongoing mission to make memories that would promote smiles. But when Rosa thanked him while the play was being made, he reprimanded her.

"Bitch, we still in the trenches! This just happens to be a more enjoyable part of our job. So don't thank me for doin' what I'm 'posed to do," Manny said as he shared a plate of fried oysters with Tookie.

$$$$$

One day, back in Salinas, Manny was on his way out of a little motel called The Wagon wheel when he passed a room with its door wide open. Music poured loudly from the inside, and it wasn't the carnival-type of Spanish music that he heard most often in this city.

Manny glanced inside as he walked by. His curiosity was met with the sight of a couple who seemed to be having some type of disagreement. He stayed out of their business and continued on his journey to the gas station in search of the super-sweet coffee he and Rosa thrived on.

As Rosa's workday began with her morning rush, Manny found himself trying to play the background without actually leaving the premises. And while walking to the lobby to pay Rosa's room for the day, he noticed a thuggish guy with a doo-rag on his head storming out of the room that had caught his attention earlier.

The guy hopped into a big white Chevy Suburban and left the area. The truck wasn't anything special, so Manny figured he was seeing some domestic dispute between a boyfriend and girlfriend taking place – nothing worthy of his interest or concern.

Then, later on it became clear to see that the flow of customer traffic was splitting itself up between Rosa's room and the room that came to his attention at the beginning of the day; the same room that he'd assumed was occupied by a couple of squares.

From behind his tinted windows, Manny discovered that there was a good-looking mixed girl peeking out of her window to catch whatever stray clients Rosa missed. And from the look of things, she wasn't doing too badly.

Manny sent Rosa a text. "Uh oh! U better not leave no money waiting out there for too long or UR competition a few doors down gonna scoop it up!"

A short while later, Rosa sent her reply: "She can't fuck wit me!"

Remembering the disagreement, he'd only halfway paid attention to earlier made Manny curious about something else. "Checkin' ain't cheatin'" he told himself as he decided to poke at this new face to see if he could get her attention.

After watching a date leave the room in question, he started his car and let the motor growl loudly. Then he turned up the volume on his sound system so that the bass from the huge woofers in the trunk would be sure to draw the attention he was looking for. The next move he made was to steer slowly out of the parking lot, taking his time to pass the room his actions were aimed at.

He saw Rosa peek out of her window. *There's one ho doin' what hoes do. Now for number two*, he thought to himself as he glanced at the room the other girl was working.

When she peeked out at him, Manny smiled to himself and put on a show. For the benefit of those watching, he did the gas-brake-dip that made the car do a little dance, then he "toot tooted" his horn and continued on his way.

Manny looked into his vibrating rearview mirror and saw that his audience was now leaning out of her wide-open window looking curiously right back at him. As he waited for a break in traffic with the music still bangin' loudly, he thought to himself, *My, my... Ain't we outta pocket today...*

$$$$$

Shortly before lunchtime, Rosa called Manny on his cell phone. "Hello. This is your conscience speaking," he answered playfully.

"Hey, conscience, I'm tryna catch my Daddy so I can ask for a smoke break when he comes to get his money. Do I have the wrong number?"

"No bitch. Don't try to be funny. Yo' Daddy and yo' conscience are one in the same. Let me go grab a Swisher and I'll be there in a few minutes. You'll hear me when I pull up," Manny said in a no-nonsense tone.

"Oh yeah! And speaking of hearing you, I see that girl down the hall been standin' outside her door all of a sudden since you left. Look like she tryna be outside whenever you come back."

"You mean the bitch ain't workin'?"

"Oh no, I'm not sayin' that. She workin' for sure. But between her dates she been findin' her way out there to smoke her cigarettes.

"You already know I ain't 'bout to let her get my dates before they can see me, so I took my add out there, too. just bein' nosey and choppin' it up wit' the bitch. First thing she asked was if you was my folks. She sprung off how Bay Area niggas do that flashy shit y'all do with the pretty cars and stuff. She from Fresno and her name is Natalie."

Trying to play it off like it was no big deal, Manny limited his response. "That's cool. If the ball bounces my way, I'ma bag that ho before her peoples get back and do some ol' rescue-ranger-type shit."

"All I know is that if you get at that bitch, you'll probably take her if he ain't up on his shit," Rosa said, showing no hint of the jealousy she felt.

Changing directions quickly, Manny took the conversation elsewhere. "Well, whatever the case may be, I'll be around in a minute. You need me to bring you somethin' else while I'm out here?"

"Ummmm... Yeah, I actually need more condoms. Oh! And since you 'bout to give me the munchies, can I have a bag of Cheetos? Please and thank you."

"OK, boss! I got you."

The few minutes turned out to be more like a half an hour before Manny finally pulled up at the motel. Rosa had a few hundred dollars to give him with the promises of more to come. They smoked a little bit of weed and enjoyed each other's company for a few minutes before Manny put her back to work with a plan in place to have a late lunch of Mexican food from the taco shop after her midday rush.

While he was walking back to his car still blowing big clouds with the blunt, he was careful to take his time in case of unfamiliar eyes watching. He was rewarded when Natalie stepped out in front of her door casually trying to be noticed.

She didn't even hide the fact that she was looking in his direction, and Manny wasn't sure he liked that about her. It was a major break in protocol for a prostitute to look openly at a pimp when she was already spoken for. The offense was called "being out of pocket" and could lead to all kinds of trouble for the woman in question.

To avoid the possibility of rapes and robberies, or even a full-blown kidnap scenario, girls made a show of looking in some opposite direction of any pimp she didn't work for.

Anything less was a noticeable issue that would surely lead to harassment under the pretense of her not respecting the pimpin' of whoever she'd given her unapproved attention to.

So, in acknowledgement of this general principle, Manny used her transgression as an excuse to approach her, but his mind wasn't set on chasing her back into her room with a whole tirade of tough talk he was well within his rights to deliver. Instead, he decided to use finesse to pull her further into his direction.

First, he made a show of clearly putting his blunt out so she could see him doing it. Then he walked right up to her and said, "I don't know if ya folks is on some stalker-in-the bushes-type of pimpin', so play it off like you givin' me a light off yo' cigarette and we won't look too crazy out here talkin'. While you at it, let a real nigga know what's up wit' all that reckless eyeballin' you out here doin'."

Manny took her cigarette from her hand as he said this and it established that she would allow him to assume control of the situation. It also served to draw a small giggle from her smiling lips.

She was taller than expected, with a silky mess of curls reaching just past her shoulders. It was pulled back into a ponytail that allowed a good look at the pretty details of her face. She had light brown eyes that weren't quite hazel, but still lighter than normal. And her whole aura just screamed that she knew how good she looked.

"I been seein' you all in my mix like you want somethin' to do wit' this Ism. Hope you know curiosity killed the cat and satisfaction brought it back," Manny said smoothly as he hit his blunt a few times before continuing. "I'm guessin' you already know you outta pocket, so you must be tryna see 'bout a pimp. That's cool, too, 'cause you got a right to choose up if what you been doin' ain't takin' you where you need to be. So speak on it and let a pimp know if yo' voice match yo' face. Start wit' ya name if it's cool."

Still smiling, she answered him. "OK, I'm Natalie. And yes, I know enough about the Game to be sure that ya girl probably told you that much already.

"I also know I ain't 'posed to be lookin' at you like that, 'cause you obviously a pimp. So, yeah, I'm outta pocket. But I like what I see since you make it so hard to ignore you." She paused to hit her cigarette, and once she saw that Manny wasn't going to pass the weed, she went on with her statement.

"Anyway, you got ya'll shit lookin' real official, and ya folks say she ain't even been with you long. That's how I want my shit to look, but my nigga been on some other shit."

Manny took it all in then said, "Hmmm... So are you sayin' you only want the good, but when it's bad, you like to jump ship?"

She shook her head, but before she could answer he hit her with another series of questions.

"How long you been wit' ol' boy? Sorry, but I don't call him no pimp because you not actin' like a ho who got a P in her life. No disrespect to either one of y'all. I'm just sayin', it sounds more like maybe you got a boyfriend who don't know all of what it takes to do this the right way. Am I wrong?'

Natalie slowly nodded her head to affirm his observation with a small touch of shame. "It's somethin' like that," she said. "He talk the shit, but don't walk it like you do."

Manny looked at her closely for a moment. "Well, loyalty is like royalty in my world, girl. So how do I know you won't dip out on me if I bring you home? One day shit might not by all gravy and we need to dig ourselves out of that to bounce back. You gonna stay down wit' a pimp, or just keep choosin' a better-lookin' situation?"

He paused to intensify his look and said playfully, "Let me find out I'ma have to change yo' name from Natalie to Choosy Suzie!"

She giggles self-consciously and spoke in her own defense.

"OK, I do feel where you comin' from on that one. But it just feel like I'm goin' backwards compared to what I see you got goin' on."

But Manny still pressed his point, even in the process of accepting her words.

"When a ho makes a choice to bust a move after less than ten minutes of conversation, I would guess either you or yo' situation must be real fucked up.

"But I ain't no desperado, though, so here's what I can offer you. Work through the rest of the day while you think on what you want to do. If ol' boy come back to check some dough, you can just give him a little bit and claim it been slow for you because of the competition. Tell him to let you keep goin' and you'll get it right, then you run some drag every time he come back. If you decide at the end of the day to rock wit' me and mine, you should have a cool lil choosin' fee stacked up, you feel me?"

Natalie giggled again and said, "Yeah, I feel you, Mr. Bossman. I see you got it all planned out, don't you?"

Manny took a long, drawn-out pull on his weed, then said, "This is what I do. Pimp don't need no plan when he sticks to the script. Now, if you tryna fuck wit' me, you better get at it and call my folks on ya room phones to give her yo' number and get mine. That way I can coach you through any surprised. You'll be cool."

Natalie was already nodding her agreement when she responded. "OK, but what's her room number?"

"It's 4-1-5," Manny said over his shoulder as he made his way back to his Impala.

Natalie went back inside and immediately did what she was told. Rosa answered her landline as the sound of Manny's music faded away to signal he was leaving the motel.

"Hello?" said Rosa.

"Hey, girl, this is Nat, from down the hall. I was told to call you and give you my number. That sure is some kind of nigga you got there. Do you mind if I join the team? I swear he just walked up to me and started talkin' like he been knowin' me forever!"

Rosa wasn't surprised at all, but she wasn't as excited as Natalie was either. Yet, she kept her response as diplomatic as she could.

"That's cool... but if you come home, can you please not be on no bullshit? That's all I ask. The rest is up to him, and that's y'all business, not mine."

"True talk. And I got you on that. He told me to keep workin' and get some more money before I choose. Ain't that crazy? Most niggas would take whatever I got just to get it, right?"

"Yeah, bitch, but that tells me you better have a certain amount or he ain't gonna fuck wit' you. So you better get busy!" Rosa told her seriously.

After exchanging phone numbers, both girls got back to work. One to make sure she added up, and the other to make sure she was not outdone....

$$\$\$\$\$\$$

Rosa wondered what Manny's goal might be. She didn't expect Natalie's contribution to lighten the load for her, but she hoped that whatever the next level might be, it included living happily ever after. She would play her part for that result, but it would not be a very cheerful effort.

And yet, her sense of reality led to enough acceptance that she would go with the flow of this girl coming into the picture, at least until she saw something going wrong.

$$$$$

Later that day, Natalie sent Manny a text message. "Hope U come ASAP! He just left. Gave him 200 N got 400 left 2 choose U."

He read it as he sat smoking a blunt with Rosa after checking what money she had. "Damn, Rosie, it's crazy to see just how much money is really out here. This bitch is less than two hundred behind you, and you killin' it as always. Makes me wish I had two or three more of y'all out here gettin' down," he said offhandedly as she hit the blunt.

"Oh, OK, and then how much time would I get with all these hoes expecting you to keep them company?" she said while still trying to hold in the smoke.

Manny sensed a hint of jealousy, but decided to pimp past it. "Awwww, don't worry 'bout that. You know you my lil Mexican magic! Ain't nothin' gonna fuck wit' what me and you do. Bitch, I thought you knew!" he said sweetly before getting more serious and saying, "To keep it real, I'm gonna move us to Vegas. So you can use the help. Just enjoy the assistance because I ain't even sure how solid this bitch is gonna be in the long run anyway. Only way you need to worry is if you plan on faggin' off on me."

Rosa took reassurance with another puff of weed smoke before passing the blunt back to him and smiling at what he'd said.

"Well, maybe I'm just high, but all that sounds real good to me, so I feel better. I don't know what you and that bitch is up to, but it must be some sneaky shit 'cause I just saw her soon-to-be-ex-folks leave in that truck before she texted you. Do what you do, Mr. Mindbender," she said with a little laugh and a shake of her head at the clever way Manny did things.

Manny received a text from Natalie and his role immediately switched from counselor to coach. "Don't worry," he texted Natalie. "It'll be greater later! We can cut him off B4 he come back. Stay in touch w/ him until he say he on his way."

She replied almost immediately: "OK, sounds good!"

"When he on his way back, U go down to my room N stop answering UR phone," Manny texted in conclusion to his instructions.

Manny then went directly into his next move. Talking to Rosa now, he said, "OK, check it out! This bitch gonna call you a little later, so be ready so she can come hide with you with a choosin' fee before that sucka come break on her. Make sure her phone is off, then hit me so I can be on the scene. You got me?"

His excitement was contagious and Rosa's nervousness was clear to see. Especially when she said in a wary voice, "Yeah, I got you, but you better be here in a flash and don't be too far away with all this goin' on."

Manny smiled at her and smoothly delivered the promise she needed to hear. "Awwww... I got me a scaredy cat, huh? I'ma stay close just for you, then, OK?"

That was all it took to soothe her. She laughed at herself and they each went to play their parts...

$$$$$

A little while later as he analyzed the entire plan, Manny passed judgement on the unwitting victim who drove the white Suburban.

Now, if the boy had any sense, he'd stay close to keep an eye on his game, or maybe pop up on the bitch with no warning so he can catch whatever got his money all funny, he thought to himself. *But he mad at the shit he can't understand, so he'd rather pout instead of pimp,* he concluded.

Manny was sitting in his car, parked at a 7-Eleven, sipping on a bottle of beer as he discussed things with himself that he knew very few people were qualified to hear. When it came to the game he was in, he was usually pretty private about what move he would make next.

A few hours had gone by since he'd set his plan into motion. His phone was filled with updates, and he kept a flow of inspiration going out to maintain the momentum. Natalie had caught cold feet twice, but Manny spun a web of words that kept her motivated to make the move.

Under the pretense of playing it safe, Manny instructed her to hide her money in the room with Rosa to avoid having her disloyal act prematurely discovered be her soon-to-be-ex-pimp. She added to what was stashed away, and there was no doubt that she would follow her money. However, having the situation already so far gone in his direction did not stop him from thinking of what his opponent could've done better to offset such an outcome. Manny knew it could've just as easily have been him in this position, and at the end of the day it was not in his nature to wish bad on anybody who played this game.

That said, the law of the jungle still stood, so he wouldn't hesitate to benefit from a flaw in a fellow player's game. Sympathy played very little part in the art of pimpin' at its best. Therefore, no mercy would ever be shown when it came down to deciding winners and losers.

$$$$$

As the night came near to its end, Natalie nervously came through the door to Rosa's room. All she had was her few belongings and a lot of anxiety, but she was ready and willing to follow any and all instructions.

Seeing someone else's life possessions stuffed into a pillowcase brought back memories to Rosa's mind of being in that same situation. After directing Natalie to take her cell phone apart, a text was sent to Manny immediately.

"She's here. Wish U were 2!"

Manny replied quickly: "OK. On my way. C U in 2 minutes."

Rosa was relieved when she read the response. Then she turned to Natalie and said, "OK, we good. He promised not to go too far and said he on his way. From what I see, it looks to me like you had good reason to choose a winning team," she added with a little laugh to lighten the tension her reference to the pillowcase might cause.

Natalie laughed it off and explained her position.

"Girl, I can't even lie! They say misery loves company, and that shit might be true. Because it sure feels good to know that somebody else was doin' just as bad as me not long ago. Especially now when I see how much better it got for you."

That statement brought another question from Rosa. "Oh yeah? Is that why you decided to come home?" she asked casually.

Natalie answered as honestly as she could.

"I mean... I been havin' problems wit' ol' boy for a while now. I met him when he was broke with no hustle, but he fucked me good and I wanted a man, so I turned him into a P.

"The problem with that is, he got a baby mama who I saw he in love wit', so whatever I do for him, I'm really doin' for her. But that bitch ain't no ho, and if he can't get her to turn a trick when they got a whole-ass family to feed, I don't see why either one of them deserves my money.

"I'd rather be number two next to you than be the number one dummy comin' last after a broke square bitch. Because I can rock wit' a real bitch, but I refuse to ho for some broad while she sit on her ass, talkin' shit about me. So I'm out!"

Rosa was caught off-guard with the wave of authentic information. Her heart went out to Natalie as she spoke, because she too had come across so-called pimps who were really lust lazy men that wanted to take her money and live a lavish lifestyle without her.

These bums would use what she gave them to impress a bunch of non-hustling women who were never even asked to become prostitutes. But toward her they were hypersensitive about putting her in her place for even the slightest infraction. This was why so many girls were now working with each other or for themselves. Because men with real character were becoming hard to find, which is why she was single when she met up with Manny.

"Damn, girl... I feel you on that shit for real. You got me over here happy our Daddy is a serious weed head, because fuckin' with you, I really need to smoke right now," Rosa said somewhat sadly.

That's when they heard the music from Manny's car as he pulled up. Natalie rushed to the peephole in the door while Rosa peeked out of the window. They both made audible sighs of relief at the sight of the big Impala circling the parking lot once before pulling into the spot right in front of the room they were in. And by the time he'd made it from the car to the curb, Rosa already had the door open for him before he could knock.

He cracked a crooked little smile as he took in the whole scene. Natalie looked stressed out, and Rosa wasn't much better off. But they both sat at the little table with their money out in front of them in the way for which duty calls. Experience taught Manny that whenever Rosa rushed to give him her money like this, she knew it was a good amount, and she wanted to smoke.

"Awww, shit! It looks like hoes in here tryna handle they bidness today, huh?" Manny said in their general direction as he pulled a bag of strong sticky weed out of his pocket and handed it to Natalie. "How 'bout you roll us each a blunt to smoke while I check that money you got? Let's see if it's as correct as it looks."

Both girls went to work as he went to relieve them of their money. He put Rosa's contribution into his pocket uncounted, but the stack Natalie offered got more scrutiny as if he was trying to guess the amount.

"So how much are you givin' me lil lady?" he asked casually as he watched her break down the weed on the table.

She looked up for her task to be sure it was her he was talking to before answering the question.

"Ummmm... it should be about seven-fifty altogether," she said. "Woulda been almost a rack, but you told me to give away a couple hundred to my lost cause. But I'll put more with it whenever we get back to work, though."

Manny kept his face empty of any expression and addressed Rosa with his next questions.

"Hey, Rosie, do you know that as my ho your opinion don't got a damn thing to do wit' my pimpin'?" he asked unexpectedly.

She acknowledged that she knew this. Then he asked the next question.

"With that said, do you think that's enough for this lil pretty muthafucka to get on the team on a trial basis?"

Catching on quickly, Rosa played along and said, "Hmmm, I don't know, boss. Let's just say I think it's a good start."

Turning his attention back to Natalie, Manny said, "OK, we rockin' from here on out. But I'm holding you to what you say about adding to it."

"Thank y'all sooo much for the leeway since we all know I wouldn't make it through the night if you sent me to go get the rest right now!" Natalie chirped cheerfully.

And with the ice officially broken, the blunts were smoked while light-hearted talk established a comfort zone. After a while, both girls laid passed out on the bed as Manny sat on a chair at the table counting their money.

The day turned out to be a pretty good one, judging by the profits. But outside the motel room, the situation was taking a different turn.

Nobody took notice of the white truck pulling up outside, or its driver beating on the door to the now-empty room that Natalie had been working in. And nobody noticed this extremely agitated individual suspiciously eyeballing Manny's car as he talked to the old man behind the checkout counter in the motel lobby. Nobody saw it when this individual came out of the lobby with a look on his face that had taken on a deadly intensity as he locked eyes upon Manny's car. So nobody knew that this same individual got back into his truck, parked out of sight, and settled in to wait while he kept the Impala in clear view.

Before Manny drifted out of consciousness, he thought about giving a courtesy call in the morning once he was already safely on the road to inform the unfortunate ex-pimp that he had been separated from his income.

CHAPTER 10

MACKIN' GANGSTER

"I gotta keep a weapon, I need it for protection. So Lord please forgive me, it's time to apply pressure."

– Philthy Rich

The next morning, early enough so that the stars were still in the sky, the world was starting to wake up, yet still sleepy enough not to notice much. It was at this time that Manny got his team up and in motion, planning to reach Las Vegas as early as possible. His goal was to avoid being the only car on the road at late-night hours, which was an open invite to get pulled over by police looking to spice up their shift.

He turned in the room keys through the mailbox and warmed up the car as the girls got ready. Since all seemed to be going well, he allowed himself to start feeling comfortable with his position. But as soon as he did that, his years of street experience kicked into gear, and a feeling of being watched invaded his comfort zone as the two girls got into the car.

Glancing around revealed no one, but he had used his gun enough in his life to always expect that someone was hiding somewhere waiting to catch him by surprise. So when he got into the car, the chatter of the excited girls was only background noise to the narrative of his focus.

$$$$$

The owner of the eyes that were now aimed at Manny and his team was hyped up after hours of snorting cocaine to stay awake and alert. He smiled wickedly as he started his truck and slammed it into drive with intentions to ram into the beautiful car that caused all his problems. But the drugs had him moving so fast, he over pushed his plan and only managed to block the entrance of the parking lot.

Instead of trying to rearrange the position of his vehicle in order to achieve his goal, he grabbed a cheap little small caliber pistol from where it laid on the seat next to him. Full of courage from the controlled substance, he bounced out of the truck with no idea about what he planned to do next.

Pretty-ass pimp niggas think they can floss they way through shit without puttin' in no work. I'ma show this fool 'bout fuckin' wit' a gangsta, he thought to himself as he closed the distance between where he stood and the target of his anger.

The two girls looked terrified, and their driver looked like he was trying to duck down out of sight, according to the distorted perception of the drug-induced individual. He mistakenly read this to be the reaction to his sudden appearance and the gun he was holding. This encouraged his approach, increasing his pace in crossing beyond the point of no return.

While unbeknown to everyone else present at that moment, Manny went into a deadly kind of trance as soon as the big white truck appeared. *Uh huh*, he thought to himself, confirming his instincts as he quickly reached down beneath his seat. His gaze never left the fast-approaching man Natalie

82

had so recently decided to leave. He never showed a single shred of hesitation, surprise or fear. He just opened his door and waited, while collecting a stainless-steel revolver from its hiding place and wrapping it in a hooded sweatshirt he had in his immediate reach.

As the individual got himself placed directly in front of Manny's car, he aimed and squeezed the trigger of his gun.

But nothing happened.

Again, he squeezed with more force, this time as if he could force the shot to come by willpower alone.

But still, nothing.

In his rush to get things going, he'd foolishly forgotten to cock his weapon, leaving him unprepared in a situation where preparation made the difference between life and death.

Manny flew into action in a blur of motion as the individual's expression melted from fury to folly before it settled into pure fear. From the bundle of the sweatshirt in his hand, Manny popped a muffled shot off that no one would've ever thought was the sound of a gun.

A hole exploded suddenly in the individual's shoulder as if by some kind of viciously harmful magic. Self-control is all that saved him when it was clear to see he was no longer a threat.

Instead of shooting again, Manny skipped up close and delivered a hard punch to the face before picking up the pistol that the injured man had dropped. Then he savagely stomped the fallen form into unconsciousness and dragged the limp figure into some nearby bushes.

After that, he hopped up into the big white truck and carefully moved it out of the way for purposes of making his escape. The entire episode of bloody violence took no more than two minutes, and nobody in the early morning traffic noticed what took place behind the truck that blocked their view from the street as they passed by.

Manny calmly got back into his car and pulled off into the flow of traffic. He noticed the tense energy in the atmosphere of the Impala's interior, so he broke the awkward silence with a little comment.

"I bet he won't be tryin' that again anytime soon, huh?" he said in a gravelly voice. Natalie was the first to respond.

"Maaaan, just remind me not to ever make yo' crazy-ass mad at me," she said. "It look like you a little bit too good at that kind of shit."

When Rosa noticed Manny laugh at what he'd heard, she decided it was safe to make a request. "Can we please smoke, or somethin'? I'm about half a step away from havin' the shakes right about now."

"Yeah, go on and roll up," Manny replied.

Manny kicked the bloody shoes off his feet and reached them up from the floor back to Natalie. "Toss these out the window and make sure no Highway Patrol sees you do it."

Both girls followed the instructions and did what they could to help bring him the rest of the way out of the dark place he'd slipped into. But neither one would ever forgot what they had just seen him do.

$$$$$

It would be naive to ever believe that any one place or person had a monopoly on being worthy of respect in the streets. So the biggest mistake a man could ever make would be underestimating another man in this game.

Underestimation can take many forms, and this is the truth about many details to the universal laws of the jungle. And in spite of Manny not breaking any of its laws, the jungle creed still found him guilty of overlooking a critical detail.

An enemy left alive could become a deadly threat to a player in a game where episodes of murder are thrown back and forth like balls on a playing field. And having a higher score means nothing when a single point against you can take you completely out of the Game.

Such was the situation that began to take shape when the individual left mangled in the bushes finally opened his eyes. Some form of retaliation was a must in his mind, and murder became his agenda. He wanted to kill somebody; and anybody would do as long as they had a connection to what he'd just gone through.

So as the paramedics worked on his body, he worked on his own personal plan. His mind was numb to the pain, occupied with plotting out what he would do once the opportunity presented itself...

CHAPTER 11

LAS VEGAS

*"Dusted and disgusted, these bitches can't be
trusted, you know the rules. They underhanded,
she planned it, you fuckin' fool!"*
– Tupac Shakur

A few weeks later in Las Vegas, Nevada, Manny was right
next to the Vegas strip off I-15 highway on Tropicana as the
sun went down. The lights of the strip started to twinkle
while hot chocolate was sipped in a small cafe, and Manny
was deep in thought.

Still being unsure about Natalie made him hesitate to get
an apartment right away. He wanted to break her in without
letting her know where he lived before he knew if she'd stick
around or not.

It wasn't anything she did or didn't do, it was just an
overall feeling after the drama of the first day they met,
which was hard to shake. There was something about the
way she who was unconcerned about what he'd done to
someone who was so recently teamed up with, and how she'd
so obviously joined his team because of how enjoyable it
looked.

If his guess was right, she would be gone as soon as times
turned even a little bit bad. So in spite or her getting along

well with Rosa, all Manny could see was a girl who had no interest in any permanent position for herself.

Manny's mind recalled something his uncle had once told him about fly-by-night hoes.

"Every bitch don't come to a pimp with her heart set on contributing to his come-up. There's a lot of hoes out there only tryna win off the light of your shine for a moment in time before they fag off on another mission they fail to complete.

"These fly-by-night hoes leave a long trail of short-term attachments that never turned to nothin' because they just scattered their energy in too many directions. Small minds pay small attention and usually only get small results."

Manny sensed just a condition in Natalie's demeanor because of how little resistance he ran into when he got her. He knew that any good provider would have enough pride to at least act unsure about if she wanted to choose someone new, because investments and reputations should always be considered, and the only people who don't observe that rule are the ones with no business concerns or zero respect for the game they're in.

These were old lessons being kicked around in a new situation by a pimp over a cup of hot cocoa as his prostitutes practiced their profession.

Until a text from Rosa buzzed him out of his brainstorm: "Hey, just heard 'bout a cowboy event in town. Should be good, huh?"

"OK, where is it at?"

"Bottom of the strip, I think."

He could tell she was already wanting to try it out, so he decided to support her.

"Sounds sweet. How is UR wifey?"

"She cool. I like her so far."

This was no surprise at all. Natalie wasn't a bad fit in any way. She just happened to be of questionable character. So he kept his thoughts to himself and offered instructions instead of private opinions.

"OK, then, come check UR dough in. Get fresh N get back @ it. Maybe catch us a big fish," he replied.

Landing a big fish was Manny's term for describing the act of robbing a customer who had a lot in his possession. Expensive items and large amounts of cash were the desired targets in this kind of situation. But it could go badly for a girl if she was caught in the act.

The risk would have to be outweighed by the reward, or Manny would usually advise against making such a move. But in coming to Las Vegas, most players had high hopes for an opportunity of the overnight riches landing a big fish could provide.

$$$$$

Freshly dressed and rested, inspired greatly by the speech they were given before coming back out to play, Rosa and Natalie were both serious about getting as much as they could that evening when they started their mission. From the top of the strip, they worked their way down to the bottom where the cowboy convention was in full swing. So when they arrived, both girls had enough money earned to have room to hang out and mingle once they found the right bar and casino where most the cowboys were.

Slot machines made the chatter of background music as the girls searched through the selection of potential victims. As each new man approached them, both separately and together, certain questions were asked, observations were made, and decisions were reached.

Rosa kept a specific preference in mind as she led Natalie through each encounter, bypassing casual solicitations and focusing on the goal of a more involved opportunity. The target they were trying to hit had to fit a very narrow description. So by the time the evening started to get late, Natalie thought her co-worker must not even want to actually find what she claimed to be looking for.

Then, suddenly Rosa returned from one of her many trips to the bathroom with a two-man escort. Natalie watched from the bar as they caught eye contact with each other. This gave her a chance to cut short a fruitless conversation she was having at the time, and make her way toward the approaching trio.

"Hey girl! I thought maybe you went home without me," Natalie said as she approached Rosa. "Who are these two big stud muffins?"

"Oh, this is Jerry and his uncle, James," Rosa replied sweetly. "They're here from out of town. And would you believe they've never tasted Mexican before?"

Eyeballing the younger of the two gentleman who was obviously interested in her, Natalie put on an exaggerated show of surprise.

"What? Oh, we can't have that now, can we?" Natalie said. "Sounds like somebody needs us to feed them all they can handle!"

That was the beginning of how the two girls skillfully led the two men down the road to becoming the "big fish" that each woman was hoping for. Drinks flowed freely from that point on, but Rosa and Natalie somehow managed to spill most of every drink, acting far more intoxicated than they really were.

The men were encouraged to drink every drop of what they got as quickly as possible under the belief that they were impressing their dates with the show of machismo.

The talking never stopped, the drinking never stopped, the touching never stopped, and the calculating observations of everyone's condition on Rosa's part never stopped. She was the director of the play, while Natalie was just a character and the two men were their audience. Little cues given here and there were readily responded to, and when circumstances were at their best, Rosa steered the action toward the motel room the guys were staying in.

"Sweetie, I think I wanna see what you workin' with in those sexy Wrangler jeans," Rosa whispered into the ear of the older Mark as she watched Natalie flirt with his nephew. "Maybe you can tie me up like a calf and show me how you ride it?"

"Ma'am, I reckon you might be onto something with that thought," he mumbled back to her as she pushed his hand down between her legs.

"Well, then let me take a last trip to the ladies' room before we go. I gotta bring my cousin so I don't fall down or get lost. You guys can meet us there after you take care of the bar tab, OK?" Rosa said as she grabbed Natalie's arm and made her way out of the cowboy's earshot.

Once they were far away enough to talk without being overheard, Rosa quickly gave Natalie the game plan.

"OK bitch, we got us a good one! These dudes are part of a ranching family from Wyoming. The uncle owns it and the nephew is the spoiled son of the old man's sister who I think is the co-owner.

"Anyway, they 'bout to take us to their room. Soon as we get there, I need you to get yours in the shower. Make sure you can hear ya phone, though! I'ma put the old one to sleep, clean they asses out, and text you when I'm done. You just make sure you get the pants off yours before you go to the shower, and I got the rest, OK?"

Natalie struggled to keep up in the midst of her excitement.

"Damn, ho! How you know all that?" she asked in awe of what she'd just been told.

"I ask the right questions, and I peeped that fat-ass watch the old one is wearing. That's why I snagged 'em for us," Rosa mumbled to her as they entered the bathroom with the two drunk marks already trailing behind them.

When they were out of sight, they went over their plans again, touched up their make-up, and smiled at each other in the long mirror before stepping back out on stage to continue their play.

$$$$

The tricks were so drunk and horny that they were just about ready to do anything the girls asked, as long as it kept them from leaving. Once they were back at the cowboy's motel room, making out on each of the twin beds in the dark, Natalie went into playing her pre-planned role...

"Oooooh, baby, you got me so hot I think I need a shower, and you should wash my back. You're about to get very lucky in there, mister," she murmured into her victim's ear after she got his pants off on the promise of a blowjob that would never quite take place. She was down to her bra and panties, so it wasn't hard to believe her sincerity as far as her inexperienced date was concerned.

When they were up and safely out of the same room, behind the closed door of the bathroom with the shower on full blast, Rosa made a show of being relieved that she was finally alone with the man she had in her clutches.

"Mmmmm... Now I can really feel free to rock your world without an audience," she said seductively as she took complete control in preparation of wearing the man out.

"Little lady, all I ask is that you have mercy and patience on an old fella," he said as he laid back to let her have her way.

She got up for a moment, only to return without her clothes. Wasting no time at all, she knelt down in front of him and removed his pants before pushing his legs apart. When she peeled his boxers away from his dick, it was as hard as nails and ready for some serious action.

Rosa took his dick between her lips and deep into her mouth. The cowboy enjoyed the sensation of this sexy young exotic woman face-fucking his manhood.

Carefully making sure that he didn't shoot his load off into her mouth, she switched up her attack to make things start to really get interesting.

She climbed up into a sitting position with his face as her seat. He accommodated her as if it had been his lifelong wish all along. He began licking her clit while playing with her wet pussy lips as she spun around in a reverse cowgirl that could've become a sixty-nine at any moment. He continued his attentions and she jerked away at his joystick.

She drew her nails up his shaft, scratching the skin lightly. He gulped at the feeling and twitched at the way she tickled his stem. Then she increased the pressure of her pussy on his face as she opened her mouth, leaned over, and swallowed his entire length in one go. She completely devoured him down to the balls and he gasped against her pussy while she deep-throated him for a short time.

In doing this, she skillfully rolled a condom onto his pulsating penis without him even knowing it. And now with that done, she pulled away only to throw herself back in the saddle. However, this time she was slamming herself down onto his dick.

She pulled him in, powerfully clamping him by the waist with her knees. Their hips slammed into each other hard and fast with an aim at overwhelming him. She let her nails rake his chest, she pulled his hair, and she slapped his face.

He thrust himself into her as fast as he could, his hands groping her breasts roughly as their strokes met in the middle. He moaned loudly as he lost the power struggle they were engaged in, but Rosa wasn't after a submission, she was going for a knockout. So she fucked him and fucked him, and after five more pumps, he came.

The alcohol and intense exercise worked like a tranquilizer pill, and in no time he was sleeping like a baby. Snoring loud with his pants pulled inside out, down around his ankles, he never stood a chance.

Rosa sat still for the time it took him to slip into the deep sleep on an intoxicated blackout. Then she slowly untangled herself from her victim and silently got dressed before going to work on the next part of her mission.

After sliding the pillowcase off one of the nearest pillows, she filled it up with all the money in the pockets of both men's pants, and both of their gun belts, complete with bullets and revolvers.

She went through their luggage and found a bigger stash of cash in each man's bag along with car keys. She took all she found before returning quietly to the sleeping form of her victim. Then, ever so slowly, with the utmost care, she took the huge, eighteen-karat gold watch off the wrist of its unconscious owner.

Upon hearing the ring of her cell phone over the noise of the shower, Natalie giggled her way out of the extensive episode of foreplay she'd been dragging out and made her exit with one last lie.

"Hmmm... I think I got us a condom in my purse, and you're gonna need it for sure, you beautiful man. I want you to give it to me right here in the shower. Wait two seconds and I'll be right back, OK baby?" she said in a sing-song voice as she left him in the shower with his head spinning.

The trick was in heaven as he waited happily in the shower with his manhood at full attention. Never in his wildest dreams would he have ever expected to be so lucky. But it would've taken that same stretch of his imagination to ever conceive of just how unlucky he and his unconscious uncle were about to discover they both turned out to be.

$$$$$

Off location at a late-night dog fight, Manny smoked a blunt of some good Purple Kush as he watched two pit bulls quietly locked onto each other, wrestling for a deadly advantage. He passed the blunt to a White guy who happened to own one of the dogs in the fighting ring.

"Is that bud called Granddaddy Purple, bro?" the White guy asked as he strained to keep from choking on the smoke he was holding in while he spoke.

"Yep!" Manny said, distracted by the bloody action in front of him. "I like it all, but it gotta be at least this level or better."

"Man, I grow some shit even stronger than this myself. You should come check me out sometime. I'm Jesse, and if you like that black dog we're watching, I can show you his brother and sister, too. I own the mother."

That got Manny's attention, and their conversation increased from that point on. After introductions were complete and contact information was exchanged, the text message Manny was waiting for came through.

"Got one, Daddy," Rosa texted. "A real goody! We R N taxi now 2 get away. What 2 do?"

"Switch cabs ASAP! Then meet me @ the room."

"K. Will do!"

With that, Manny left the dog fight early to go check his trap. But as he turned the key in his ignition, his mind flew through all the possible outcomes of this situation. By the time he pulled out and aimed his Impala toward the motel where he'd meet the girls, he had an entire plan in place on how to approach them.

$$$$$

When Rosa and Natalie hopped into the second taxicab, Manny's reason for telling them to do so became clear as the new driver carried them further away from where he'd picked them up. Now the distance between them and the scene of their crime felt greater, and the only connection was left behind at the switching point.

On the way out of the hotel, Rosa had stopped in the parking garage and chirped the alarm button on the key ring as she walked around until lights blinked on a big Ford pickup truck. Both girls quickly searched the truck before they continued on their getaway. They found an additional stash of cash, another large handgun, and some credit cards. Rosa tossed the cash and gun into her bulging pillowcase and left the credit cards behind with the car keys.

Now, as they approached the motel, both girls looked around for Manny's car, which was noticeably absent from the area. Excitement blended with anxiety in their hearts when they paid the cab and made their way up to the room to wait impatiently for Manny to show his face...

$$$$$

On the other side of that same situation, Manny sat behind the cover of a slot machine in the minimart across the street from the motel. He watched the girls exit the taxicab, knowing they'd be wondering where he was. But he also knew that before he went anywhere near them, he needed to be certain that no law enforcement was on to their location.

He sat there for a while after his team went inside and watched all the traffic around the motel to be certain they were not followed. When he was sure that it was safe, he slid off the stool cautiously to walk over to the room instead of driving. He left his car parked at the minimart out of sight so as to not announce his arrival.

It was a very tense walk that had his eyes everywhere as he made his way as indirectly as possible to the motel room where his team was waiting.

The text alert on his cell phone was going crazy, but he knew it was them, so he didn't do much more than glance to make sure it wasn't a warning before returning his attention to watching everybody's back.

Before using his own card key on the door to let himself in, he stood there silently for a moment, listening to see if he caught any noises from inside that he should not be hearing. But Rosa was also on high alert, peeking out of the window to see him, and she opened the door for him with no though of what he might be trying to do.

"Whew! I'm do glad to see you, Daddy!" she said with extreme enthusiasm.

Both girls went into a chatter as they gave Manny the play-by-play on how the move was handled. He listened closely to get a clear picture of the situation before he spoke on it.

"OK, sounds like you played it right," he said slowly. "I bet those tricks never woulda guessed they was fuckin' with two real hyenas on the hunt when they came across y'all, huh?

"Maaaan, you shoulda saw Rosie steer them fools like they was puppets, Daddy! This ho been around you for waaay too long. All I had to do was keep mine distracted while she peeled 'em like some bananas," Natalie declared as she continued to count the money for the fourth time.

Manny glanced over at Rosa and said playfully, "Yeah, this bitch think she be peepin' game so she can do her thing the way I would do it. Ol' slick-ass muthafucka... But I kinda like her, though."

Rosa beamed with pride while she helped count the money and met Manny's gaze smugly. The smirk on her face wasn't quite a smile, it was just enough to show that she was feeling good about herself.

$$$$$

Success brings its own brand of intoxication that leaves little room for anything else. Out of habit alone, a couple of blunts got rolled up, but remarkably none got smoked.

Instead of weed smoke, conversation and compliments filled the air for the rest of the night.

When their energy was finally spent, the whole team ended up tangled together on the bed with Manny in between his two paper chasers. He had a big gold Rolex watch now on his wrist, and close to twenty-thousand dollars in cash tucked away.

On the floor next to the bed were two forty-four magnum revolvers and a forty-five automatic pistol. The handguns laid there in a row like a deadly set of power tools ready for use.

$$$$$

Early the next day, the weed got smoked, the room got paid for, and the girls got sent to work like any other day. But those guns sent Manny up to Jesse's secluded property under the pretense of seeing his dogs, with a real plan to hide the weapons rather than having them in that motel room waiting to become felony charges.

$$$$$

Having Manny so far away in another county an hour up from Las Vegas allowed for confidence to work against Rosa and Natalie. They worked at a slower pace and then recklessly drifted back into the area where they'd robbed the cowboys to make up for their unimpressive results.

It wasn't long before they were spotted in a crowd by their victims who then made a citizen's arrest on Rosa while Natalie ran away from the confrontation.

The last thing Rosa saw of Natalie was her leaving the scene before a group of angry cowboys surrounded her and tackled her to the ground. She never saw her attackers coming and would forever wonder if her co-worker chose to escape without warning her in order to remain safe.

Her next stop was the police station, and her night ended early with her going through the booking process...

$$$$$

Natalie wasn't much of a fighter, so fleeing the scene was her only option when faced with the unexpected threat of danger.

When she felt sure she'd gotten away from the enraged crew of cowboys, she paused to think. The goodness in her wanted to call Manny at first, but with the phone in her hand, the image in her mind of how he'd react to her leaving Rosa like that made her hesitate.

Women's intuition had already let her know that Manny wasn't overly fond of her as of yet. He was always cool, but remained distant and watchful with her for some reason, so her connection with Rosa was what she'd been thriving on.

Now she had just destroyed that bond in a major way and didn't want to face Manny alone with such a truth about herself being known. So when she finally found herself at the Greyhound station, her fingers dialed the only number she could think of...

$$$$$

Petey Rock was the name of the man Natalie left when she teamed up with Manny and Rosa.

He wasn't really from Fresno, but when she turned him on to the Game, that was where they got their start together. He was actually from a rough little town called Tulare, a few miles outside of Fresno, and Natalie knew him well enough to be sure he'd want to get back at Manny more than he'd want to punish her for leaving.

"Who the fuck is this?" he growled into the phone in the place of a polite "Hello."

"It's me, Nat," she replied after a brief hesitation. "Can I come back, or is you gonna fuck me up when you see me?"

"Ho, you know you need yo' head busted! But where that nigga you was wit'?" he asked, just as she knew he would.

"Maaaan, I'm not tryna fuck wit' dude. You just be havin' me hot at you sometimes with yo' baby mama. But I got you some money, though. So... what's up?"

"Yeah, OK. But I still need to see ol' boy, though."

"Well, I can tell you what I know about him when I get there. Is it cool to call when my bus arives?"

"Naw, bitch! Just get the ticket while I'm on the phone!" he said desperately trying to keep this opportunity from slipping away.

With a small smile in place, Natalie did what she was told. Running low on loyalty left her feeling no remorse about what she was doing, because all she saw was the next beneficial situation.

But Petey Rock's vision was showing him a whole other set of possibilities...

CHAPTER 12

SEPARATION & REUNION
"Chicken one day and feathers the next."
– Old Pimp Saying

During the following few weeks, life flipped completely from what it had been. On the night Rosa was arrested for the robbery of the two cowboys, Natalie ran off, never to be heard from again. And to make matters worse, the cops called Manny on his cell phone from Rosa's cell phone trying to connect him to the crime. But he was smart enough to play like there was a bad connection, and then remained where he was, in the small town two counties away from Las Vegas.

It was impossible for him to know if Rosa had in any way implicated him in the crime or not. It was torture to have to guess about it as it unfolded beyond his control. But those were the cards he was dealt, so his only decision was to make no decision at all.

He refused to set himself up by going anywhere near her, but he also refused to leave her in Nevada all alone in case she found a way to contact him needing him to pick her up. The next month was spent in limbo where he was stuck between his duty to Rosa and his duty to remain free.

In a lost fog of confusion, he spent that time up on the mountain with Jesse, drinking beer and smoking weed until their minds went blank each night. He slept on the couch and helped with odd jobs Jesse had each day as a general handyman around the town.

The days were a nightmare of living in fear of what Rosa might be telling the police, so all his waking moments may as well have been tossing and turning in his sleep.

$$\$\$\$\$\$$

In the meantime, Rosa was just as lost and confused. She was just as unsure of what she should expect Manny to be doing as far as loyalty was concerned.

After the detectives took her phone and searched the text messages to zoom in on Manny, she felt a sense of doom when she imagined what he must be thinking once they called him. And never being to jail before gave her no points of reference about what the outcome of this mess would be.

Deep down inside she was scared to death, but she held on and did her best to stay strong. While she was surrounded by girls who were falling apart, trying to convince her that it was OK to put it all on Manny like they were doing with their men, Rosa chose to believe in something else. She chose to remember the better times, lay on her bunk and stay to herself. She pictured Manny eating giant oysters with Tookie on their trip to Disneyland, and she held onto that.

As far as the east is from the west, she was a long way from letting him go. She closed her eyes at times to remember the sky, and she wondered if he saw the same sun or moon that she imagined. This sustained her with a feeling in her heart that they were somehow still connected. So in spite of them being apart, the realness of their intentions proved to be stronger than any reason to have doubts.

It wasn't easy in the face of Manny missing court dates and not coming to visit or answer his phone. She never even knew if he was still in the same state or not. But her hope was all she had to go on, and if memories served to soothe her like this, then she would make a vow to create more in the future.

Then, finally the lawyer came with a plea bargain from the District Attorney that would set her free. All she had to do was plead guilty, and they would suspend her sentence if she would agree to do probation. This would get her released on her next court date, and she was all too happy to make that happen.

But there is a level of heartbreak that no shield can save you from which is widely available in jailhouse situations. It will do its damage undetected, sinking into the soul as sadness plays its games with your mind.

Over time it lives and grows, keeping score in a game nobody knows is being played. And no matter how much sweeter the situation was about to be in the immediate future, that pain would keep some degree of bitterness dwelling in the heart of whoever had to suffer from it.

$$$$$

Even though Manny refused to make himself available to any undesirable possibility, he still kept up with every court date without actually attending them. So when Rosa's mother contacted him on Facebook to let him know the news about the importance of the upcoming appearance, he knew he would need to show up for her.

It was the only way she would know he was there for her, so when she got out, she would know he had not left her stranded.

$$$$$

On the morning of Rosa's court date, Manny sat parked in front of the courthouse in downtown Las Vegas, watching the many people going about their business. Being a true student of human nature, he calmed his nerves by absorbing his surrounding population, trying to distinguish between the people who worked there and the ones that had legal issues.

He was alone in the midst of a moving crowd as he made his way through the maze of finding the correct courtroom. And once he did that, fear crowded his senses as he began to think every other man he saw was a detective there to arrest him.

When the bailiff finally called for court to begin, the prisoners shuffled in slowly to sit in the jury seats that were separate from the audience. One by one they entered, until at last Rosa walked in looking both sad and angry at the same time. Looking around at the spectators in general made it hard to tell if she'd seen him in the group at first, but then she looked up again and her eyes came straight to Manny, remaining on him until they called her name.

The judge asked her some questions, her lawyer spoke on her behalf, she agreed to everything, and the moment was over. She sat back down and it was somebody else's turn to be heard. But she would be released, and when she looked up to see Manny leave the courtroom, she knew all she needed to know.

He would be there when she walked out of that door, because he would always be around at the times that mattered most. And she took a grudging comfort from that fact as she got herself ready to wait for her release.

$$$$$

Meanwhile, Manny was outside trying to find his way to the back of the building amidst all the one-way streets. His mind kept coming back to how Rosa had looked as him from the restraint of those shackles, while his memory played out words to a song about not always being there when called, but always being on time.

It was crazy how life seemed to work so that you think you understand something, all the way up until the moment you realize you're just beginning to figure it out as your reality fits perfectly into the words you heard.

Manny found where he needed to be and parked near the curb, thinking these thoughts while somewhere in that building Rosa was thinking thoughts of her own.

But there was now a bruise upon their bond that would not show until it became a problem beyond repair. And their reunion would only serve to distract them from this, so that in ignorance, they would continue their journey together.

CHAPTER 13

BACK AT IT
"Don't pump ya brakes, bitch, break ya pumps!"
–Philthy Rich

"What you over there thinkin'?" Manny asked Rosa as she stared out of the window while they drove down the street.

She let a moment pass before answering. He noticed this and wondered what it meant. Then she said, "I wasn't sure you was gonna be there today. Didn't know what to expect after no word from you this whole time."

Manny digested her response before saying, "I can feel you on that, because I can put myself in your shoes. But it don't sound like you put yourself in mine. I ain't mad at you, but ask yourself a few questions, though.

"If it was me in there instead of you, what would you do? When the police called yo' phone, would you have stayed around, or got outta town? Keep it real. And remember, the whole time you would be stressed out about wondering if I would tell on all the other shit I've seen you do. Be honest and tell the truth; what would you do?"

She kept her gaze averted with tears in her eyes, seeing nothing, but looking out the window. "I wasn't throwin' you under no damn bus. But when they called you, I knew you was gonna wonder. That's why I wasn't sure about what to expect today."

"Well. . . I was spooked fa sho, bitch, but I came anyway. So let's don't doubt each other over a cup of cold confusion."

With that said, he reached into the center console and pulled out an eighth of weed with a Swisher Sweet. He handed both items to Rosa and said, "Now, if I got my co-pilot back, can you process this so we can smoke?"

She smiled, poked her lips out, and proceeded to produce a fat blunt for them to smoke. They pulled into one of the many weekly-rate motels found all over Las Vegas and sat parked in the car, finishing the blunt.

Manny looked over at Rosa and said with all the sincerity he could squeeze from his heart, "Look, I know you ain't no damn psychic, so you can't see the future. But we gon' be OK if you allow that to happen. You just can't let this lil bump in the road scare you outta the Game, you feel me?

"Our money ain't funny, and these rooms pay by the week. So we got time for you to get your mind together, but when it does come time for you to get down, I don't want you to hesitate on yo' hoin'."

Taking his words in, letting them soothe her fears away, Rosa nodded her head and said, "You must've read my mind. I was hoping we didn't have to go right back to work, but I don't want you to feel like I'm holding back on you, either, because I ain't tryna lose you. So, I was just gonna see where your head was at. But would you be mad if I said I didn't want to ho no more?"

Now it was Manny's turn to nod his head. "Yeah, I think I would. But not for the reason you'd think. Because if I thought you hated this shit, I would tell you to quit. But if I felt like you was lettin' yourself be scared out of somethin' you are actually good at, then that's a different story. We can't have you backin' out on somethin' you can be the best at for a reason that ain't real.

"Does that make sense? I would never push you against your will, but I'd never sit there and watch you play yourself, either."

Rosa was no stranger to Manny's talent for saying more than one thing at a time, but she knew his words were true because he didn't sugar-coat them, and that was clearly appreciated.

When he saw this, Manny decided to throw her a curve ball with his next question, just to put her on the defense again.

"Since we're bein' all cute and curious, let me ask you this. What if on the day we met I would've said I don't want a ho in my life? What if I woulda said no thanks and walked off on you?"

This brought a smirk to Rosa's lips as she said, "I wouldn't be here now because I wasn't done doin ' what I was doin'. I woulda went about my business."

"So you sayin' that if I didn't choose a ho on that day, I couldn't have had you, right?"

"Yeah. At that time, that's what it was," she admitted.

Manny laughed out loud at that, completely confusing Rosa with his reaction. When he saw the question on her face, he shook his head and said, "Bitch, you so damn selfish! You lucky I got a lil bit of love for you, or I'd drop yo' ass like a hot potato right now. It's sad that you don't even see how fucked up you sound.

"How you gonna force me to choose a ho and then take that shit away on a change-up without thinkin' 'bout how far I had to go to accept you in the first place? Or is it that you feel like it's only about what you wanna do and fuck whatever I'm goin' through?"

With his point made, he hopped out of the car and made his way up to the room. Rosa jumped out after him and he paused to chirp the alarm so the doors would lock.

"Did you grab the weed?" he asked her when she caught up with him. His sudden change of mood left her not knowing what she should say, so she just nodded her head and followed him inside.

$$$$$

The only thing Rosa wanted to do at first was take a hot bath and relax. And maybe even cry a little bit. Manny ran her a tub full of sweet-smelling bubbles, then gave her a big hug before slowly undressing her.

When he got her naked, he took her by the hand and walked her into the bathroom to the tub. After sitting her down in the water, he knelt down beside her to wash her back. Extra attention was paid to her neck and shoulders, massaging her until she started to go limp. Then he kissed her ear and whispered in it.

"I'ma go roll us up some more of that real relaxation while you soak yourself. I'll be back, OK?"

Giving her some time to herself, he went to go roll up a few blunts for the night and ordered a pizza. He was in no rush, since he knew she needed room to get her mind right. And when he finally found his way back to the bathroom, he had a blunt lit so he could come bearing gifts.

Rosa had dipped her head into the water and her soaking wet hair rippled down her back like a black waterfall. The top of her breasts peeked out over the suds and the moisture had her shining as if her skin was made of silk. Her eyes were closed as she leaned back, and her face looked peaceful now that it was free of the stress and frustration that had etched itself into her features.

Manny hated to break the spell, but he didn't want her to fall asleep in the tub, so he spoke.

"You alright in there, cutie? I got some pizza coming, and if you go to sleep, I'm just gonna have to wake yo' sexy-ass up later. Plus, the water gonna get cold."

He held out a towel for her to dry her hand before he passed her the blunt. She hit it and inhaled the smoke deep into her lungs before letting it out slowly and repeating the process.

She was happy to be free, and she was feeling very good in that water at that moment. She could not imagine being anywhere else or doing anything else if it meant she had to be with anyone else right then. She glanced at him through the smoke and knew who she belonged to. With him it was all or nothing, but for her it was him or no one.

As for him, when he looked at her, he knew he would play his part. But only so she could prove he had a good reason to feel the rest of what he would never tell her he felt...

$$$$$

Three blunts later, with all the pizza gone, they were both high out of their minds and all over each other. Knowing the pussy would be good after sitting on the shelf for a month, and actually feeling his fingers touch the smooth, freshly shaved heat of it were two different things.

Manny could barely get the first knuckle of the two fingers inside her, but she melted onto them as he worked them deeper. He slid his other hand across her ribcage and up to cup her breast. Rolling the taught nipple between his fingertips, he was as excited as she was.

Rosa kissed him passionately and mumbled something meaningful into his ear that he never heard clearly. She tried again, and once more her words were muffled beneath his mouth.

A smirk tugged at the corners of her lips as she grabbed for his dick and undid his pants. When she pulled it out, she murmured something to herself in a husky voice and took him into her mouth.

Manny leaned back on the bed and she climbed on top of him, straddling him. Her pussy was already soaking wet from his fingers. She sank down onto his dick with one deep thrust of her hips, and her eyes rolled with pleasure at the penetration.

She rode him hard, and when he reached up to stroke her clit at the same time, she pushed his hand away, intent on finishing herself off on his dick instead.

Moments later, Rosa kissed Manny as she came breathlessly, and the feel of her tight pussy gripping him, along with the animalistic sounds she made, pushed him over the edge as well. He came so violently his vision blurred as he burst inside of her, and all he could do after was lay there panting with her draped across his chest until they both drifted off into a deep, satisfied sleep.

$$$$$

A couple of weeks later, the sound of her shoes could be heard by anyone she passed who cared to listen as she walked her way down the street, waving and winking and blowing kisses at the cars that drove by.

She couldn't hear the click-clack of her own heels, though, because her ears were filled with music from the MP3 player on her phone as it came through the Beats by Dre earbuds she was wearing.

Most of the people she passed would be more moved by what their eyes showed them when she walked by than anything their ears could hear. She was a seductive image of pure temptation in hip-hugging stretch pants that barely came up over her ass and left a gap of bare skin visible between them and a tight little T-shirt she wore beneath a waist-length mink coat.

Her make-up was flawless as always, with her eyebrows perfect and her lipstick making her lips shine with a color that looked like candy. Her hair laid straight down her back and over her shoulders, blending into the black fur of the coat she wore.

Pausing at the bus stop as the cops passed by, she tapped her feet and wondered what her day would bring. It was hard to guess from moment to moment out on the track because anything could happen with so many people trying to handle their business.

There were other girls trying to do their thing, and a lot of different kinds of pimps driving around, showing the many different levels of success. She noticed the latter from a distance and made a show of ignoring them as best as she could, while the former provided her a sense of pride when then grudgingly saluted her with their obvious approval or her man's car.

Manny passed by slowly with his music up loud, bumping the bass and causing the other girls to either whisper about how nice it looked, or dance a little bit to whatever song he was playing. A few even showed interest in her and Manny's program, but she was reluctant to bring anyone home after her recent experience with Natalie.

And yet, even in receiving all the attention she got, she was anonymous here, because none of the attention was given to her. It was given to what she showed of her body, the fake name she gave, or her man's car. But as far as who she was, that person remained unknown. But she just counted it as part of the hustle, and she didn't let it bother her too much.

$$\$\$\$\$\$$

Without knowing it, Rosa did have the undivided attention of someone that day. And as Manny's car disappeared from view, blending into the traffic, this person positioned himself to intercept her when she reached the corner.

Had she known what she was walking into, she would've gone the other way for sure. But watching her all day revealed to her stalker the best way to catch her away from where witnesses could see what he had in mind.

He waited at the top of the block behind the side of the building for her to come around, walk by, and let him approach from behind to block her from running back the way she'd come. It would've been better if the driver of that black Impala would pull over at some point to interact with her so he could catch them both together, but on this day, he wouldn't be so lucky. That particular target was too slippery

113

with how he faded in and out of the area so unpredictably, leaving just as soon as it was clear he'd come around.

The grudge that was held against them was far too engulfing to keep sitting on it without doing anything now that Rosa had finally been located again after the first time he saw her. She needed to know she had not gotten away with getting on his bad side; and through her, a message would be sent to Manny that could not be ignored.

$$$$$

Meanwhile, Rosa decided to call Manny to take her mind elsewhere for a moment. He answered on the second ring as if he'd been waiting for her call.

"Hello. You've reached the Therapeutic Pimp Project of Rosa's private paradise," Manny said playfully. "Please leave a message at the sound of the beep – Beeeep!"

She knew it was him and not a voicemail, but his off-the-wall antics got a laugh out of her before she asked, "Oh, so you the answering service now? I thought I was payin' the CEO. Can I come smoke whenever you become the boss again?"

Manny didn't like how slick she was getting, but he had to admit her comeback was kind of funny, though he kept it under wraps.

"No, you can't come smoke, because it ain't time for smoke breaks, bitch! But since you kinda cool, we can go out to lunch right quick. You hungry? I know all you really tryna do is rest yo' feet anyway."

"Yeah, well, don't blame a bitch for tryin'. What you gonna feed me?"

"Catch another date while I figure out what I got a taste for, OK?"

"Uuuuuggh! Let me call you when I get it, then, since it sure won't come while I'm yappin' with you," she said with a small sense of satisfaction.

She only needed that little bit of a boost, and he never did fail to provide it. After that, she regained her focus and continued toward the side entrance of the casino she was approaching with more purpose.

Rosa looked down to make sure she put her phone safely into her pocket and was not looking where she was going. So when she lifted her gaze to the path she was on, fear followed the surprised shock of seeing who was reaching out to grab her.

"Yeah, I bet you didn't expect to see me again, did you?" the lead detective who investigated her case grumbled through gritted teeth as she clamped his hand like a vice grip down upon her shoulder.

"You think nobody knows what you're out here doing? You bitches make me sick!" he said, snatching her arm roughly, pulling her toward him and putting his face right up in front of hers. "Come here, you fucking idiot! Don't you know I could make you disappear right fucking now? That goddamn pimp isn't here to protect you! You're only safe because I'm allowing it! This is my fucking city! Not his! So you let that motherfucker know that I'm going to catch him or kill him if he stays in Las Vegas! This is my house. And the house always wins!"

Rosa could smell the alcohol on his breath and said not a single word as he delivered his threats. She knew not to push her luck with a man so clearly on the edge, and anything that came out of her mouth would only be fuel to the fire, because she knew a trick when she saw one, and the presence of his erection poking her in the leg when he pulled her close left no doubt in her mind that he was nothing more than a trick.

He slammed her into the wall of the building and stormed off, leaving her relieved that she'd been spared any physical harm. But then the scandalous part of who she was found his hard-on humorous and she smiled at her proven power over this man.

She never even bothered to mention the encounter when she spoke to Manny again.

$$\$\$\$\$\$$

Later that night, while eating dinner at one of the buffet restaurants in one of the casinos, Manny dropped a bomb of a surprise on her.

"I think I got us an apartment or a house deal goin'. But I don't know which one we gonna get yet. I do know that this is our last week in a motel, though." This was good news to Rosa's ears.

"Ooooh, for real?" she said excitedly. "Why don't you know which one we gonna get yet? You waitin' to see which one they let us have?"

"No, it ain't that. We workin' wit' enough money to pick and choose, so it's just what the best choice gon' be. But we might just do it like some bosses and get 'em both so you can do yo' probation at the apartment while we live worry-free at the house."

"Oh, so we gon' be good no matter what, huh? That's right on time, too, 'cause I got this old man named Joe who gives me a whole lot for not doin' shit. Now if he try and play the boyfriend with me, I can let him think I live in the apartment, right?"

"Oh yeah? Joe, huh? You think he got some real money? Or do he just like you enough to make yo' job easy?"

She had to think about her answer for a second before she gave it. Joe didn't really dress too flashy, and his car was pretty basic even though it was a newer model...

"I'ma have to get in his business to know for sure, now that you askin' me about it. I just figured he was a good regular because he come spend with me every day. Was that wrong?"

"No, you not wrong, but when you make plans based on an outside muthafucka, you gotta get a real idea of what he workin' wit', you feel me?"

"OK. I'll know for sure by tomorrow. But for right now I think I need some more of that Chinese food before I go attack the Italian food. I got the munchies tonight!" she said with a giggle before skipping over to where the food was.

Manny watched her go, glad to have said something that made her so obviously happy. Little things like that made a big difference with his conscience, because there were other times when he didn't always feel so good about what he had to say or do.

But he had the munchies too, so with that in mind, he went to go grab himself something from the Mexican food section before indulging in the dessert dishes.

$$$$$

When something outside of yourself becomes worthy of your effort, it justifies all the things you do no matter what those things may need to be, because the ends will justify the means.

Manny realized this as a major truth when he pulled up into the yard surrounding the house he had just signed the lease to. The entire property was about two acres, and the house itself wasn't very big.

When they walked in the front door, Rosa was met with an image of herself in the mirror that ran along the wall of the living room. It was neat and clean with a lot of room and a fireplace.

"Is this really where we gonna live, Daddy?" she asked Manny in a voice that sounded far away to her own ears.

"Yes, this is ours," he told her.

Rosa walked from room to room, slowly exploring their new home. She stood in front of the China cabinet, flushed the toilets, and ran the water in the sinks. When she came back to where Manny stood, he handed her a key that was freshly made with a little cartoon face of a monkey smiling from the end where the key ring would go.

"That goes to the front door and the back door. Don't lose it," he said matter-of-factly.

The fireplace had little glass doors trimmed in brass. The kitchen had a breakfast bar like an island separating it from a den with sliding doors that opened into the front porch.

And the only view in the distance were mountains in every direction.

It was beautiful to Rosa, and as she wandered around taking it all in, her heart was touched by her surroundings in a way it had never before been touched.

Manny could see that she was deeply moved without her having to say so and he spoke on it.

"Well, you been runnin' the hell out yo' race, so you deserve this," he said. "We might use hotels and motels to handle our bidness, but we won't ever live in one, though."

She looked up at him, walked over to him, and gave him a hug. "Thank you," she whispered into his ear.

It was all she could think of to say...

$$$$$

Over the next few weeks, they enjoyed their new place, getting all the necessary furnishings and appliances. Rosa used her probation as a reason to start catching the Greyhound back and forth to California so she could work Salinas since it was safer for her to stay off the front lines.

Now Las Vegas was just an enjoyable home base, and her new out-of-town hustling status put a new polish on an old profession as she and Manny prospered.

CHAPTER 14

MINOR SETBACKS & MAJOR COMEBACKS

"Send 'em on automatic, I ain't gotta stay much.
They know what time it is, I ain't gotta say much."
                                                    - Pimpin' Tre

There was another arrival taking place as Manny and Rosa were coming into their own as a financial force, but it wasn't based on anything constructive.

Petey Rock had just made his way into Las Vegas with a very nervous Natalie and a mind full of malicious intent. When Natalie showed back up in California, he was there to pick her up. And with his shoulder yet to fully heal, he played the role of a nice guy, biding his time while Natalie patted herself on the back for the scandalous moves she made.

Over the next few weeks, Petey Rock picked her brain for all the information she could give him about how to find Manny. Before long it was clear to him that his adversary had been careful to make sure he kept Natalie in the dark about where he laid his head. However, she did know a lot about the places he went to get money, so she was tolerated until she revealed these spots.

But bosses move fast while bullshitters move slow, so after enough time went by without seeing Manny or his

Impala even once, paranoia poisoned the environment for the trouble-seeking duo. They began to bicker and fight about trivial matters as Petey Rock's shoulder healed and his patience wore thin.

He began to think Natalie was giving him the runaround, but the truth he never knew was that Manny was starting to go national.

$$$$$

Manny Fresh was emerging as the type who didn't have to go outside much in pursuit of his profits. He picked up money daily from Western Union, smoked his weed, and stacked his cash.

Every few weeks Rosa would come home and he would show her yet another unbelievable bankroll he'd saved up. His main motivation was her amazement. They complimented each other's ability with their mutual performances. Life was good and it steadily got better for them.

Then, one day, when Rosa was out of town, Manny got a call from a friend that would chance his life.

"Bro, you need to come to my barbecue tomorrow!" Manny's friend Gerald said to him. "My nephew out here and he be talkin' some shit I know you need to hear. What you know about the east coast?"

Manny was caught off-guard, but not completely. He'd heard all about the east coast and going cross-country before. All the old pimps he ever knew swore that a participant in this game had never really played unless he'd played on the east coast.

But Gerald wasn't a pimp, though. He sold weed on a large scale, running it back and forth from California. So now Manny had to question the source of his information.

"Oh yeah? I know a lil bit 'bout it, but I might have to come check you out, though. Make sure you ain't switchin' yo' hustle up on me, since you know pimpin' ain't yo' thang."

Gerald laughed at that and clarified himself.

"Naw, bro, you know know I stays in my lane, but my nephew got his lil potna wit' him and you came to mind when I heard them talkin'. I know you been sendin' yo' work outta state lately, but why send her back to the land when other spots do you better?"

Manny and Gerald talked a lot about general-hustle-type things on a regular basis, so there was no doubt about this being worthwhile.

"Yeah, I'ma slide through fa sho, big bruh. Good lookin' out. Tell ya boy don't bounce 'til I get a chance to holla at him."

They ended their call and Manny thought to himself that this was destiny reaching out to him. On his own he'd been looking into details about the east coast, but he had a real tendency to stick with what was working, so the little bit of info he'd gathered was unused as of yet.

But now it felt like he was being called to it instead of seeking it out. So maybe it was about time for him to make some real power moves...

$$$$$

That next day, Manny drove over to Gerald's house on the east side of Las Vegas. He was dressed casual with expensive accessories in colors that matched his Impala. He had on the gold Rolex watch Rosa had stolen from the cowboy, because he could not bring himself to sell it. It glittered so extravagantly upon his wrist, it made wearing any other jewelry unnecessary.

When he pulled up with his music bangin', people came from inside that party to see who it was that demanded to be noticed. All eyes were on him as he stepped with pride and purpose into the house.

Gerald enjoyed cooking, and the aroma in the air made it clear that he was having a very good time. There was a table in the kitchen with all kinds of food already on it, while the grill was going in the backyard and fish was frying on the stove.

Manny held a big bottle of Privilege Hennessey in his hand and raised it up to show Gerald when their eyes met over the small crowd.

"My nigga! Come crack that damn bottle," Gerald said loudly when he saw Manny. "Was that you out there tryna disturb my neighbors with all that noise? Half the bitches in here found an excuse to walk out there and now they all back inside. You might just knock you a ho in here if you ain't careful."

He reached into the cabinet and pulled out two tumbler glasses while he was checking on his fish. Manny uncorked the bottle and poured them both a drink, then he sat the bottle on the table for everyone else.

"Bruh, you got shit smellin' like a restaurant up in here. You tryna compete wit' the buffet or somethin'? Don't tell me those is hush puppies I see on that table! Man, you need to be sellin' this shit instead of givin' it away for free!" Manny said.

Gerald took a big gulp from his tumbler before he answered.

"Man, you ain't the only slick one in the building. Most of who you see in here buy weed from me, so in a way I am sellin' this shit. Get you a plate so you can hurry up and eat. My nephew in the back blowin' big already."

Manny got to work on stuffing himself and sat down in the kitchen out of the way. But a few of the ladies were still curious and found their way in there to catch a peek at him or try to get noticed.

Gerald had a cute little girlfriend named Shawn who seemed to know all the women in the party. Manny was tempted to pull her to the side and ask about a few of the girls he saw, but more than anything else, his mind was on the information he came to collect.

Manny ate everything on his plate but left room for the Barbecue that was next on his agenda.

"Look at Mr. Manny Fresh, all up in here Gucci'd down just so he can come pig out!" Shawn said to him as she held the platter full of ribs and links up for him to attack.

"This ain't all I came for, sis," Manny replied with his mouth still full of fried fish. "I'ma snatch a few of yo' friends up, too, so point out the go-getters so I can go get I em!"

She had to laugh even though she often tried to act like she didn't notice his antics. "Sorry, Mr. Fresh," she said, "but my friends ain't hookers. You don't want none of them."

Manny smiled, wagged his finger at her and said, "Not yet they ain't, but that's 'cause they don't know me! Let yo' lil bro work his magic and we'll see who's who when I get through."

He went back to his food while Shawn sat down the barbecue, shaking her head and trying her best to hide her smile.

A little while later, with most of the food gone and the bottle of Hennessey almost empty, Manny sat in the corner of Gerald's back yard with Billy Banks. Billy was Gerald's nephew, and he was a younger pimp from Sacramento, California. They exchanged information that filled in whatever empty spaces existed for each man in their area of knowledge and experience.

Other people were in the yard smoking blunts, but Manny and Billy remained apart from the rest of the partygoers. Gerald kept them in the rotation, passing the blunts between them and the rest of the people. Nobody else had access to their private conversation.

Manny: "So where you think the best place is out of all the spots out east?"

Billy: "Man, what if the ho don't wanna give you all the money?"

Manny: "What's the difference between D.C. and Maryland?"

Billy: "How you get them bitches to get along wit' each other?"

Manny: "You ever heard of Milwaukee?"

Billy: "It's more parts of New Jersey than a lot of people know."

On and on, the questions and answers went back and forth between them. There was a million dollars' worth of Game being discussed at a backyard barbecue through a cloud of weed smoke.

When they parted company, each man felt more confident in what they could do than they did before they had that talk. The Bible best explained what took place on that day: "As iron sharpens iron, so does one man sharpen another."

$$$$$

The next time Manny saw Rosa, he had a new plan in mind ready for presentation. He picked her up from the Greyhound station and headed to the apartment they had on the north side of town. They talked a little as they rode down Las Vegas Boulevard, with Manny mainly listening as Rosa reported on the details of her trip.

Communication was the most important part of Manny's hustle. Because without the understandings that can be reached through communication, there can be no relationship. And the relationship is the foundation upon which all else is built. That's why the old pimps say, "You gotta like who likes you." Because if there is no mental/emotional "click," you won't get very far with each other at all.

One thing Manny noticed in what he was told was the fact that, whenever Rosa got bored, she took all kinds of pictures of herself with her camera phone. So when they got back to the apartment, that was the point he chose to dig into the most.

"Hey, you know what? I need to see those flicks you been taking of yourself. You might have already been workin' on some shit that I was gonna introduce you to," he said vaguely.

They sat on the small couch in the living room and she leaned over into his lap with the phone, pulling up pics for him to see. Together they went through what she had with her pointing out the ones she liked the best.

"So what you been commin' up with in that monster of a mind you got, Daddy? I'm 'posed to sell pics out my phone or somethin'?" Rosa asked after a short while.

Manny pulled up a particular website on his phone's internet before answering. "Well, you almost got it right, except hoes sell pussy, not pictures. So the pictures are just a tool you use to help sell product."

Manny showed her the different classified ads on the site where girls offered their services as "escorts." She caught on immediately.

"Ooooh, I heard about this shit! These bitches be online with their phone number and pictures so the tricks just call who they like the most. Money come to them while they chill in the motel room."

Rosa was completely consumed by all the different photos she saw. Manny saw this and knew what he needed to say next.

"Them hoes ain't got nothin' on you. Some of 'em got professional photos done, but other than that, you can hang with the baddest bitches on there, you know that?"

She looked up from the screen to see if he was serious.

"You think so? I mean... I just take pics for fun. What if nobody calls me?"

Manny pointed back to her photos and said, "Do you see what I see? I see the same bitch who gets a stack a day in Salinas from doin' nothin' but standin' in the window so a trick can see her. So I know a whole lot of the people that see you is gonna want what they see. You just make sure you say the right thing when they call you."

"But how am I gonna know exactly what to say so I don't fuck it up?"

"I'm glad you asked me that because I want you to go undercover with me. I'ma call every ho on this site and act like a trick so you can hear how they talk. Just use yo' ho sense to pick up on how you need to play it from what they say, feel me?"

Rosa giggled at the idea and said, "Yeah, I gotta hear this shit. You playin' a trick? I wish I could record this!"

"Uh huh... You can laugh if you want to, but you better be listenin', too, bitch, because this is bidness," he said seriously.

They spent the rest of the night sipping pink Moscato and making phone calls to learn more about what they needed to know. And the next day he gave her the assignment of figuring out how to make her own account and upload the pictures to create an ad.

Within two days, they knew all they needed to know. But what Rosa didn't know was that this knowledge was not for local use. She figured she'd be able to rest her feet and still make her money, but the west coast didn't have the same cash flow that the east coast did, and Manny was more concerned with making it worthwhile than he was with making things easier.

$$$$$

One day Manny took Rosa to the movies before grabbing some drinks at a casino bar. She could tell that he had something on his mind, but had the wrong idea about what it might be.

"You OK, Daddy? You need me to get to work or somethin'?" she asked him.

Manny just looked at her, shook his head and said, "I want you to set up your ad online in the D.C. area. And every day until I tell you to stop, I want you to pick another spot where a lot of hoes post ads so we can see where you get the most calls from."

Rosa wasn't thinking big enough yet to understand what he was up to. "But we in Vegas, Daddy. I know you not stupid, but let me in on what you thinkin'."

He granted her request without any fuss.

"OK, here's the move. Wherever you hit the most is where we about to catch a flight to."

The flood of adrenaline she felt was like her stomach reacting to the sudden drop on a roller coaster ride. Things were about to get real, and Manny was ready to jump in on the deep end. That made her nervous.

"Oh... OK, Daddy. Can a bitch get another drink? And will you please promise you won't leave me out there by myself? That shit ain't like California."

"I got you like always, so don't trip. I ain't ever left you nowhere before I made sure you knew the spot and I ain't 'bout to start now."

"I trust you and I'ma do whatever you tell me to do. But I can't even lie, though... I'm kinda juiced that we 'bout to go national with our shit."

"Yeah, but let's get paid before we claim the fame. There's more to it than just sayin' we out there."

She watched him as he ordered them another round of drinks. Nothing seemed like it was beyond him, and she never knew what to expect next. The only thing she was sure about was that it was obvious he had been thinking about it for a while before speaking on it.

No time was wasted on wishing she could think and function at the same time like he did. Instead, she was just glad that he filled in that blank spot for her, because it was better to complete each other than compete with each other.

$$$$$

When the flight was booked, Rosa was pleasantly surprised to hear that they were flying first class. He told her that each of the fully-reclining chairs sat tucked inside their own private little cubicle. It would be her first time flying, and she couldn't wait to experience such luxury surroundings.

$$$$$

About an hour into the flight, after the lights were dimmed so passengers could sleep the four hours until breakfast, Manny rose from his seat and snuck across the aisle.

Nervous that someone would see them, Rosa quickly pulled him down and tugged a big fluffy blanket over them both.

"Good thinkin'," he muttered against her neck.

The grainy stubble of his goatee scraped against the delicate skin just beneath her earlobe. She writhed beneath him, rubbing her thighs together to try to stop the pulsing of her pussy.

"Oh... Allow me," he insisted as he traced his thick fingers along the line where her thighs met, tickling the sensitive skin through her spandex leggings.

When he reached the seam that bisected the crotch, he followed it up until he hit the bump of her cut. And although she tried to keep quiet, she couldn't help but gasp. Clearly, he didn't need to be able to see her body to know exactly where she wanted to be touched.

She pinched her bottom lip between her teeth, desperate to contain the sounds of pleasure she made as his thumb circled her clitoris. His hand moved a little higher, and his fingers curled into the waistband of her leggings.

"Let's get these out of our way," Manny said huskily.

He rolled her pants and underwear down her legs, pausing only to free her feet from the fabric. Then he nestled his head between her thighs.

"That's what I like to see," he murmured as he trailed a finger along her freshly-trimmed landing stip.

He nuzzled his nose against her pussy. "You smell so sweet," he whispered. "Just like candy." She reached down and pressed a finger to his lips.

"Somebody gonna hear you," she said softly.

He chuckled, puffing warm air onto her bare skin. "Ain't nobody gonna hear me," he promised. "Trust me; everybody either wearin' earplugs or earphones."

His hands moved over her slit. Using his fingers, he parted her folds, exposing her pussy to the cool air of the airplane, but he didn't allow her to remain cold for long. His tongue dipped inside of her, tracing its way up one moist pussy lip and down the other. On the first pass, he was careful to avoid her pulsating cut, but the second time around he hit the bundle of nerves head on.

Rosa bit back another moan, and Manny knew he had her. He teasingly asked, "Why are you so wet? Is it because I keep doin' this?" He sealed his lips around her clit and hummed a little tune, the sound creating a buzz that felt like heaven to her.

At that point, she didn't care who might catch them. She was so completely aroused that she was more likely to ask a passerby to join in than she was to stop him from doing what he was doing.

Deciding to just give in all the way, she rested her hands on his head and rocked her hips against him. Since he still had his lips wrapped around her clit, he released another long song that vibrated into her body.

"Mmmmm..."

The effects of that intoxicating rumble were similar to that of a sex toy, but he felt so much better. His mouth was warm, soft, and pleasantly pliant. He molded to the shape of her mound, ensuring that every nook and cranny was tended to.

Having his tongue dancing over her clitoris was maddening enough, but then he had to add his fingers into the equation. It only took two to fill her, and her reaction reflected how wonderful it felt. Growing impatient, she thrust her pelvis against his hand, leaving no question about what she desired.

Always attentive, he delivered. He worked his mouth and fingers in tandem to finish her off. As she came, she pushed the fluffy blanket against her mouth to muffle her groans. But if anyone heard, in that moment, she didn't care.

The second her body stopped shaking, he wiggled his way up her torso, bringing them face to face. He brushed his lips over hers. She could taste the tangy flavor of her juices. She loved the rare occasions when he ate her out. Having her unique flavor on his lips afterwards was a bonus – a not-so-subtle reminder that her man had seen to her needs.

His fingers caressed the tender skin at the back of her knee as he hiked one of her legs over his hip.

"Come on, baby, roll wit' me," he said seductively.

He reached behind her thigh and curled his fingers into the fleshy underside. In one smooth motion, he flipped their bodies so that he was now lounging on the recliner and she sat on top of him. He'd magically positioned her so that she was straddling his hips, with her knees resting comfortably on either side of him. It was the perfect position to enjoy an undeterred fuck on an airplane.

He reached down and took his hard dick into his fist. He moved it like a joystick, seeking the best angle to thrust it deep into her pussy.

The crown of his manhood entered the threshold, stretching her wide to accommodate his thickness. He gripped her hips, holding her steady as he pumped himself through the opening.

With him fully inside her, she groaned again. This time, she pushed her face into the flesh between his shoulder and neck, dampening the sound.

Using his hold on her hips to guide her, he bounced her up and down on his lap. He tried to keep the motion small and discreet, but their hunger far outweighed their fear of getting caught.

By the time she reached the finish line, he was lifting her so high that her head was undoubtedly visible over the little privacy wall surrounding her seat.

Cum shot forcefully from his dick, gushing into her pussy as it warmed her from the inside out. He dipped his face down, burying her breasts so that they absorbed his moan.

When he was finished, he looked up at her to pin her awareness down with a big, megawatt smile...

CHAPTER 15

KEEPIN' IT MOVIN'

"And you ain't done it unless you done it like in five states."

– Lil Wayne

Not knowing yet what the best place was to start on their money mission, they flew into Washington, D.C. since that seemed to be the center of the best area to come. Over the next few days, they got hotels all over town, one after the next, but soon figured out that the surrounding areas were where it was at.

Maryland showed to be better than D.C., and Virginia proved to outshine them both. The whole experience enhanced their hustle tremendously, and when they came back home, they were ten thousand dollars richer.

After resting up in Nevada, they paid their bills and made another trip straight to Virginia this time. City after city, they came and went, adding thousands of dollars to their bankroll whenever they departed. And it wasn't long before they found certain spots they both knew would become repeat destinations on their money route.

Then, one night, Rosa was told about New Jersey by a client who was in town from New York. Since Manny had already heard about a few places out there from Billy Banks, they decided to try it out.

They caught a short flight into Newark and got to work immediately. The first week was great and the weeks that followed seemed nonstop.

Taking a break one Sunday, they rode a bus over into Manhattan. They spent the day like tourist a couple, and New York was even more beautiful to them than either one had ever imagined it would be. They wanted to see the city all lit up at night, but didn't want to get stuck on that side of the bridge due to business concerns, so they left a lot sooner than they would've liked to.

When they got back, they ordered Chinese takeout and enjoyed the skyline of New Jersey through the huge window of the hotel room, as the evening rolled on by and the scene brought them closer together.

They ended up in Secaucus, New Jersey on their hustle, where Manny found a pawn shop that had some Tiffany jewelry in stock, so he bought Rosa a souvenir from Jersey to add into her growing collection to Tiffany & Company.

They tried out a few more places over the passing of the next few days, picking their favorites and collecting another fifteen thousand dollars. It made the west coast feel like they were doing too much in return for too little when one made a comparison.

In the eastern part of the United States, Rosa took being "Olivia" to a whole new level. She had not stepped outside to work one single time, and even if she went to sleep on the job, her money would call on the phone. It was almost too easy.

$$$$$

As the plane took flight from Newark, New Jersy, heading west, Rosa looked out of the window and saw everything from New York, clear up the Atlantic coast. In her mind, it felt like half the world was beneath her, all stretching out to be conquered by her and Manny.

It was the biggest and best she could ever recall feeling about herself. She looked over at Manny and caught him watching her as if he could read her thoughts.

He smiled and winked his eye at her before saying, "Did you know that you're beautiful when you're successful?"

"I could say the same to you, Daddy. But all that money in our bags probably already got you feelin' yourself enough.

"I can't lie, though; I do love you for all that you show me, and I think I'm proving it to you," she said, unsure if she had said too much.

Manny, being true to form, never failed to surprise her with the things that fell out of his mouth. "Well damn, bitch. You sure did say that shit, huh? Since you talkin' square bidness, why don't you go on and marry a pimp, then, how 'bout that?"

When he saw the confusion on her face, he filled in the blanks for her.

"I mean... Since you provin' it, feel me when I say I love you, too, and don't wanna be without you in this life if I don't have to. So, what's up?"

This was the last thing Rosa expected him to say. For some reason, it almost embarrassed her.

"You would marry me?" she asked him. "I'm your ho. And you made me a bigger and better ho since you found me."

"This is true, but I don't need to turn my ho into a housewife, though. Just my wife who happens to be my ho. I don't fuck wit' square bitches, so it's me and you, kid. Far as I'm concerned, we can make it official, if you want to."

With that said, he closed his eyes and dozed off for the rest of the flight. She was stuck with a lot to think about, but she'd never know that Manny wasn't sleeping at all, he just didn't know what else to say so he played possum to leave the conversation alone.

A few days later, they were at a little chapel in Las Vegas getting married.

$$\$\$\$\$\$$

The upward momentum of Manny and Rosa's life was a direct contrast to the downward spiral being experienced by the driver of a white Suburban who endlessly crawled around Las Vegas looking for them. Petey Rock often missed them by mere moments without ever knowing he had been so close. As they were getting married, he was on the other side of town fruitlessly scanning his surroundings in hopes of spotting the object of what was becoming a real obsession for him.

The pressure of his growing frustration gave way to violent outbursts that eventually sent Natalie running off again. This time she got with a young pimp from Texas after reaching her limits of tolerance for being beaten more and more each day.

Petey Rock didn't care. His hunger for vengeance consumed him in a hot, hateful fire that burned away all other concerns. And when the guy from Texas called to inform him about Natalie's latest defection, he flew into a fit of curses and threats to earn himself an abrupt disconnection.

All he had left was an old Springfield 1911 .45 caliber automatic pistol that he lovingly caressed every night before he went to sleep. That was his only friend and all the partner he needed. Nothing else mattered to him except catching up to this Manny Fresh and feeding a whole clip to him for what he had done. Only then could life continue to be lived again.

One day he sat in his truck, parked out of sight, watching the passing traffic, when he was suddenly sure he caught sight of the black Impala going by. This was finally his chance! But as he started to navigate the maze of turns and one-way lanes that led to the street from the casino parking lot he was in, it became clear that he wasn't about to be catching up to anybody anytime soon on that day.

Far from being daunted, this experience only served to stiffen his resolve. He knew now that it would only be a matter of time before he caught Manny somewhere slipping in these streets...

CHAPTER 16

THE GOOD, THE BAD, & THE UGLY

"They ain't wrote the book yet about what a bitch is gonna do next."

– Old Pimp Proverb

Less than two weeks later, Rosa was taking trips to the east coast on her own. At first it was just weekend runs that lasted from Thursday night until Monday morning. They would hang out all week and do it all over again on the weekend.

Manny thought things were going great, but Rosa privately began to hate the weekends out of love for the time they spent together during the weekdays. And when this became an obvious issue, Manny just kept her in Vegas, letting her work in the apartment they had while he stayed an hour away up at their house.

Rosa did not know how to tell him that she just wanted to be at home with him. She knew they had enough money put away to make it OK for them to be together more, so her unfulfilled desire turned her realness into something rotten, and she went the indirect route of allowing her performance to raise questions she didn't want to answer.

This is how love destroyed the growth of a good situation between a gifted pimp and what could have been a great whore. Manny wasn't too hard on her because they weren't hurting for money, but their savings suffered enough for him to notice the change in Rosa's level of enthusiasm.

Lies began to creep into their relationship to excuse the lack of good results. But the bad thing about lies is that they're only a temporary fix for a problem that will remain if unresolved, so before long, Manny caught on to what she was doing as well as what she was not doing anymore. When things should have been getting better, they were getting inexplicably worse.

Manny knew that somehow the "love" that he'd allowed into his program was now working against him, and that really hurt his feelings. But that was something he kept to himself, along with all the other secrets about emotional damage that existed between the two.

Smiles became strained, and trust was a difficult thing to maintain, as dishonesty became detectable without a clear understanding of where it came from exactly. For Rosa, the natural conclusion was that Manny must have a girlfriend on the side, since she was thinking from a more square perspective lately. This deflated her motivation even more than it already was, causing her lies to make even less sense in an indirect effort to draw Manny's attention.

One afternoon Manny called Rosa to address the issues more directly. When she answered, he knew it was time for the whole situation to come to a head.

"Hello?" she answered hesitantly.

"Sup, slowpoke? What you lookin' like over there?"

She didn't want to tell him that she hadn't even gone out at all yet so she lied. "I got about four hundred right now, but I'm on my way to another date for another one-fifty in a minute, so I guess it's moving along."

"Oh, yeah? That's cool. Go on and send me that on Western Union so I don't gotta drive down there. I'm tryna bust a move without goin' in the stash."

"OK... Let me get this other date out the way and I'll send you the five hundred."

"Yeah, OK," Manny said sounding unconvinced.

He hung up without saying much else. Her story sounded as weak as her actions were looking. And to her he sounded like he was onto her game. The last thing she wanted to do was answer for the lies she'd been telling, and if he showed up anytime soon, she'd be doing just that.

Rosa had been talking to her mother about the emotional side of what was happening in her life. Her mom lived in Texas and she was starting to consider jumping on a bus to escape the mess she was making for herself.

$$$$$

Manny knew something wasn't right, but he was trying to keep his cool. It wasn't easy when the lies were so obvious, and as time went by, the pressure continued to grow in his heart.

After a couple of hours went by with no word from Rosa, he called her back.

"Hey, let me ask you a question," he said when she answered sounding like she had bad news. "How much longer do you plan on tryin' yo' best to shovel me as much shit as you possibly can?"

There was a silence on the other end because Rosa was stuck for a response, so Manny drew his own conclusion. "Yeah, that's what I thought. I'll see you later, bitch," he said ominously before hanging up on her.

There was no use in arguing or listening to another lie, so conversation seemed pointless to him. Therefore, when his phone rang numerous times with calls from Rosa showing up on the caller ID, he just went out into his front yard and handwashed his car to occupy his mind. He figured it would be better to pick back up after she had handled her business.

But on her end, Rosa was in a panic zone, wondering why he wouldn't answer the phone. Was he on his way to beat her up? What should she do? The thoughts came as quickly as she could think them up, and each time she called without getting a response, her fear created its own answers.

She convinced herself that Manny wasn't answering because he was driving from the house to do her harm. He had real reasons to be very angry, so she was probably about to be hurt badly when he got done with her. She had to get out of there!

After making one last call to say good-bye, she made her way to the bus station in a hurry. She was going to her mom's house in Texas to hide out.

This all took place without Manny ever imagining that things were going so far. When he woke up the next morning and checked his voicemail and text messages, he found a mishmash of one-sided communication that made him seriously wonder of Rosa had lost her mind.

As angry as he was, he couldn't help but laugh to himself at how silly she was on her own. *This bitch done sat her stupid ass over there and chased her own damn self outta town*, he thought as he got up to roll himself a blunt.

Manny figured they would talk whenever one of them broke down and called the other on the phone. In the meantime, the Impala would need an oil change, and the rent was due on the house. A decision was made on the spot to let the apartment go since Rosa wasn't using it. Hating drama, he took his mind to practical matters that forced his focus on to what would count the most at the moment.

There was a redhead named Michelle working at the gas station who kept giving him the eye. It was now starting to look like the time had come to turn her out onto a new job...

$$\$\$\$\$\$$

A couple of days later, Manny had Michelle's phone number freshy saved among the contacts in his cell phone. He felt good about the possibility for turning her out, because there was a level of anticipation in the air when she gave him her contact information that bordered eagerness.

He refused to let Rosa's issue lead to his downfall, so suffering in her absence was out of the question. He had to keep pursuing his profession regardless of how he felt, because he'd been taught to not let one monkey control the show.

She called him on the phone, but it seemed like that was only to air out her built-up list of frustrations. This was OK, but it wasn't productive, and Manny wasn't going to sit and wait for her to get her mind right, so Michelle was a gift that the Game provided, and he was determined to make the most of it.

$$\$\$\$\$\$$

As Manny screwed the cap onto his gas tank, preparing to leave the gas station, he decided to let life be whatever it was, taking it how it came. He hopped into the car, charged up on positive thinking and a knowledge of being watched, turned up his music, and poured the Impala into the flow of traffic toward whatever the day would bring.

$$$$$

A few hours later, Rosa called him from Texas as he was getting ready to drive into his attack on Michelle's day-to-day existence. He started to ignore the call, but he felt like he owed her for the times that she did her best even while she was at her worst, so he picked up.

"Hello, this is the Abandoned Pimps of America headquarters. You've got the most abandoned pimp of all speaking."

His effort at humor paid off with a giggle from her. "Very funny, Mr. Abandoned Pimp. What you doin'?"

"If you wanted to know that, you shouldn't have put a whole time zone between us, you big dummy."

"I felt like I had to! I thought you was comin' to fuck me up!"

"Well, that was an issue between you and the lies you was tellin'. I ain't have nothin' to do with that. Anyway, though, why you callin' now if you need to be gone so badly?"

"I'm just callin', that's all. Life don't feel the same."

"Yeah, I hear you. Before you can think you know what you want, you gotta know what you don't want. You moved too fast without thinkin' 'bout where you would end up. That's backwards, bitch. Now the moment has passed and you find yourself fucked up."

"Well, I sure wish you woulda told me all that before I left! I didn't know what else to do!"

"Look, Rosie, I gotta bounce. You left a pimp with bills to pay. Figure out what you wanna do, and I'll be here doin' what I gotta do."

With that said, he hung up on her, and almost immediately she sent him a text message. "I luv U," it said. He didn't bother with responding so she sent another: "U don't luv me no more?"

To that he responded with, "I'm learnin' that luv makes pimps look stupid."

CHAPTER 17

COP & BLOW

"And now I never see your face, but that's OK,
I've adapted anyway..."

– The Weekend.

That night, Manny went to pick up Michelle so they could talk and hang out. He met her at her job when she got off and waited in his car while she showered and changed at her aunt's house.

When she came back outside, she looked sexy in a pair of skin-tight jeans that showed off her hips, and a little button-up shirt that showed off her cleavage. Her long, straight red hair was pulled back into a ponytail, and when she got into the car, she smelled fresh and sweet. She wore no make-up except a light lip gloss that made her mouth very noticeable in a natural, enticing kind of way.

She had a splash of light freckles across her nose and the tops of her cheeks. They could also be seen attractively upon her cleavage, disappearing down into her bra. Her eyes were a hazel green, but more green than hazel, with dark-red lashes that looked like they'd been brushed.

Manny liked what he saw and made a show of taking in the sight of her. She blushed under his attention, smiling brightly to show off a small gap between her two front teeth.

"Damn, Manny, you make a girl feel like she's on display when you look at her like that."

Manny smiled back and asked, "Does it make you uncomfortable? Because I can stop if you want me to, but if I don't have to stop, I think I could stare at you all night."

Michelle enjoyed the attention and didn't want his eyes on anything else but her. "Well, I had to let you see that I look different when I'm not in my work clothes."

"Baby, you better please believe that I already knew there was a whole lot more to you since the first time I saw you. But damn, girl!"

She looked at him and twisted her mouth in disbelief. "Then why did it take so long to get at me?"

He played as if his answer took some deep thought before saying, "I mean... I saw you look my way a few times, but I ain't so full of myself that I automatically think that meant I could get you. At first I just figured you never saw a guy like me before. Out of respect, though, I couldn't just run up on you like that."

His words caught her off guard with their unpolished sincerity. He strutted his stuff in a way that led her to never expect him to be humble. She thought he would be cocky, but he wasn't like that.

"OK, I can appreciate that respect. But come on, Manny! You gotta know you're hot when you look like you make sure every girl who sees you is gonna like what she sees. From your car to your clothes, you stacked the deck on being noticed."

It was good to hear such a candid description of the effect he had on a woman, but he started the car and got moving before he responded to her in order to not get too caught up in the conversation right then. Not that it would be a bad move, but he'd rather be in a better place when he made the kind of connection he could see they were on their way to.

Michelle did more than just spark his interest. She made alarms go off in his head that let him know he had someone who would follow his lead. That stimulated him into being more conscious of how he delivered his game because he knew what it could do.

After a moment he asked her a question. "Hey, tell me somethin', cutie. How is it that you're single? You seem smart and you're obviously attractive, so what am I missing?"

She gave him a sideways glance and said, "I don't have an appetite for the lame-ass dudes in this small town, and everybody down in Vegas is fake. There's not a lot of black guys here, and most of the white guys are into some hillbilly shit. What I'm into just hasn't been available, so I'm solo."

"Hmmm... That makes me want to know what you're into. You like space Martians or somethin'?"

"I knew you'd ask that next. But now you're trying to be funny. All you gotta do is look in the mirror and see who I'm with right now. Look at your car and how you fixed it up. That is all the answer you should need."

Manny liked that response. She seemed straightforward and solid enough so far. "I wanna take you out and enjoy something with you, Michelle. But at the same time, I feel like we need to sit down and talk ourselves into a good long conversation. Which one do you wanna do most?" he asked to see where her head was at.

Michelle looked lost in her thoughts for a moment before answering. "It's really funny you should say that, because I'm down for whatever you wanna do. You got me curious to see where this goes, though, so we can sit down somewhere to talk."

"I'm glad you said that. Because as beautiful as your body is to me, I really wanna just use your ears and mouth right now," he said enigmatically.

They drove on in silence for a short while until they pulled into the yard at Manny's house. A small smile played across Michelle's lips when she saw where they were. She was definitely OK with this, but her experience was too limited to ever imagine what all Manny had planned for her.

Pulling up to the house, he asked, "Is this cool? We can go somewhere else if you want to."

"No, I'm OK. It's good to see you trust me enough to bring me here."

Out of the car and up to the front door, he came up close to her as she walked in front of him. His nearness from behind turned her on a lot more than she wanted to admit to herself. He gently grabbed her by the ponytail and pulled her back into him, causing her breath to catch in her throat. Her heart missed a beat when his lips brushed her ear as he whispered into it.

"You smell so good to me, girl... Mmmmmm..."

Then he let her go and pushed past her into the living room. "You can have a seat on the couch for now," he said as if they had not just had a moment. "Do you drink or smoke?"

He was across the room on his way to the kitchen. She was still trying to catch her breath and calm down the sudden throbbing she felt between her legs. There were butterflies going crazy in her belly.

"I'll take a drink. What do you got?" She sat down to try and get a grip on herself. "Don't even trip, I got you," he said, winking his eye and disappearing into the kitchen.

She heard a loud "POP!" and the twinkle of glasses as they touched. Then he returned holding a bottle of pink Moscato and two glasses. He sat on the opposite end of the couch and placed the glasses between them. He snatched up the remote control from a nearby table and turned the TV on.

"Have you ever seen the movie, A Bronx Tale?" he asked her?

She said she had not ever heard of it. This seemed to surprise him. "It's a good movie," he said as he got up to put the DVD into the player and pressed play.

Michelle was very confused at this move, thinking at first when Manny grabbed her hair, she was sure that sex was on his mind. Then this champagne and now a movie instead of the talking he said he wanted to do. What did it all mean?

He saw the question written all over her face. He poured her a glass of the wine and offered it to her, saying, "This is to celebrate us getting into something new."

She took the glass and sipped it. She'd never had pink Moscato before, but she liked it a lot. They watched the movie and drank the whole bottle of wine, only to have Manny replace it with another.

When the movie was over, Michelle noticed that she was touched beyond what she thought possible. It spoke to her heart in a way that made her want to cry.

The racial issue addressed in the movie were so powerful that it sent messages to her subconscious. Wow! She looked over at Manny and saw a little bit more that she did at first. She also found herself wanting to know more about the mind that would choose such a movie, as well as show more of herself to such a mind.

"So what was I supposed to gather from that movie, Manny?" she asked. "Did you not get anything from it?"

"Yeah, I did. But that's why I feel like you had to have that in your plan. It seems too meaningful. So, what were you trying to show me?"

The sparkling wine had removed whatever inhibitions she may have had. And Manny had to look at her to convey his meaning in a million different ways before saying, "It was just a movie that I was hoping you enjoyed as much as I do."

He saw the slight disappointment in her with that answer so he added a little more to it. "If I had to get all deep wit' it, I would say that the black girl and the white boy each thought that their world was complete, but without each other they would've never known the beauty that they brought to one another's lives. And that beauty came from something separate from what they came from. You can also say that, just because a person is different, that don't mean they're bad, and just because they're bad, that don't mean they not still cool, you feel me?"

Michelle gulped down some wine before saying, "That was kinda beautiful in its own way. I see you got levels to you that people don't see on the surface."

Manny turned the bottle up and finished it off before going into the kitchen to return with another. Michelle's eyes opened wide with surprise.

"Damn! You got it like that? That's the third bottle in a row!"

Manny laughed at her loudness. "Baby, this just some Barefoot Bubbly. I only costs seven or eight bucks a bottle. I love it, so I drink it instead of the other shit."

"And here I am thinking we were blowing big money without even going out. I must admit that it is good, though. So... What is it that you're up to, Mr. Manny?" she as she sat back and looked more directly at him.

Manny poured them both more wine before responding. "OK, check it out, Ms. Michelle.

"I'ma call you Shelly, if you let me. But that ain't all I wanna do. I been watching you at work for as long as I been in this little town, and I know you caught my attention for a reason.

"I represent a level of life that can lead to a very beautiful form of loneliness. The material things that you see in your dreams will be yours, but most, if not all of the people you run into will be fake as fuck, so you'll be alone in your heart if you don't find somebody who can feel you. I guess you can say that means I'm tryna bring you into my life on a level that won't leave me lonely."

He could see that she didn't know what to make of his words, so he continued: "I got a space in my life that's just yo' size, Shelly. You think you wanna try it on and see how it fits? Or are we gonna just hook up every now and then on some fuck shit? Because I promise that would be nothing compared to what I'm tryna do."

It took her a moment to find her voice again before she asked him, "How is it that you're alone and some lucky girl hasn't already loved you in whatever way you need?"

Manny could tell that she liked what she was learning about him, so he went in with the timely truth. "Who says that hasn't already happened? Nobody ever said there was no love. I'm just sayin' it ain't filling in all the gaps, so whatever it is, I still got room for whatever you could bring into it."

"But what could I ever bring into your life? I'm just a small-town girl with a small-town job. You might like my looks, but that's all I got to offer."

"That's enough to start with for me. The question is if that's all you ever want your description of yourself to be?"

She was serious now. This talk was taking on some turns that she wasn't prepared for. "Now that you mention it, I guess not. It wasn't a big deal when it was all I knew. But what else can I do, though?"

Manny almost felt sorry for her when he saw the despair develop in her as her awareness increased. It was sad to have to bear witness to someone being so lost. The wine was forgotten for the moment, because he was now like a cat watching its prey, carefully moving with a hunger in his belly that had to be fed in a way that should be impossible to achieve.

One wrong word could kill his chances completely. But he was good with his words. "Well, let's ask ourselves why you would change anything about your life? Is it because of your own ambition, or because you want to be with me?"

She thought for a second before answering. "I think it starts with you. But to be honest, I have to include the ambition because I want to be important to you, not just some girl in your life. Because I wouldn't want you to ever throw me away or replace me."

They talked long and deep into the night with Manny exploring all there was to know about her, and she got more comfortable with each new revelation. The hours passed by and the wine poured and they knew each other better as time went by.

Michelle was ready to turn her back on everything she knew by the time their talk was over. She didn't even want to give a two-week notice at her job. Somewhere along the line, the subject of what exactly she'd be doing came up, but by that time she was already a believer.

He was clearly successful with what he did, so she had a hard time thinking badly about the role he wanted her to play. She didn't expect it to be fun, but talking to him about it made her see how she could be worth it. And the more she learned about him as a person, the more she wanted to be with him as her man. She was right where she needed to be until he took her to do what she needed to do, so she would take the chance and stake her claim.

Then a small measure of disappointment began to peek into the atmosphere as unsatisfied sexual curiosity let them both know what was wanted. Manny grinned at her and looked down at his own crotch. Michelle followed his gaze and saw the bulge in his pants. All she could think of after that was his obviously formidable size and the warm damp patch between her thighs.

Maintaining eye contact made any further words unnecessary and he leaned over to plant a tender kiss onto her lips. She kissed him back, closing her eyes as he wrapped his arms around her and pressed his tongue into her mouth.

Her heart fluttered, which was like pressing a button that made her clit throb. Sliding her hand down, she touched his bulging erection through his jeans. He sighed and pushed his crotch forward, encouraging her to stroke him through the material. She did that, feeling the outline of his hard dick as his hands wandered all over her body, pausing to grope her ass.

She felt a huge buildup of sexual tension throbbing in her pussy, and she shivered with pleasure as Manny pulled her closer to him. Fingers fumbled with buttons and zippers in order to remove pants from being able to cover private parts, and once they were both properly exposed, they maneuvered themselves so that he was positioned between her parted legs.

His dick stood magnificently, rearing up from a nest of dark curly pubic hair. It was an absolute whopper, and Michelle's mouth watered as she thought of how wonderful it was going to feel digging away inside of her.

When she pursed her lips, Manny got the idea and rearranged himself so she could reach the object of her attention. She quickly reached for it and helped him get it into her mouth, running her tongue around the heavily swollen tip.

His hands cradled her head and his fingers moved in her hair, massaging her scalp as she took as much of him as she could into her mouth. It wasn't possible for her to consume the full length, so she squeezed the root of his dick while sucking on the head.

After a while, Manny grunted and lifted her up so that her legs were wrapped around his as he straddled her. Grasping both her wrists in one hand, he held her arms above her head. Her heart beat wildly at being handled in such a way. His authoritive vibe excited her, and her pussy ached to feel him inside of her. She could hardly wait for him to push open her legs and enter her, so she pushed her pussy toward him invitingly.

Nudging her thighs apart to expose the wet folds of her pussy, Manny positioned himself between her legs, pressed

156

his rigid ramrod against her inner opening, and pushed gently into her.

Her pussy gripped around his thick shaft, and she arched her back as the friction of his manhood moving deep inside of her sent her body into spasms. His breath came faster with each thrust as his big beam-of-a-penis created a heavenly pulse in her cubby hole.

Slipping a hand between her thighs, he began teasing her clit, smoothing back the slippery folds of her hood as he thumbed her tingling love bud. It throbbed with pleasure and she knew she wasn't far from climaxing.

Her hips worked overtime as she slammed her pussy into him. Manny's back stiffened and his hands moved under her. He gripped an ass cheek in each hand as he plunged himself fully into her. Then his body gave a mighty jerk, and he exploded a warm shot of his semen deep inside her pussy, grabbing hard onto her ass as he pumped out every last drop.

The pressure on her pussy popped right after that. She screamed out loud, unable to help herself as she came really hard. With the orgasms achieved, the chemistry was verified and their situation was set in stone.

She was satisfied with surrendering who she was to this man, and the new existence he would introduce her to...

CHAPTER 18

STILL PUSHIN

"A steak ain't a steak without the A-1, so I stay
dipped in sauce and they come."
– Mac Dre

The next week, Manny had Michelle completely turned out. He watched her through the windshield of his car from the parking lot of the casino on Boulder Highway. She took to it like a fish to water and seemed to be enjoying herself.

He pulled out of his parking spot as she walked toward him and slid up next to the curb where she was. Without missing a beat, she hopped into the car with him and they took off toward the next casino. His plan was to drop her off as soon as he checked whatever money she'd made since the last drop off.

"I can't lie to you, these shoes are killing my feet, but I don't ever have to stand for long before another car stops to get me! I can't wait till we hit that next level you were talkin' 'bout, though," she said enthusiastically.

Her mood lifted his spirits even though things with Rosa were still going up and down.

He smiled at her as she handed over her money before replying. "You doin' good, girl! And we already to the next level. I just needed to run you through this week to be sure you serious, so give me these next few days and I'ma have us outta town by next week. From there it'll be all call-girl work so those feet will get that rest, OK?"

"That's gonna be what's up for sure! You OK, though? You still goin' through it with my co-worker, or is she comin' around finally?"

Michelle knew all about Rosa and wasn't bothered at all. She just wanted Manny to have all that he needed in order for their plans to work out.

"She'll be alright. She just feels stupid right now so she needs a way back into the mix without bruising her ego," he said as he steered them into another casino parking lot.

As he pulled the car into a space, she leaned over and kissed his cheek before saying, "Oh, well. . . keep at it. You'll make it happen, and if not, you got me regardless and I'ma do my part." And with that, she hopped out the car on her way to the money.

Manny watched her walk out to the sidewalk and only make it about fifty feet before the daisy dukes she wore with a little tank top caused yet another car to stop for her. She leaned over into the window for a minute, then got in.

As he thought of how glad he was to have her, his cell phone rang. It was Rosa, so he pressed the green button to accept it without saying anything.

"Hello?" she said into the silence as he just listened. "Yeah, I'm here."

"You don't got no words for me now?"

"It ain't that at all. I figure I'll just hear yo' words since nothin' I say has any effect on you or what you do."

"You act like I don't listen, but I do. I just been confused. I know my probation is coming up, though, and I got into it with my stepdad, so I won't be here too much longer because he threatened to call on me. Can I come home still?"

"It's your home, dummy, of course you can come. But I'm outta here next week, so when you come, just chill out until I get back or send for you."

Rosa paused at that to process the meaning of the news he'd just delivered, so he filled the void with more news. "I gotta go handle my business. Text me, though," he said before disconnecting.

He then sent a text to check on Michelle's well-being, but before she replied he got a text from Rosa: "So U ain't go no more time for me now? Got U a new bitch?"

"U trippin. I do what I must. I didn't tell U 2 leave."

"U Rite. Can't B mad @ U. Hope she cute!"

"U will see 4 URself soon Enuff."

Michelle finally sent her reply. "I'm OK. On my way back now."

$$\$\$\$\$\$$

Manny's day was going pretty agreeable for him. His continued text with Rosa confirmed that she was coming back, so he now could say he had two providers on his team instead of one. But he knew he couldn't quite trust Rosa as much as he wished he could. Those lies would be hard to forget, while his real problem was what he really needed to remember about her, which was something he never knew in the first place.

$$\$\$\$\$\$$

Michelle did really well in the different suburbs of New Jersey after Manny got her settled into a rhythm of working the fast flow of internet attention he promised to introduce her to. She was enjoying herself, and Manny was enjoying her to the fullest.

They grew close and had a very-nice-sized bankroll by the time they made their way up through New York and back down into the Washington, D.C. area, so Manny bought a newer model Cadillac that was silver and black and had vogue tires wrapped around some chrome rims.

He got the windows tinted lightly to set it all off, and Michelle felt like it was their trophy for winning the game of playing the east coast successfully on their first try.

"Oh, my God! Manny, did I pay for that on my own? That's the biggest thing I've ever done in my life!"

She didn't even care how much they had left over because she knew she would gladly put the money right back before they left for home. And that's exactly what she did.

CHAPTER 19

DUTY CALLS

"Shove your feelings in your ass and just do your job!"
– Delancy Street Foundation

Driving back to the West Coast with the music playing and the Cadillac floating over the road like a big pretty boat was an adventure. The car ran like a damn dream and they could hardly feel any of the bumps in the road at all with the new luxury tires and the cushioned air-ride suspension.

Michelle seemed to get a kick out of flashing the truck drivers that passed by as they drove down the highway. Her breasts were enjoyed for miles at a time in this way, and that entertained her for a while, but going through the long lonely stretches of cornfields in the Midwest bored her out of her mind.

"Uuuugh! Manny, I swear we gonna have to fly when we travel from now on, because this driving is the worst thing ever!" she said one evening in a rush of pent-up energy.

"You just gotta find somethin' to do with yo' mind, cutie. Somethin' besides moan and groan. Do you wanna drive?"

"Hmmmm... No sir! I want you to be the captain of the ship around here. But I'm not moaning and groaning, either.

Now let me do something with this brain that'll have you moanin' a little bit."

Before Manny realized what she was up to, Michell had her hands in his lap, undoing his pants. The look he saw in her eyes when their glances met kept him from scolding her for distracting him while he drove.

He put the car on cruise control and tilted the steering wheel to give her all the room she needed to do her thing. When she got his pants undone, she made a quick work of her seatbelt so she could lean over and replace her hand in his lap with her head in his lap.

She slowly slid the length of him into her mouth with a new level of expertise born from the extensive practice provided by her recent change of job description. Her hand gently cupped his balls as she bobbed up and down on his dick, the gagging sounds she could not contain only turning him on ever more. Before long, she grabbed his base in the fist of her free hand to more comfortably cover every inch of him. Then she really got down to the serious business of making him moan and groan, lavishly licking his manly extension with her mouth and milking him madly with both hands.

Focusing on the road with only half his mind managed to make him last longer under the erotic pressure of Michelle's oral exercise. The partial distraction went both ways against concentrating too much on any one thing, so she gave him a long example of what she could do with her head. She was so intense with it that when he finally did explode into her throat, the size of his load forced her to come up and catch her breath. But her hands remained dedicated to their job, and the spurt of his satisfaction shot a lot of itself onto her face as she pumped him through the full extent of a glorious orgasm.

"Look how wet you got my face!" She cheered as she rubbed his cum all over her glistening lips and flushed cheeks. "To be honest, my pussy is probably super soaked the same way. I can feel my panties squishing down there!"

By the time they reached the next rest stop, she'd attacked him once more, but denied him the climax. So when he got the car pulled over, he put her on her knees in the big back seat and pounded himself ruthlessly into her pussy from behind until they both shook with sexual release.

The thrill of being out in the open added itself to each episode, and every opportunity to make another memory was seized with a gusto that could never be forgotten. Rules did not apply to them on this trip, and their Mile High Club membership was earned at the upper most part of a mountain in Aspen, Colorado instead of an airplane. Needless to say, they had a very good time on the highway together...

$$$$$

When they finally made it back to the house, there was a fine coating of dust over the Impala sitting there parked in the yard. The whole scene was one that brought to mind a look of being aged and unused. Manny registered this as he remembered experiencing the same feeling at other times when he returned from being on the road, but it never stood out to him the way it did now.

The symbolism of old things being left behind seemed to nibble at the back of his mind as he directed the Caddy around the house to park nose-to-nose with the Impala. And looking up at the dusty screen on the front door, he could see that the door itself was open and the bluish light of the television was shining through it.

Rosa was home, and a slight degree of guilt poked at the person he was beneath the armor of the pimp he chose to be. Then, for a split second, he allowed himself to feel the human happiness he knew not to give in to before remembering to perform according to his profession, because his wife was also his ho, and sitting next to him was his other ho who deserved to feel comfortable and appreciated for her recent contribution to his cause. So he did one of the many things he got paid to do: He did his job... Without involving his feelings.

"Do me a favor, Shelly," he said as he pulled some money out of his pocket and handed it to her. "Go to the store for us while I do a meet-and-greet with your co-worker. Grab us some of that pink Moscato, some Swishers, and whatever you want me to cook for a nice dinner, OK?"

She took the money and asked, "Do you want me to hurry back or take my time? I know you guys got some talking to do, huh?"

"Yeah, but don't drag yo' feet on account of that. Get the stuff and come on back home or I'ma worry about you. Ain't nobody tryna ditch you just because a runaway decided to come back."

"OK, Mr. Fresh! I'll try and hurry then. And you don't ever have to worry about me, I got you!" she said before scooting over into the driver's seat and driving off on her assignment.

Manny walked into the house, curious to see what was waiting for him. Rosa was sitting on the couch, eating a bowl of ice cream. She was all curled up with her feet folded under her, and her knees up to her chin.

There was a dab of ice cream at the corner of her mouth and she snaked her tongue out sideways to catch it while she looked up at Manny.

"Did somebody just drop you off?" she asked for lack of anything else to say.

He walked over to her and slowly took the spoon out of her hand. He lowered himself down

to one knee in front of her ever so slowly with his eyes never leaving hers. His expression was blank as he scooped a spoonful of her ice cream into his mouth. Then, leaving the spoon in the bowl, he got back to his feet and walked into the master bathroom to run Michelle some bathwater.

After setting some towels out for her to use, he grabbed one for himself and went to the guest bathroom to start the shower. As the water was running, he came back to reply to Rosa's question.

"You don't question my pimpin' about events that took place at any time between the day you left me and the moment I walked through that door to see you come back. But it's good to see you, though. Hope you got yo' mind right. I think I might have really missed you if I wasn't so busy pimpin'."

Rosa sat up straight on the couch. "Well, hello to you, too, sir. I wasn't tryna grill you or nothin'. I just thought the car was pretty and decided to be nosey. My bad."

"Well, I'm glad you like that car. I like it too. And it's mine so you'll be seein' a lot of it," he replied as he began to undress.

Walking into the bathroom, he said over his shoulder to her, "Get these clothes up and set me out somethin' to wear. When that Caddy pulls up, my bitch will be drivin' it. Help her get settled into that bath. She earned it for sure, so you need to respect it."

He cut short any possible response by closing the bathroom door behind him. "And don't let the bathwater run over!" he yelled through the door over the sound of the shower.

Rosa looked down at the floor for a moment to absorb all that she'd just heard. Then she took a deep breath and said out loud to herself, "Well, at least he's honest...."

CHAPTER 20

ON THE ROAD

"And a jealous muthafucka would love to see me fall."

– E-40

The next few days were full of unasked questions and unmade accusations as everyone was on their best behavior.

As far as Manny could see, the girls got along with each other. But when it came to dealing with Rosa's real intention, he knew that there were unseen things to be concerned about, because no matter how hard he tried, he could not completely trust the ticking time bomb that she represented.

Being his wife earned her the benefit of the doubt, though. So he figured he could at least have eyes on her when he wasn't around with the way things were now set up. And in the process, she could feel like she was in charge since there was no dispute about her being more experienced.

But in regards to allowing this, he had a valuable lesson to learn...

$$$$$

At the airport, on their way to Baltimore, Manny told the girls to act as if they were not together so as to not draw unwanted attention. He'd been hearing about a federal operation that was targeting pimps, and wanted to avoid at all cost the enthusiastic cops who would gladly plant evidence to make sure a felony charge would stick.

He remembered the words of an old pimp named Dr. Silk from the Oakland/San Francisco area he used to talk to...

"Pimps is hated in one way or another by everybody, mane! Jealousy, envy, spite or suspicion, the world will hate you. They'll smile in your face, but as soon as they get a chance to bust your game up, they'll do it almost every single time.

"And no matter who it is, I promise you that, in the end, they'll show you how much they hate to see you win. They feel like you gettin' over too easy, or yo' hustle ain't tough enough to deserve all that respect. And a lot of 'em just know secretly that when they pay a ho, they really helpin' a nigga like you.

"Ain't nobody gonna wanna admit to it, so you gotta stay on ya toes and not get caught up in how good it feel. Because out of nowhere, they'll turn on you."

At first it sounded like paranoia to Manny's young ears, but the older and more experienced her got, the more he was seeing the truth of those words.

Shaking off the unpleasant thoughts, he changed his focus to the people around him. In this way, he learned how to carry himself and blend in with successful people through knowing what to wear and how to wear it.

After landing at the BWI airport and recovering their luggage, they met at the passenger pick-up part of the airport where taxi-cabs and charter buses were to be found. They all hopped into a van-sized cab and headed to their hotel. The sights in Baltimore, Maryland let a person know immediately that the West Coast had been left far behind. Brick buildings were everywhere, and everything seemed more urban.

It was like a refreshing drink of water when Rosa took it all in and broke the silence.

"I can't lie; I love my home, but whenever I get back out here if feels like I'm where it's really at. I don't know about y'all, but I'm glad to get a break from the desert."

Michelle understood her point. "Yeah, I see where you comin' from with that, now that I've gotten a chance to compare both places. It's more alive out here."

Looking out through the windows as the cab moved along, they could see people making money in countless ways. It was no wonder that this place made more for them than just about anywhere else in the country. It was like a true economic mecca for anyone who cared to apply themselves to the paperchase.

Arriving at the hotel, they were met with the presence of company trucks from moving companies, construction crews, and out-of-town contractors on one job or another. There were easy sources of money for any girl who could catch the eye of a man when she passed by, and Manny had not only one, but two he knew could do just that without a doubt.

The days and nights were going good as days went by. The girls stayed busy and Manny continuously counted all that they collected.

There were no complaints, but he soon grew bored and became a tourist to occupy himself.

He shopped and sampled restaurants, spoiled himself and his team, wandered around the whole DMV area, but yet, he was still bored.

One day while cruising the many social media sites, he came across a girl in Philadelphia are named Valerie who seemed receptive to his charm. They talked through texts and phone calls for a couple of days before he realized she was a prospect for his professional pursuits, so during one of their calls he got more direct with the way he was talking.

"Let me ask you something. Are you sure you really ready for the answer to all these questions I've been side-steppin' that you insist on askin' me anyway?" he said when she asked him again about being able to afford to be on the road like he was.

"I can handle anything except a lie," Valerie said confidently. "So how do you pay for all these days in a hotel, plus still pay your bills back in Vegas like it's nothing."

Manny was glad to see that he had her thinking, and his answer was already prepared.

"See, you can only look at things up to the point that your own experience allows you to understand. Beyond that, things get hard for you to believe because it's more than you know.

"But if by some miracle you did know without me telling you what I do, you would say that my life is based on being able to accept steps and choices. And most of these have some kind of sacrifice involved as the main ingredient."

Valerie laughed before replying to his evasive answer. "You're really somethin' else! Most guys got jokes, but not you. You got riddles instead of direct answers. I can't tell if you're explaining what you do, or avoiding the subject. But you got me curious."

"Yeah, I can feel that. But I promise you I ain't tryna confuse you. I'm just sayin' people usually think my life can be narrowed down to a deed or an activity that I'm into, when in reality it's a circumstance that demands a certain state of mind.

"A person with a limited outlook on life wouldn't be able to wrap their mind around the concept behind the deeds and activities that my daily routine consists of, because they've never asked themselves how or why they're willing to live with a daily existence that don't make them happy. So now I'm curious to know if you're proud of how your life is going?"

"Well... I don't think I would say I'm proud of it. But not like in a way that means I'm ashamed, though, that's for sure."

"Shit, baby, I sure hate to break the news to you, but any lack of pride represents some degree of shame. That's just the facts. But if you've been dealing with that on even a small level and accepting it as life, how on earth have you never conceived of a situation that would make it worth your while?

"My life is about doing just that. Like how show biz pays people to play all kinds of parts, I represent that on a more reality-based level. But my business don't have the same discriminations that show biz does."

The day after Manny had that particular conversation with Valerie, he was booking a flight to Philadelphia with a promise in place that she was willing to give his lifestyle a try.

He arrived later that same week and had her take a taxi to the airport where they met in person. She showed up wearing a little V-neck T-shirt and stretch pants. The only other thing she had on was a pair of glasses that added an attractive intelligence to her appearance.

She was only five feet tall with blue eyes and long brown hair that reached her waist. She brought not a single other item with her when they made their way to a motel room that night. Her feeling was that if she was going to become a new person in a new life, she didn't need or want any reminders of what she had left behind.

They made it to the motel room without incident, and after a short while it became impossible to ignore the sexual tension in the air. It started with a hand placed lightly on a thigh and a voice slightly hoarse with the acknowledgement of a mutual desire. Then he leaned in for a random feel, and she touched him back, growing moist in the panties as her body reacted to his hands on her.

She reached for him again, then looked into his eyes as her arms wrapped around him, placing her lips onto his. She pushed her tongue into his mouth and her breasts rubbed against his chest. He felt her nipples harden beneath her shirt, so he unbuttoned her and eased it back over her shoulders. He'd fantasized about seeing her naked breasts, and as he hastily unsnapped her bra, he bent down to suck a nipple before flicking it with his tongue.

A moan escaped her and she laid back on the bed while he leaned forward, kissed her cleavage, and enjoyed her natural aroma. His hands travelled down her body, stopping between her legs. He moved his fingers across his crotch, causing her to squeal as she ground her pussy against his hand and slowly moved her pelvis up and down.

Her breathing became more rapid and she softly moaned when he proceeded to peel her leggings down. Removing her G-string, he them explored the glistening folds on her pussy lips before removing his own clothes.

They were both naked, and the feel of her hot skin against his was sensational. He returned to sucking her large heavy breasts; his warm breath dancing across the taught buds of her nipples as they stiffened even more from him wetting their sensitive surface with his greedy tongue.

After a few minutes of him orally exploring her ample orbs, she spread her legs and motioned uncertainly for him to go down to her pussy.

"Lick me there," she sighed. "I wanna see how that slick-talking mouth feels on me."

His tongue darted in and out of her inner core, tasting every tiny ridge and furrow of her love hole. He savored the flavor of her juices as her muscles began to contract and her lips began bucking.

With a sigh of pleasure, she pushed his face into her crotch, gripping his head tightly with her hands, grinding her sex box hard against his lips. Opening his mouth wide, he covered her entire pussy as she climaxed and her deep groans of pleasure filled the room.

Once she'd finally caught her breath, she wanted to continue. But first she had another request: "kiss me. I want to tase my cum from your lips," she pleaded.

Obligingly, he moved up and put his wet lips upon hers. She flicked her tongue across them, licking and exploring his mouth. Her muffled moans told him that she enjoyed the taste of her own juices.

They continued locking lips as he eased two fingers into her soaking snatch. He rubbed his fingers inside of her, moving them around so she could get the full effect. This brought her a second orgasm that was even hotter and wetter than the first.

He sensuously licked her inner thighs, his tongue wet and warm against her skin there. Her twat was oozing as he teased her mercilessly, darting his tongue over and all around her clitoris, then he clamped down on her pussy and it clenched and contorted through yet another climax.

When he came up for air, his face was so wet with her juices that, when she kissed him, it was like eating herself out. That's when she realized what a truly exotic experience it was to taste her own sex on someone else's mouth.

But he wasn't done with her yet. He went down on her again, barely touching this time, just to very lightly lick her clit while fondling the folds of her vagina. He teased her by running his fingers around the rim of her anus before slowly sliding one inside. He wanted to see if she was up for a bit of anal, and was pleased when she moaned ever so slightly. Her asshole tightened as his finger slid in, and relaxed as he drew it out again. It wasn't long at all before her whole body tensed and she shuddered into another surprising climax.

"I've never done it like that before," she groaned when she pulled herself together again.

"But you liked it, didn't you?" he demanded in return.

Without waiting for a response, he turned her onto her knees, pointed her ass up in the air, and aimed his swollen mushroom head toward her rear. He gently pressed the tip of his dick into her and found that she was so relaxed he was hilt deep in seconds. He began to slide in and out, slowly at first, then faster as she really got into it.

She clearly wasn't in any pain because she started talking to him. "Harder! Faster! Fuck me in my ass! Deep in my ass!"

She moved one hand between her legs, keeping herself steady with the other one, and started to play with her clit.

That was all he could stand, and he shot his entire load before collapsing on top of her, exhausted with his dick still burned deep in that lovely ass of hers, and her greedy nature was pleased with the full feeling of being possessed so completely.

$$\$\$\$\$\$$

Virginia was sweet as always for breaking Valerie in to her new hustle, and Manny had the other girls come up from Baltimore after her introduction was complete.

They worked the town for a couple of days and caught a train to New Jersey, but that location didn't seem to agree with Valerie as much as Virginia did, and she tended to think that while the other girls were busy, Manny should be giving her special attention instead of trying to pinpoint the problem.

His refusal to indulge her expectations brought a real resentment toward the other girls who she blamed for being the reason, and after a few days of unexplained struggle, a decision was made to go back to where she'd done well before.

But what Manny didn't know is the New Jersey wasn't Valerie's problem. Rosa was where the true issues were coming from...

On the surface, thins were great, but beyond the surface, nothing was what it seemed at first glance. As soon as the girls were ever out of Manny's sight, Rosa turned into a completely different person.

She was very subtle, so it was hard to tell on her. When they were in New Jersey, Valerie was left in the dark while her co-workers worked regular clients they were previously familiar with.

"Don't let Daddy think you need a babysitter or he gonna start gettin' mad at you," was the kind of info Valerie got in response to her questions.

Michelle was cool, but she followed Rosa's lead for the most part, so Valerie was alone and started to lose her initial enthusiasm as time went by.

"Yeah, it ain't what he made it sound like it was gonna be, huh? I wonder what story he sold you to make you come so quick. I swear, I feel sorry for you hoes sometimes," Rosa said to Valerie during one of their conversations.

Comments like that started to take a toll on Valerie after a while, and it soon began to have the desired effect.

Once they were back in Virginia, it was hard for Manny's newest recruit to know what she felt, and she wasn't sure how to approach the subject verbally. Rosa took her time and slowly poisoned her new co-worker's entire outlook on the whole situation, while Manny had no clue about any of this at all.

He thought that, as a husband-and-wife team, it would make sense for Rosa to run his stable in a self-serving desire to minimize the need for as much personal participation in the physical work on her part, so the more he added to the team, the less she would need to do. And when it started looking like Valerie's was having a hard time, he decided to leave her with Rosa on a crash-course while he took Michelle on a scout-mission to Texas. It seemed like a good idea since Michelle and Rosa worked so well together, but it never crossed his mind that he might be making a very big mistake.

$$$$$

Manny and Michelle arrived in Texas among many other passengers on a flight headed into the southwest for countless different reasons.

They caught a cab to the Motel 6 in Houston and decided they may as well get to work on an ad just to see what the area could provide.

Losing patience with waiting on a call to come, Manny didn't want to let Michelle sit around, so he sent her to the convenience store across the street to check out the surrounding area. As he settled into watching TV, she called him within five minutes of leaving with some good news.

"Hey, Papa! I'm sure glad I don't mind listening to you! I got a call as soon as I hit the parking lot. He'll be here in about an hour. Then I ran into three Mexican guys on a landscaping crew who all want a quickie at sixty bucks a pop for ten minutes each. I'm on my way back now and I need the room," she said cheerfully.

"OK, trooper! That's what's up. A real ho gotta get her energy to circulate for the cashflow to go. That don't happen if she just sit still like a lazy bitch, because then she only gonna get lazy results! Call me when you done and I'll be outta yo' way when ya get here!"

"Of course, you're correct as always. But I didn't make it to the store. Could you grab us some lunch while you're out? I'm starving already."

He agreed to get the food and they ended the call. This was the beginning of a good day for Michelle, and Manny found himself making numerous trips to the store that day.

On one of those trips, he caught sight of some familiar activity next to a nice silver Dodge Charger on big 24-inch rims. And since he had time to waste with Michelle being on another date, he made his way in that direction to get a closer look.

"What it do, bruh-bruh? You on point with those rims fa sho, mane. I like how you got this thang fixed up, so I had to come check you out. No disrespect, I'm just glad to see somebody who ain't no square," Manny said to the semi-suspicious owner of the car.

The man was tall, in his thirties, with a mouth full of gold teeth that twinkled when he spoke. After pausing for a moment, he responded agreeably to Manny's approach. "Yeah, mane, good lookin' out. Ain't much on this end, but you in H-Town so you fa sho gon' see somethin' slick wherever you go. I peeped you when you first came outside. Where you from, dog?"

"I'm out that California Bay Area wit' it, though. My name Manny Fresh. Just doin' it like it go, tryna pimp on a ho."

"Oh, OK, OK, that's what's up. My name is Moe, and I'm up outta that Memphis Ten. You in the right spot for what you doin'. Just stay on the low. I got that good green if you tryna get yo' hands on some bud."

Manny smiled at that. "Bruh, you musta read my mind for real. What you want for an eighth of that shit?"

They did their business and exchanged numbers for future reference. Texas was looking good already. After a few days of tightening up with Michelle, the rest of the team was sent for so that they could all be in one place instead of Rosa sending him the money through Western Union.

Manny anticipated a little bit of a struggle with Valerie when she arrived because the reports told of her attitude taking a turn for the worst. But when the two girls first arrived, it was like a little family reunion for the whole day. Nobody talked much while they were all together, so Manny got himself a room that next day to rotate his one-on-one time with each girl.

The first night was spent with Rosa in a effort to get an idea of the situation. It was the first time they were able to be alone in a while. They ordered a dozen of the barbecue blue crabs Manny discovered at a local soul food restaurant and relaxed to enjoy the meal over a blunt.

"So, what do you think about our new friend Valerie and her adjustment to our program?" he asked her casually as he carefully molded the weed-filled cigar into the desired shape.

Cracking the seasoned crab shell and smacking her lips at the taste, Rosa looked up at her obvious enjoyment to speak with her mouth full. "To tell you the truth, I don't know about her. She seems like she thinks she's here to do somethin' other than just work. I can get along with her, but not all the shit she be on, though."

"Oh yeah? Do she actually be sayin shit that make you think this, or is that just how she actin'?"

"A little bit of both. But I don't kno, I just care about her pullin' her own weight. She don't seem like she tryin' to really put that effort in."

"Damn... I notice she been havin' some issues that nobody else be havin'. But then again, her orientation wasn't as extensive as everybody else's either, so maybe she just needs more time to fit in. We can't make her the oddball, though, and that's probably what hit her once she realized she wasn't the only bitch on deck, you feel me?"

"Just give it some time then, I guess. She'll show you what it is eventually."

Manny thought on his own about it and felt like there was something missing from the equation for sure. He couldn't put his finger on it, but he knew it had something to do with the girls being around each other. However, he didn't want to treat Valerie unfairly, and in his mind, it was hard to overlook the fact that she left all she knew to come give him a shot.

For the moment he put his conclusions on hold until he had a chance to feel her out for himself. To change the subject, he asked Rosa about something else. "Besides all that shit, how you like that crab? I told you it was super-duper, didn't I?"

"Yeah, this shit is fire! Don't worry 'bout me, though, Daddy. I just wish these bitches didn't need a damn babysitter all the time, 'cause we don't ever really get a chance to do our thing."

"I thought that's what we was doin' now? And speakin' of doin' our thang...come smoke this weed with me instead of givin' all my attention to those crabs."

"Oh, please believe," Rosa said as she hurried over to him, "you the only thing I wanna taste when it really come down to it. Just let me know when I can put you in my mouth and I'm on it!"

Lighting up the weed, he hit it hard before he passed it to her. "Let's start with you puttin' this in yo' mouth. I wanna see you work them lips on it to keep it lit for me."

She giggled and followed his instructions as he murmured into her ear, "Stick wit' a nigga like me and I promise you we gon' be OK. Only way we can lose is if we beat ourselves. Because every move I make is about us gettin' as far as we can, as fast as we can."

As the smoke took effect, they enjoyed each other throughout the night. But beneath the beauty of what they experienced, there was the beginnings of proof that jealousy was starting to show its ugly head.

As the next few days went by, Manny got more familiar with his surroundings. He saw other girls working their hustles for other pimps who he never saw, or just didn't recognize. But there was one who seemed to be an independent provider, and for some reason he came across her quite regularly.

She couldn't hide that she liked what she saw, and he couldn't ignore that she appeared to be working out of two different rooms on opposite sides of the building. That made no sense to him, but sure enough it turned out to be the reason he kept crossing her path.

She was a tall, freckle-faced strawberry blonde who wasn't ugly, but wasn't exactly as cute as she seemed to be at first glance. Her body was stacked with a set of beautiful breasts, generous hips, and a rounded rump. The over-all effect was an athletic physique on an amazon frame that was sure to arouse interest.

The ice-breaker between them came along when one day Manny passed her as she entered the elevator he was coming out of. She had a Mexican guy with her who was clearly caught up with her charms, and amazingly enough they were fluently speaking Spanish.

Manny froze in surprise and looked back at her with confusion clearly etched across his face. As the doors to the elevators closed, the girl met his gaze and winked at him with an amused smile on her face.

Encouraged by her boldness, Manny hung out in the pool area until he saw her again. He figured that if she'd go as far as to wink at him, she'd surely come to him when he called her. And he tested his theory as soon as she showed her face and looked his way.

When he waved her over to him and got up to move in her direction, they met at the gate surrounding the pool. Manny immediately went to work on making sure he said all the right things.

"I see you stay busy, but give me a minute to kill my curiosity right quick. I'm Manny Fresh the Best – at yo' service, by the way. I be coast to coast doin' the most with this shit on some pure pimpin', though – just so you know. But anyway, you gotta be the whitest Mexican I ever saw in my life, or was I hearin' things when I heard you speakin' Spanish like it was yo' native language?"

She smiled at him while coming inside the gate to speak. "Well, hello, Mr. Fresh. I ain't no Mexican, but you heard me loud and clear speakin' Spanish. Most my dates are Mexican dudes, so I gotta get that money. Here in Texas, that's the money language. I'm Heather, by the way... Just so you know."

They sat down at one of the tables under the big umbrella next to the swimming pool. Her southern drawl was so strong that without seeing her a person would think she was a Black woman. But Manny wasn't confused about anything at all once he had her finally in his reach and he fell naturally into his zone.

"OK, Heather, it's good to meet you. At least, I hope it will be good. Time will tell me that much, but I see you be doin' what it do and it don't look like you got no folks. So I'm curious 'bout two things. One is, what got you rockin' so hard like that? And two is, why you got two rooms if you out here solo?"

"Well, I see you do pay attention, and I'm glad I wasn't the only one lookin' outta pocket 'round here. My situation is complicated, but I don't have no man, though. The folks I do have is on a page I'm sure you ain't even talkin' about. Maybe I'll tell you 'bout it if you come see me one day, because I can't talk here for long. Is that cool?"

They exchanged phone numbers so they could text and Heather made her way back to her room. As they went on about their business, they kept in touch to continue getting to know each other.

Heather turned out to be from Louisiana and was on the verge of going back there soon. She came to Texas when she got turned out a few years prior, and had been drifting back and forth between the two states.

The man who turned her out had developed a drug habit, so she left him. She was now alone because her most-recent ex-boyfriend had gone to prison on robbery-related charges.

Manny hated to admit it, but he knew Valerie wasn't going to work out, so he may as well recruit Heather to replace her. From what he'd seen so far, Valerie didn't really want much out of life. He didn't judge her for that, but in her case, he knew that not having much when he met her was clearly a result of not doing much. Her focus just didn't seem to be where he needed it to be. And her lack of improvement showed a lack of income that made it not worth his while to keep trying with her.

After a few days of texting Heather with a few quick chats here and there, the familiarity between her and Manny became more of a mutual curiosity. The question about her "folks" still remained unanswered, but instead of asking, he just let the communication flow. As a result, he was able to pull her comfortably into his direction on an ever-increased basis.

Beyond that, there was a very noticeable sexual overtone finding its way into their daily dialoge. But Manny frustrated himself by not taking advantage of the chances he had to end up in bed with Heather.

No matter how much she turned him on, he could not let her have him for free. Being an active prostitute subjected her to rules he knew would be suicidal to ever break while he had three other prostitutes paying him on a daily basis.

Then, one day, as if thoughts could give birth to the subject being brought up in conversation, Heather asked him on the phone, "So, when you plannin' to come get in my pants, Mr. Fresh? I know you can tell that I'm liking you more than I should. What are we waiting for?"

"See, you over there confused because you tryna fit me into the same trick bag you put every other man into. But those dudes is squares and I'ma a cross-country pimp on duty, so you can't expect to fuck wit' me the way you fuck wit' them lames. Even if you tryna offer me the pussy for free... it don't work like that in my world, girl.

"I respect you as a bonified ho, so I never thought about havin' sex with you unless I was in some way making your life better. Not like a trick who gives you money, but like a qualified pimp who has an obligation of making sure I don't waste your time. So if you like me how you say you do, I'ma need you to sock it to my pocket, and I'ma show you it's the right thing to do."

Heather was quiet for a moment, then she somewhat sadly said into the phone, "But we ain't even been talkin' on that page. I thought we was just two people who liked each other. Was I wrong?"

"Nope! You was right on the money. But your thinkin' was incomplete. I ain't no monster and you ain't either. So yeah, we are just two regular people, but that don't mean our proper principles don't still apply. It ain't a damn thing on earth that should ever make you forget what you stand for in life.

"Don't get me wrong! I'm dyin' to know what you got goin' on inside those pants. But I gotta wait until you come correct with the rest of it. So whenever you ready to choose to support what I stand for, I'll be more than ready to sample them sweets and wear yo' lil fine ass out."

The silence was drawn out even longer this time, as Heather processed what she'd just been told. She understood the words, but the full meaning was unclear at first. Then she had to be honest enough with herself about how obvious it was when she thought about it. He wanted more than just sex from her and wasn't interested in any offer of sex on its own.

"But how do you know you want to connect your life to my life, Manny? I mean... I'll follow your lead, but can I make a suggestion?" she asked thoughtfully.

"Yeah, you can suggest whatever you like as long as you know it's all or nothin' wit' a nigga like me."

"OK, but I ain't trying to play you short or nothin' like that at all. I just need you to get a good look at my whole package before you decide you want me in your program. And I'll give you five hundred for ya time when you come see me tonight. If you still wanna get down after I explain my situation, then we can take it wherever you wanna go from there."

"That's cool, just text me yo' room number and I'ma hit you up when I'm on my way to make sure you ain't busy. Sound like a plan?"

She agreed to his idea and they ended the call. He immediately got a text from her with her room number and a smiley face.

Manny smiled to himself and went on about his business, knowing that unless Heather's news was about being a drag queen, he would be having another girl on his team very soon.

Valerie better pick her game up or she 'bout to find herself stranded in Texas for tryna sink my ship, Manny thought to himself. *If I can't get the bitch with talkin' sweat, talkin' tough, or givin' her attention and takin' it away, then I'm outta options. The bitch better get right or get gone...*

$$$$$

After spending the rest of the day with his team, smoking, eating pizza and talking as much as possible to be sure nobody's needs were being overlooked, Manny collected their daily contribution and got them in gear to go all night.

This was normal procedure, but since he planned to be gone, he wanted to put a specific idea in their minds. Pulling Rosa to the side before leaving, he did just that. "I'm on a mission tonight, so I want you to drive the car until I get back. Just gettin' a few extra dollars for now, pokin' at a possibility. You'll know the details if it turn out to be a reality. In the meantime, think about what y'all want me to bring back for breakfast."

Rosa looked at him with a curious glance before responding. "I'll take I-HOP, then. Just call when you get there and we'll order on the phone if you read the menu to us. That cool?"

He said it was and she wished him luck with a half-hearted sincerity that he didn't notice. His mind was already on his upcoming mission and what moves he would make to ensure his success.

Out of the door with a mind working on overtime, Manny sent Heather the text she'd been waiting all day to receive: "On my way unless U changed yo mind."

Her reply came before the elevator did: "I'm ready, so come on!"

The room smelled fresh as if she had sprayed some Febreze into the air. The bed looked freshly made up, and the sheets were visible under the turned-down blanket to reveal baby blue satin that clearly were not standard motel issue.

Heather had answered the door completely naked with a twinkle in her eye and a small wad of cash in her hand. "Hey, sexy man, here's that five hundred for ya. I'm glad you came through. I was just about to take my bath, so you can join me, come keep me company, or watch TV while you wait for me. It's up to you," she said enticingly before skipping to the bathroom.

Manny heard the bathwater quietly splashing as she got into the tub. Then he counted the money she'd given him and stuffed it into his pocket. After that, he locked the door to the room and checked the interior to be sure nobody was hidden away anywhere waiting to rob him.

Satisfied that they were alone, he took off his clothes to join Heather in the bathtub. When he entered the bathroom, he noticed sweet smells coming from the steam that rose from the bubbly suds on the water. Heather was on her knees, soaping herself generously all over her upper body.

Stepping into the water, he saw raw hunger come over her face as her blue eyes locked onto her manhood, which was already reacting to the sight of her.

"Just 'cause we takin' a bath don't mean I forgot what I told you on the phone. This is just a pimp acknowledgement of you puttin' those few chips in my hand like you supposed to," he said as he slid down into a sitting position behind her.

Her then took her wash rag to continue applying the sweet-smelling soap all over her upper body as if this was a daily routine for them.

"Now stand yo' sexy ass up so I can get the rest of you," he ordered her casually.

She obeyed him without hesitation and he lovingly took his time soaping her body down. From top to bottom, in the front and the back, taking special care with all her most intimate areas, he put her into a daze with how much attention he so naturally lavished upon her.

When he switched over to cleaning himself, Heather just stood there for a moment, stuck on the expectation of more to come before she sat down and rinsed herself off. And when Manny was done washing himself, he reached down around Heather to flip the plug on the drain, letting the water out of the tub.

She was facing him when he did this, and the look in his eyes as he held her gaze the whole time made her think he was going to kiss her when he leaned in her direction. Then he did it again, scrambling her expectations even further when he turned on the shower this time.

It was like he was intentionally teasing her by not acting upon the intentions he aroused and encouraged in her.

He grabbed her hand and led her to rise up to her feet again, standing under the warm spray that cleansed the last traces of soap from their bodies. She looked down to see he was now fully erect and possessed an impressive size and shape. He was slim with a chiseled chest and noticeably defined abdominal muscles. The corded contours of his arms and legs was surprisingly attractive to her.

Getting out of the shower, they both dried off and made their way into the room wearing nothing at all. Manny sat on the edge of the bed and motioned her over to kneel between his legs. She thought it was a summons to come and suck his sex into satisfaction, but when she eagerly knelt down in front of him he gently corrected her position, turning her around so that her back was to him.

He then sat her down on the floor and started to massage her neck and shoulders. Her eyes rolled into her head with the unexpected pleasure of what she felt from what he did to her.

"You feel like you been tense all day if not for a lot of days in a row. Why don't you tell me all that stuff about you that got you not so sure I'm gonna accept you into my program," he said in a soothing voice.

It took a effort on her part to come back to reality in order for her to get the facts together so that she could reveal them conversationally.

Talking was the last thing on the list of things she'd been thinking about doing since the moment Manny had stepped naked into the bathroom. Especially after he started touching her in the bathtub.

His hands moved the massage up into her scalp as if he planned to run the thoughts out of her mind. She felt like jelly as she relaxed into him and moaned her way into the story of her life's most relevant highlights.

Their nakedness seemed to work against holding anything back, as if it was all just as visible as her body, so she may as well tell it all. Her attraction to him made her want to connect, and his hands made her comfortable in a way that reached down deep, tapping into a truth she would never normally want to share.

She told him of being molested as a child by her older cousin, and how she grew distrustful of men from her own race as a result of this. That was what led her into associating more with Blacks and Hispanics.

She told him of dropping out of school because of a high school pregnancy in the 11th grade, and her parents being so ashamed that her boyfriend was Black, making the baby a bi-racial child.

She spoke of the times her heart had been broken and how she lost faith in the idea of real love. She shared the experience of being raped and robbed and ending up pregnant again as a result. How no one understood her love for her child because of how it came to be, and all the pain and confusion this caused in her life.

Most of her life choices landed her at odds with the people she thought she knew the best. Therefore, she learned to find comfort with those who she didn't really know at all. The only thing unchanging in her world were the two kids she had who seemed to have no one except her to count on. They were two little girls, and these were the only "folks" she had.

Heather was twenty-seven years old, and her little girls were ten and eight. She was doing her best to take care of them however she could, and they were the reason why she had two rooms. The other room had two beds and they were there at that very moment either sleeping or watching TV.

She explained how she never could expect anyone to ever accept the difficulty of her package deal; she couldn't leave her babies, so where she went would have to allow them to come as well.

She was in tears by the time she got to the end of her story. Not actually crying, but just overcome with real emotional overload.

Manny never once interrupted her as she got it all out. He just listened and rubbed the words from her for as long as it took. Now she made much more sense to him, and in spite of what many people might think of her, he respected her reasons for deciding to sell herself day after day. He never really judged any prostitute as a general principle, but this one he judged even less than the ruled demanded.

In the brief quiet that followed the things that Heather had said, Manny could feel in her shoulders the physical relief of releasing the burden she'd been bearing on her own for so long. And he was glad to have helped her achieve this, even if only for a distracted moment in time.

He was then pulled out of his thoughts with her next question. "So now you know my situation. You came up here to see if I would choose you, but the real question is if you want to choose me."

She had turned to face him, still on her knees between his legs with her arms now resting on his knees. It was not hard to be distracted by how good she looked in that particular position, so he looked her in the eye to keep his focus off her mouth.

"If I choose you, it's gonna mean you can change that independent outlook on life that you got. For a lot of years, you trained yourself to not care what anybody thinks, but I need my thoughts to really matter to you – like on a life itself kind of level.

"The only way I would take a chance on you is if you take one on me first. So even though I understand you tryna take care of your little ladies, you gonna have to trust that I'm tryna be responsible for you in the same way. But I'm seein' them as part of that because they're a part of you. So don't be tryna keep most of the money and only give me a little bit. Go hard to cover yourself and them too, so I can keep all of you cool as long as you don't ever lay down on my pimpin tryna use them to get no free rides," he said seriously.

"Yeah, but I keep them separate from what I do. I don't want them to know anything about this life."

"Well, as it stands now, I can promise you it ain't separate enough. With me, you'll be away from them while you're at work instead of in the same building. So you gotta play it like I'm just a friend and our team is just your little family circle so they see it as an uncle and some aunties. Our personal enjoyment of each other will have to be a private thing. Can you handle that?"

"I can handle whatever I have to handle," she said as she looked down into his lap and added, "I see something I want to handle right now as a matter of fact. Can I give it a special kind of kiss?"

"That depends on if the lips you plan on using still belong to you or have been given to me. Are you trying to be mine all the way? Or you just wanna be my designated dick pleaser?"

"Oh, I'm yours for sure, Daddy. I just needed to make sure you was OK with my situation. I wasn't trying to hold back on you."

"Yeah, that's what you say, but if that's the case, then why ain't you put the rest of whatever money you got in my hand? You can't claim you not holdin' back while at the same time you still ain't checked the whole bankroll you got stashed away for a rainy day. Because we both know you done waaay mo' than five hundred dollars' worth of hoin' since I first saw you."

Heather smirked at him as if he'd just passed some kind of test. Then she took his manhood in her hand, held his gaze defiantly, and gave it a quick kiss before getting up off her knees to walk across the room to the closet. Bending over seductively, she rummaged through a couple of shoe boxes she had in there and looked back over her shoulder at Manny, who was watching her with his dick now fully erect. She wiggled her ass at him and got back up to skip over to him with her offering.

Once in front of him again, she sank back down to her knees and said, "Now, let's try this again," before handing him a fat roll of cash. "You happy now? There ain't nothin' in there less than a twenty and a lot of it is fifties and hundreds."

Then, without saying another word at all, she closed her eyes and made his manhood disappear into her mouth. That was where it all started on a long road to their finish line. By the time they were done with each other that night, it was hard to tell who had taken who, but one thing was for sure: They had done it in many different ways, and neither one of them had a drop left when it was all over.

The roll of money she gave him held almost three thousand dollars, plus the five hundred she had given him at first. She'd been saving it in case something stopped her from being able to work every day. So now Manny had himself another member on his team. But he couldn't congratulate himself yet, because he knew she was only a replacement for the one he was about to lose.

Chicken one day and feathers the next...

$$$$$

A couple of days later, back in his own room with Valerie, Manny decided to explore the issues she was having. "So tell me something, V; how you been feelin'? It seems like since we got passed the part of it being just me and you, the happiness been lackin' more and more. If I did you wrong in some kind of way, just let me know 'bout it."

Valerie looked up from her iPhone with a somewhat sour expression. "Do I really have to answer that? I'm sure you can figure it out, since you're Mr. Know-it-all."

"Damn, though, bitch. Yo' attitude won't help me figure out a muthafuckin' thang. I'm askin' because you seemed half-ass cool when it was just me and you, but keep switchin' it up on me when we ain't cupcaked up somewhere. Ain't nobody 'bout to be jumpin' through hoops according to what mood you in from moment to moment."

"Then don't jump! See if I care," she said as she directed her attention back down to her phone.

Manny walked over and snatched the phone from her hands. "Bitch, you sure are mighty comfortable fuckin' up a good vibe! Why you can't speak on the problem? Don't you know in real life you can't just go around bein' a cancer to a real deal based on how you feel? So if you ain't got a better suggestion 'bout how a thing should go, you need to fall in line as a proper ho instead of disrupting my flow. Because them head games is for suckas, not pimps."

Anger had crept into his tone, but Valerie did not notice it. Instead, she grew very still at the loss of her phone, building herself for a fight. Manny noticed this and didn't want to take it there, but she seemed to be asking for it. Yet he still refused to take the bait.

"You know what? I see you tryna play a game I'm not rockin' wit. Why don't you sit here and think about what you really wanna do. I'll be back in a few minutes to see if you ready to talk like you got some sense."

He turned to leave without even thinking about the cell phone he was still holding in his hand, but Valerie flew into a tantrum. "Motherfucker, gimme my phone!" she screamed at him as she came up from her seat in a rage, almost tackling Manny from behind.

She hit him aimlessly in the general area of his head without much force behind her blows. Manny quickly got control of her and flung her forcefully to the floor. She came at him again, trying to grab his hand and settling for the arm that held the phone.

"That's not your phone! You need to gimme my shit, dude!"

Manny pushed her away agin, quite roughly this time. "Or what you gonna do, V? You better be happy I ain't beatin' the breaks off yo' ass right now! What you better do is calm down and come back to reality before you get yourself hurt. Like I said before... I'll be back!"

As he left through the door, a shoe flew at him and slammed into the wall next to his head. He closed the door behind him, knowing that if he did anything right then it would go too far. But he was still very, very upset, to an extremely dangerous degree.

For her to have the nerve to go off like that when he was obviously trying so hard to remain reasonable was more than he could take. Especially when all she'd been doing for the last few weeks was hindering his progress.

He got down the hall from her location to a closed-in hallway between one side of the building and another. There, out of sight, he snapped. All the anger and frustration he felt toward Valerie was taken out on her iPhone. He slammed it to the ground so many times that a witness would've lost count. Off the walls, into the ceiling, and back to the ground again, until the only way to recognize it as a cell phone was the general shape.

Breathing hard from the sudden burst of physical exertion, Manny pulled himself together, put the shattered device into his pocket, and made his way to the store in pursuit of the biggest bottle of beer he could find.

On his way back to the motel, he got a call from Rosa. He didn't even bother to answer it. She called right back a second time and he picked up.

"I already know you hoes got a hotline that got you up on what happened with the bitch Valerie, so what the fuck do you want?" he asked in an exhausted tone.

"Daddy, I'm just doin' what I'm 'posed to do. I know you mad and I don't want you to hurt nobody, so I'm checkin' up on you. Plus, I'm 'posed to tell you when things ain't cool, so that's what I'm doin', too. Valerie say she is gonna leave, she just wants her phone back. But would you please come smoke before you go back over there so I can know you calmed down?" Rosa said in a diplomatic rush of words.

Manny went up to the room where Rosa and Michelle were. Rosa had a thick blunt rolled when he arrived, and

Michelle took the big bottle from his hands to pour him a glass of cold beer.

When she brought him the tumbler so he could drink, Michelle spoke for the first time. "I'll refill it as often as you need me to. Just sit down and relax... Please?"

He took the glass and had a seat as Rosa lit the blunt and passed it to him. "Here you go, Daddy. Just get your mind back right for a minute," she said soothingly.

Sipping his beer and puffing on the weed, Manny felt his nerves calming down.

"I appreciate you hoes tryna calm me down. But I'm good, though, 'cause this ain't no tragic event that deserve any kind of special attention. I just hate drama."

They smoked without saying much after that. Michelle refilled Manny's glass only once, and the cold beer felt good going down with the strong, smooth weed smoke.

He had to admit that he did feel a lot better after a while. So much better, in fact, he seriously wanted everything that didn't add to this feeling to get completely out of his life.

Today was a good day for Heather to be revealed to the rest of the team. He had not touched the money she'd been giving him in any way except to add it to what she gave him the first day, so her introduction was sure to be on good terms.

But first there was the problem of Valerie that needed to be disposed of. This was unfortunate, but he had no sympathy toward the way she'd been acting. He was going to leave her stranded, even though he knew it was wrong, because he knew the area they were in would provide everything she needed if she decided to work. So he figured one way or another, she was going to pay her dues to the hustle she chose to disrespect.

Lost in his thoughts, he didn't notice that Rosa was trying to pass him the blunt. "Daddy, you, OK?" she asked while exchanging a worried glance with Michelle.

"Yeah, I'm fine actually. But I got a smudge I need to go wipe off my program. Won't take long. Save the rest of the blunt until I get back."

With that, he got up and walked out the door, filled with the joy of acting on his conclusive decision.

Using the room key, he unlocked the door to the room Valerie was in. She was on the bed, watching TV, looking sad and lost.

"I heard you don't wanna be here no more. Is that true?" he asked calmly.

"I was mad and I'm not about to be going through all of this," she said.

"Well, yo' mad move was a bad move, and if you think that's how you need to get down with me, then I'm the wrong one for you to be with."

"Yeah... whatever. Can I just have my phone so I can gladly be gone then?"

"You know what? If all you want is yo' phone, I think you deserve just that. So yeah, you can have yo' phone, bitch! Each and every piece of it."

Manny took the destroyed device out of his pocket and tossed it onto the bed. "Take a good look at that, and be glad I didn't do the same thing to you," he said. "Consider your safety a gift, 'cause that's the last thing you gonna get from me in this lifetime."

He walked out of the room after that, followed by the sounds of her crying behind him. But he was done going backwards, and as he strolled back to the room where Rosa and Michelle were waiting, he deleted Valerie's number from his phone. Never again would she get another moment in his mind.

$$$$$

"I don't know who that bitch thought she was around here anyway," Rosa babbled off to no one in particular as she finished off the blunt.

Manny and Michelle looked at each other as she went on while they smoked. It kind of irritated him to see how this drama seemed to put a new life into Rosa. And the way she spoke about Valerie was ugly, considering the fact that he knew up to the very last moment Valerie thought she and Rosa were friends.

"Hey! No matter if she did a good job or not, she still put into our pot all the way up until she stopped. And I won't have nobody talkin' bad about that. Plus, she's a done deal, so let's talk about what's goin' on now instead of jaw-jackin' on a played-out issue," Manny said seriously.

Michelle supported his idea. "I second the motion for having only happy thoughts." Then she turned to Manny and said, "Daddy-man, I ain't trying to be pushy or disrespectful, but you been holding out on us lately."

There was a smile on her face as she said this, so Manny knew there was no negativity in the comment. It was just her way of changing the subject. He suspected he knew what she was digging at, but played it off as if he had no clue.

"What you mean? Holdin' out on what? You know I would never hold out on my hoes," he said slowly in a sing-song voice, playing the role of exaggerated innocence to let it be known he wasn't serious.

Rosa caught on and nudged Michelle to join in on the play. "Uh-oh, bitch, I see you must be onto something, because everything about him just made me think of a kid caught with his hand in the cookie jar."

Then she dropped her chin into her chest and sprang to her feet with her hands on her hips in mock authority. "OK, mister Daddy, you're surrounded. You may as well give it up!"

Both girls giggled and Manny drained his glass of the beer Michelle had poured upon his return to the room. Once he handed her the glass to refill again, he replied to their inquiry. "OK, OK, yall got a pimp pinned down. You can technically say I been holdin' out, but really though, I just been makin' sure the cookie was official before I bring it to the table to share with my team.

He then pulled the bankroll out of his pocket that Heather had been giving him, holding it up for both girls to see. "This is the cookie, and not a dime of it came from either one of you. On top of that, it been growing on a daily basis, so I know it qualifies for an introduction," he declared proudly as he got up to pull a Louis Vuitton backpack out of the luggage and unzipped it.

When he dumped the contents of the backpack out onto the floor, numerous gigantic wads of cash were piled up for both girls to see. Surprise showed in their eyes.

"Of course, the money that y'all made is waaay more than this little cookie, as you can clearly see for yourselves. Don't get shy on me now! That's us right there, so feel free to go on and count it if you want to. But don't miss the point I'm tryna make, which is that the money I just pulled out of my pocket came from another source. Now it's time for y'all to meet that source since it has proved to be worthy of the honor," he said ceremoniously to them as they stared transfixed at the pile of cash on the floor.

They'd both see proof that Manny was good at stackin' money, and they knew there was at least this same amount stashed somewhere back at the house. But it was still a lot to behold what their efforts had produced on this trip all at one time. It was remarkable, and a new appreciation of what they were all a part of came into the aura of the room.

Rosa could only manage to say, "Damn, Fantasy Island around here," while Michelle chimed in with, "Like something out of a dream."

When he saw their reaction, Manny had to gloat a little bit. "I told y'all it take team work to make the dream work. And the more feet we got marching in the same direction, the faster we can get to where we goin'. Especially when I'm stackin' this shit how I do."

He pulled out his phone and sent a text to Heather with instructions to come check in whatever money she had so far that day. Michelle noticed the move and curiosity controlled her reaction.

"So, are we about to meet our new co-worker? That's where this cookie came from?" she asked.

Manny sipped his beer and nodded his head. "That's exactly right, you lil semi-psychic muthafucka! You're the grand prize winner!"

"Oh, am I? And what is the grand prize?"

"You get to roll the next blunt or answer the door when my newest bitch knocks on it in a minute. The choice is yours!"

"Oh, wow! I'm such a true winner!" she said in a dry tone. "Can I at least add a bonus prize to my choice list?"

"You sure can, since we always aim to please on the Manny Fresh game show!"

Michelle caught Rosa's eye and winked at her before asking, "Can I answer the door, roll the blunt, and then go count our money with my wifey while she watches us? Just to make sure she knows exactly how we do it around here?"

Manny smiled at what turned out to be a very good idea to set the stage for the kind of activity he wanted the whole team's mind to be tuned in to. So he agreed without seeming to do so overly fast.

"That's cool, but who gonna pour my beer for me?" he replied just to scramble the scenario.

Rosa got up and went to the small refrigerator to bring him what was left of the entire bottle. "There you go, Daddy. Now I feel like I played my part, so I'ma start counting this money if nobody minds."

Just as she sat down to do her task, there was a light knock on the door. The plan went right into motion when Michelle answered it to let Heather in before joining Rosa on the floor to help count the cash.

They looked like kids making sandcastles there on the floor next to the pile of money. Michelle rolled a blunt and Manny made introductions.

He sat at the small table next to his beer and the bankroll Heather had been building up, so she sat down in the other chair to join him.

"This is all I got so far," she said as she handed him what she had. "It's only a little over three hundred, but my rooms are out of the way, so I can put at least five more with it before the day is over."

She couldn't help but keep glancing over at Rosa and Michelle on the floor, and the reason was obvious. But in an effort to play it off, she directed her attention to Michelle's blunt-rolling mission.

"Girl, can a bitch hit that shit when you light it up? I can smell it from way over here!"

Michelle smiled at her and replied, "Sweetie, you're part of the family from what I just seen, so I would have wondered what was wrong if you didn't stay to smoke with us."

Rosa nodded in agreement, and Heather looked to Manny just to make sure he had no objections. All he did was shrug his indifference while pointing to the stack of cash on the table.

"That's every dime of what you've given me over the past few days. As you can see, I don't need it. But at the same time, it's right where it needs to be."

He gestured toward the spectacle on the floor and said, "That's the rest of our team right there, and we been on the road almost two months. You can see the rest of what it is for yourself, so I know you shouldn't have a problem catchin' on to what we about."

Rosa reached over to pass the weed to Heather who hit it hard before responding. "Oh, yeah... I see how y'all doin' it."

She hit the weed again before passing it to Manny and adding, "Can a bitch just say, wow!"

"Yeah, you could say that, but that wouldn't give me the honest answer I need to the question I really wanted to ask, though," Manny said.

Heather looked up at Manny with a quizzical expression and fell into the trap his words had just set when she gave her response. "What did you wanna ask me?"

Manny pointed her attention back to the sight of Rosa and Michelle, then he said, "Look past all that money and at the two bitches on that floor. Can you honestly say those ain't no bad bitches, or would you keep it real and admit how beautiful they really are?"

Heather didn't answer immediately, but after a moment of thought, she admitted, "Well... I mean... of course they both beautiful."

Manny watched her as her eyes took in the details of each girl in front of her. Then he pressed even further. "Beautiful enough to turn you on at all?"

He wanted Heather to admit to the team that they were arousing her. He wanted her to say that she was horny right there where they could hear it.

"Yeah," she said barely loud enough to be heard.

The room got quiet as the atmosphere was suddenly electrified, and Manny was overcome with a desire to sick these women on each other, just to prove to himself that he could.

"Can you imagine what it would be like to feel one of them lickin' yo' pussy?" he asked.

Heather made a little noise in the back of her throat, and Rosa knew what that noise meant. Heather's mind was taking Manny's words and turning them into sensations. She'd experienced the same situation herself before, so she caught it as it took place in front of her.

She shared a glance with Michelle that included a sexy smile, and that was Rosa's cue to jump into the erotic wordplay.

"I would start by kissing your thighs and pushin' them apart so I could see that pussy," she said seductively.

Seeing Heather's legs move apart as if she was already down there, she continued. "Then I'd kiss my way up... Would you let me do that to you?"

"Hell yeah, girl," Heather whispered back with a sleepy look in her eyes.

Manny sat there smoking slowly as the scene unfolded on its own. He noticed Michelle was looking at him with the sexy smile still on her face, so he tilted his head toward Heather with a wink, and that set it all off.

They started by undressing each other, touching, and caressing as items of clothing slid to the floor. There was soon a heap of clothing on the carpet next to the pile of money.

Heather was now on the floor, stretched out with her thighs spread as an open invitation flowed from her aura in waves. She spread herself even wider as Rosa got closer, displaying a neatly trimmed strawberry-blonde bush. Her tall statuesque figure, curly tresses that matched the hair down below, and shapely limbs made her as wildly attractive as anything any of them had ever seen.

Rosa was surprised at how attracted she was to her. There was a sexual excitement that almost exploded off the scale when she brushed her the sandy bush of curls on Heather's mound. And as her arousal increased, her pretty pink labia became swollen, peeking through the hair, giving Rosa an incredibly tempting sight to see.

Michelle was kissing Heather as Rosa gently stroked her fingers along Heather's juicy pink vulva. She whimpered as she felt Rosa's touch, and Michelle sucked her tongue while playing with her tits. Turned on completely by their attentions, Heather lifted her legs and spread her thighs even wider, allowing Rosa to slide a finger into her warm, wet womanhood.

Rosa's finger slid easily between the slippery lips and she fingered the inside, trying to find the elusive G-spot in hopes of making Heather cum. As she worked her fingers back and forth, Heather became even more wet and excited. This allowed Rosa to fit another finger inside of her, and that caused Heather to moan and rise slowly up and down on the fiddling fingers filling her pussy.

Soon she became quite heated and was wiggling wildly while Michelle helped to excite her all the more by pinching and twisting her nipples, gently distending them as Rosa's fingers thrust deeper and faster.

Heather's pussy muscles gripped those fingers tighter as one initial orgasm rolled into another. She was gasping for air as Michelle pulled Rosa's fingers out and began to gently suck Heather's juices from them.

Noticing how intent Rosa's eyes were on her mouth, Michelle returned her stare and whispered, "Kiss me, and taste her."

Rosa's pussy clenched and she reached for Michelle. Their lips met in a deep kiss and she tasted Heather's sweet juices on Michelle's tongue as it twirled against her own. She was aching for sexual release when she felt Michelle caress her most personal place, so she relaxed and parted her thighs to allow better access.

She could not resist reaching for Michelle's beautiful firm breasts and squeezing the healthy softness, breaking their kiss to pushing her face between them so she could inhale her co-worker's scent. And when Michelle's fingers slid between her legs, into her pussy, she used her thumb to circle Rosa's clit, making the inner muscles clamp tight around her thrusting fingers.

She felt her back arch as she neared orgasm, with her pussy convulsing in a steady rhythm of spasms in reaction to Michelle slamming her digits harder and faster into her love nest, until she slipped over the top and began to climax extremely hard.

With their lips locked together again and her pussy still throbbing from her orgasm, Rosa really began to get into the groove when she felt Heather's fingers upon her ass cheeks.

In surprise, she broke the kiss with Michelle and looked back at Heather, fascinated by what was being done to her. Heather looked brazenly up at her and told her to eat Michelle out while she tried something different on her.

Through a haze of weed-laced sexual abandon, Rosa did as she was told, positioning Michelle on her back so she could begin fingering her slot. Her fingers dipped into the sweet little strip of softness, and she played with her pretty pink lips, sucking on her juicy labia and tickling her clit to get the juices flowing.

The whole time, Heather had begun to lick her way from Rosa's clit, through her pussy, and right on top of her anus. Her tongue danced across the pussy and then the rest of the way into the puckered little rosebud of her asshole.

Round and round, she rimmed the tight little ring while Rosa lapped and sucked harder and harder on Michelle's pussy. She'd never in her life felt to excited by anything before this.

Then Heather pushed a finger into Rosa's pussy, soaking it with the flowing juices. In turn, Rosa began to apply more oral focus on Michelle's clit. She slid her own fingers into Michelle's pulsating pussy as she felt Heather's finger running gently around her asshole, then she pushed slowly inside as the other hand found her clitoris.

Rosa shafter her fingers faster in and out of Michelle's pussy as she sucked and nibbled on the clit, while Heather teased and tickled hers.

With the double sensation of Heather's finger in her ass, and her clit being stimulated at the same time with the other hand, Rosa could not hold off or contain herself. She came again, inexpressibly hard this time, while sucking powerfully on Michelle and pounding two fingers into her pussy.

They seemed to climax in unison, squeaking and squealing with pleasure, then collapsing in a tangle of all three girls kissing each other passionately.

When they had all gathered themselves and recovered from their freak show frenzy, they were surprised to see that Manny had slipped away, leaving them to their triple enjoyment.

His mission was accomplished as soon as he saw they liked each other enough to do what they had done. They needed no further motivation....

CHAPTER 21

IN THE SNOW

*"Suffering from player stress, pimpin' through
the snow and rain..."*
— Mac Mall

It wasn't long before Manny had everyone back in Nevada, getting Heather and her two daughters settled in. He felt like he might need to invest in a van or an SUV if everybody started wanting to do things all together, but the situation wouldn't make it that far before disaster struck.

Manny explained Heather's situation to Rosa and Michelle, earning their respect for her position with an agreement to do their best to shelter the children from catching a glimpse of what was going on. This made working out of town the most reasonable way to get money, and they rotated it so that at least one of the team was always at the house with the kids.

His plan was to set Heather and her girls up with a place of their own once she returned from her first trip down the highway, and he ended up keeping an older woman named Teresa around to play babysitter sometimes. She was from Iowa, and her exposure to his lifestyle came from Chicago. With long blonde hair and big blue eyes, she looked good at forty-one years old. She had a nice shape and so much sex appeal that Manny was soon thinking he should reintroduce her to the hustle.

The interest was mutual, inspired by Teresa's front row view of Manny's success. She'd known pimps all over Chicago and Memphis who never seemed to care about the real-life concerns of the women on their teams, but somehow Manny seemed to be different without losing his focus on the bottom line. She recognized that he had no patience, but his attention to detail made him still meet all needs.

She liked him and grew into wanting to try him out in more ways than one. He made her remember why she turned her first trick over twenty years before she met him. Therefore, once things developed in his program to the point of making it possible, Teresa started working for Manny on a local basis. She didn't interact much with the rest of the girls beyond just being openly aware of each other.

Her objective was to qualify for his regular attention, and his objective was to have her follow the rules of the game if she wanted to play a part in his world. They exchanged sex, money, and conversation in whatever order they desired, and Manny was now able to honestly say he had three hoes on deck and one ho in check whenever he referred to the set-up of his situation.

$$$$$

Manny and Rosa's relationship drifted into less time being spent together and more hidden resentments on her part. Her plan with Valerie backfired terribly. Now, instead of one new girl to get rid of, she had two whose situations were so different that the same approach wasn't even possible. Heather was too focused on handling her business for her kids, and Teresa was some mystical image that everybody only ever heard about. She never even left Las Vegas, so she wasn't on the road with the rest of the team, and Manny kept her separated the rest of the time. Michelle was the only one she really had access to, and she was so loyal to Manny that corrupting her would need to be done very carefully.

On his part, Manny could not stop replaying that whole situation with Valerie in his mind. Something just didn't seem right about the whole scenario. Whenever he went over it in his mind, he always came back to the times when Valerie was alone with Rosa as the moments when he noticed the changes. He knew enough about the Game to know when salt had been sprinkled onto what he was trying to do, so he kept Rosa with Michelle to stay busy and watched her from a distance as he began to suspect he may have made a mistake when he married Rosa.

The program took care of itself, and the bankroll moved in a steady upward direction. He bought himself a Rolex watch and a diamond pinkie ring that matched it perfectly. He liked the ring so much that he bought another one just like it, but twice the size to wear on his other hand. It glittered like a big marble made of ice that was as big as a fifty-cent piece.

Everything multiplied by leaps and bounds in his life, until one night he got pulled over on the Las Vegas strip while taking Teresa to an outcall date at one of the hotels.

The police arrested him for traffic warrants, leaving Teresa with his Cadillac and a lot of rushed instructions.

The only phone number he knew by memory was Rosa's, so he called her to get all his affairs in order. She got the car from Teresa, paid the rent at the house, and organized the team's activities exactly like he needed her to.

Then she had a chance to sit back and think about her position...

Manny had to sit in jail for a week until his court date. He had no bail because he'd failed to show up for his previous court dates. That's when she realized that she was in control, and things went from good to bad as the jealousy she'd been stuffing away in her heart began to take control of her actions.

By the time Manny got out of jail ten days later, Michelle was no longer on the team. She'd somehow gotten robbed and pistol whipped in Baltimore by some guys that her and Rosa dated regularly. Now she was out of reach at her aunt's house in San Diego, and the only person who knew the whole story was Rosa.

As if that news wasn't bad enough, Manny was also faced with the new obstacle of Heather suddenly not feeling like being away from her kids was such a good idea, and it seemed like no coincidence that Rosa was now her new text buddy in a way that was much more than it was at first.

Manny didn't believe in coincidences...

Then, in the strange way that things can work themselves out, Rosa got busted in New Jersey in a prostitution sting. Her probation activated a no-bail hold on her for violation of the terms in Nevada, so there wasn't much Manny could do to help her.

All he had to remember her by was the aftermath of her destructive efforts. Her sabotage became clear to see as Heather's dedication dwindled and Teresa began to reveal things Rosa had been maliciously dropping into her ear to poison her mind.

Every single problem that he had, came back to Rosa as the source. She was a bigger enemy to his success than law enforcement was, and it didn't take any major stretch of the imagination to read that jealousy was the only reason for any of this – the blind, unreasonable, territorial jealousy of a wife. If it was not a mistake to trust such a productive provider, it was a mistake to marry one unless they were done with the Game, and retirement was the new adventure.

To top it all off, Rosa's mother was calling the rest of his team to continue the pollution with news of Rosa claiming to be pregnant. Overnight it seemed like everything he heard or knew about his number one teammate became an evolving drama-based source of bad news.

He didn't know what to believe, or how to feel, in the combined conflict of blaming himself and trying to juggle the results of this unexpected attack.

But the worst part of all was the part he didn't know about...

$$$$$

Officer Darwin Nelson had just recently been promoted to Detective in the vice division of the Las Vegas Metro Police Department. He felt it was overdue, but his inability to pass the required test delayed his promotion.

What he lacked in smarts, however, he made up for with how personal he took his job. This quality was what kept him connected to a desire for Manny's downfall after he first came into contact with Rosa back when she robbed the cowboys. Manny was the one who got away, and he could not let it go.

For a short while, he tried to track down the mysterious figure he'd spoken to so briefly on the phone, but he got nowhere beyond establishing that Rosa did indeed work for a pimp from out of state named Manny Fresh, who wasn't very social.

But he knew Manny's luck would change eventually. This was Las Vegas, and the house always wins...

Over time, he got little tidbits here and there about Manny's activities from his informants. News of different girls and cars only served to increase Detective Nelson's hateful determination to one day put him in jail.

Then, one day he received a call from a woman in Texas claiming to be Rosa's mother...

$$$$$

One rotten apple had almost spoiled the whole bunch. But lucky for Manny, the only mistake he'd made was letting love, marriage, and jealousy into his game with Rosa. Aside from that, he was ahead with a big bankroll saved up and the veteran assistance of Teresa in his corner, so he didn't need to keep going out as he planned his next series of steps...

With the new source of information at his disposal, Detective Nelson's interest in Manny intensified. Knowing now that his suspect did not live within the city limits and travelled extensively with his girls made it understandable why gathering information had been so hard. This situation was looking like it was a lot more widespread and sophisticated than what was thought as first...

$$$$$

North Dakota had an oil rush that raised the economy drastically when it was discovered. Manny took Teresa there after Heather packed the girls off to Louisiana, overwhelmed with the constant calls from Rosa's mom and all the bad things being said about Manny. She didn't want to leave him, but she didn't want her kids involved in a messy situation either, so she left.

"Don't worry about none of that old stuff. I'll hold you down for as long as you do me right," Teresa told him numerous times on those frozen nights when snow storms kept them indoors.

Manny had never been so cold in his life; but he adjusted his mood and rose to the occasion of trying to be upbeat about how things were going.

"What I like about this place is that we get time to hang out, but when the money starts coming it goes from nothing to something real quick. I can tell we gonna be OK as long as we don't self-destruct," he told her one night while they were at the bar eating buffalo wings and drinking Yaeger Bombs.

Teresa was in agreement with him about his way of seeing things. "Yeah, we got a strange schedule, but for some reason, the money comes in overdrive when it finally does come. I ain't never saw so much so fast!"

But the cold was a killer. Some nights it was as bad as twenty below zero, and when they walked outside, the ice on the ground was up to three inches thick. And that's why they were in the bar on this night; because it was attached to the hotel they were staying in.

Manny munched on a piece of chicken and looked closely at Teresa. She had been a positive presence during some not-so-great moments, and so far she was doing good.

"You standin' tall through it all, T. Don't think I don't see you. And please believe I'ma build a new team that's gonna be waaaay stronger for waaaay longer. I can't let her win like that."

Teresa swallowed half of her Yaeger Bomb in one gulp, and without meeting his gaze, decided to speak her mind. "Daddy Man, I told you I had ya back, and I do. But I see you sometimes when you don't think I'm watching you. It's alright to feel a little hurt when people turn on you, so I can understand that part of how you might feel.

"But if your girl Rosa plays any kind of part in why you wanna be successful in the future, I don't want to be used as your tool to get back at her. I'm here for you, not anybody else. So if you got ya lil heart broke 'cause y'all was in love, then please let me know so I can get out the way. I chose to get down for you because I thought pimpin' is what you do, and I like that about you. No disrespect, but this ain't a game for heartfelt memories, so either we do what we do, or you waitin' for ya girl. You gotta choose one, baby."

Manny had to smile at how real she was right then, but also not go overboard in acknowledging that she was right. "Bitch, remind me to keep yo' ass away from Yaeger Bombs in the future. You get all insightful on me like that again, and I might just feel forced to get all macho on yo' ass. But I hear you, though, and you make a good point."

Teresa smiled at him and said no more on the subject. She knew better than to push her luck, and she appreciated he let her know to watch her mouth without having to put her in her place or ignoring her input. It was just enough to set her straight without trying to defeat her.

She studied him a moment longer before coming to a decision. "Hey, you know what? As far as building something back up goes, I know a girl from back home who would really go for you if she ever met you. She's about twenty-five or twenty-six, and before I came to Vegas, she used to ask me a million questions about the Game once she knew I had been in if before."

This had Manny's attention. "Oh yeah? What she look like?" he asked as if he didn't really believe what she was saying.

Teresa ordered more buffalo wings and a Pepsi to wash down the liquor. Then she answered him. "Well, I see you must think I'm joking, but I'm not. She's almost as tall as you, with long, black hair. She's cute and got a set of the biggest titties you ever saw. She's a little chunky, but it fits her, though, and most guys that see her pay her a lot of attention. Trust me, if we teach her what to do, she'll work out. I can call her tomorrow if you want me to."

"Why not tonight?" he asked curiously.

"Because that Yaeger got me hoping I can get you to do something else with me tonight if you don't mind..."

$$$$$

True to Teresa's claim, Chloe came to meet them within a few days. When the cab showed up with her in it from the train station, Teresa ran downstairs to meet her and bring her back to the room.

When she walked through the door and her eyes landed on Manny, they never left him. He returned her gaze as Teresa made the introductions, and he noticed that Chloe had some of the palest blue eyes he'd ever seen. They were like ice that produced an attractive contrast to the darkness of her hair and eyebrows.

Teresa was right when she described her as being very attractive. And when she took note of how intensely focused the attention was, she excused herself to give them space to get acquainted with each other. Making up a reason to go to the store, she left them alone.

A few seconds after she left, Manny broke the silence. "Well, I sure do see you over there, Ms. Look-E-Loo. If yo' ears and yo' mind stay stuck on me as much as those eyes do, I can really do somethin' with you."

Chloe shook herself out of the daze she was in, then she smiled at his words. "Didn't mean to stare like that. It's just that you don't look like none of the guys I see in Iowa at all. I was told that you were different, but... let's just say I like what I see."

Still sizing her up, Manny wanted to keep the words flowing to get a feel for her mindset.

"So is that what brought you out here so quick? You wanted to get a look at somethin' real? Like I'm just a picture you always wanted to see up close?"

"No, not like that at all," she quickly replied as she sat down on the bed. "It's just good to finally see somebody who is about that life instead of just claiming it with no action to back that shit up.

"I came quick because I'm tired of seeing guys sit around drinking and smoking like bosses, but in every other way they're really bums, never going anywhere - don't even got their own cars or spots, and just want to share a girl with their friends. Then when you call them on it, they want to beat you up."

"OK, so then what is it that you want out of dealing with me? What exactly are you lookin' for?"

"I know Teresa been through it all, and if she says you're for real, then I want in on it. I know what guys notice about me and what they want. That's cool, but it don't mean I'm not supposed to get anywhere in life though. So why not get something out of it? And I hear you're good at getting something out of it. So I'm trying to be down for that."

"I can vibe with that. You'd be surprised how many people actually choose to lose with everyday human circumstances being the excuse. I've seen it happen to the best of 'em, so I'm real careful who I fuck wit'. Because this is my bread and meat, so if I don't win, I don't eat. That leaves no room for anybody who just looking for an adventure out here.

"Ain't no off-switch on what I do – and what I do is pimp, by the way – so I don't need nobody in my life who ain't as dedicated as I am, because that would injure the empire I'm tryna build. So can you commit to this cause to the point where even if you mad at me, the mission is still important to you?"

Chloe took in his words, feeling how deeply reaching the meaning of them turned out to be. She sensed his seriousness and began to fall under his spell. Not because of how good it sounded, but as a result of the way he broke down the details to his outlook on this lifestyle. His reason had more of an effect than requests or requirements, and she respected that about him immediately.

Manny saw that she was at a loss for words when she gave only a thoughtful nod of her head in response to the question he'd just asked. So he accepted that and continued on with his orientation.

"You should see that it's obvious I want you here, or I wouldn't have sent you a ticket to come. But now that you here, I need you to zoom in on what I represent. I'm here to represent my team and my team is a representation of me. So there should be no line in your mind between where you end and where I begin. Being down for me should be just as undeniable as caring about yourself. Not just to please me, but because you believe that my bottom line is to look out for you.

"I could quit all of this shit right now and be just fine for real. My bankroll has to be somewhere around a hundred thousand already. But I'll never reach a million unless I share this journey with people who will enjoy it enough to make it grow – people like you and Teresa, who would give anything to be a part of a real thing when the world is trying to use them up or treat them like nothing."

Then Manny stood Chloe up and walked her over to the mirror above the sink. "Look in that mirror and be real with yourself about what you see. Then I want you to add this into whatever you come up with. There's a person in a powerful position standing here who can really do good in life if she has a game plan on how to use what you see to her advantage. And I got a million game plans in my memory bank."

"I believe you about that," she replied. "And I'll do whatever you tell me to do. Even though I just met you, I already decided to be down when I decided to come. You just put the whole reason into words I can agree with."

"So you ready to make this shit happen?" he asked her to set the understanding in stone. She turned around to face him with a wicked grin and said, "I was born ready!"

$$$$$

Teresa got back about an hour later with a few things they could make a big dinner with without cooking. The deli section at Wal-Mart worked wonders in this area. Rotisserie chickens, potato salad, apple pie, and a two-liter bottle of the Pepsi she loved so much made for a wonderful meal.

Manny and Chloe were just getting started with pictures for her online ad, so the three of them put it all together as they munched away.

$$$$$

A couple of weeks later, Manny was over ten thousand dollars richer and on a train to Chicago. The girls were able to rest in comfort as the countryside rolled by outside. The many steps along the way made the trip a lot longer than a plane, but that was all part of the plan to rest his team.

On a stop in Minnesota, Manny hopped off to investigate something that caught his eye as the train was pulling into the station. What he found when he caught up to what he'd spotted was a small young lady in well-worn jeans and a puff coat. She had thick curly brown hair and a quick smile that still managed to be cute even though her teeth were crooked in the front.

She was from Louisville, Kentucky, on a trip to meet up with a "friend." Her name was Amanda, and she was on her way back home before her off-days were up and she lost her job a White Castle.

"I was just amazed to see someone like you using a pay phone. I thought cell phones ruled the world right about now. Was I seeing things?" Manny said jokingly suring their quick conversation.

"No, I was smoking a cigarette. Of course I got a cell phone," she replied with a giggle.

Manny swore this could not be the last time they saw each other, and they quickly exchanged numbers. When he got back on the train and pulled out of the station, he was already texting Amanda. And by the time he made it to Chicago, his phone was ringing with text alerts from her every few minutes.

As it turned out, the "friend" she had in Minnesota was a guy she'd met online who turned out to be a big fat disappointment once she got there to see him. So when Manny came along, she was very ready with an unsatisfied desire to meet someone new.

$$\$\$\$\$\$$

Hotel rooms in downtown Chicago were the starting point, but within a couple of days, Teresa took the team to the midway area. She knew the city well, so they were able to jump around without ever getting too burned out in any one place.

Chloe did well in Chicago and things were going according to Manny's plan. He kept the girls separated as much as possible to complete Chloe's transformation, and let Teresa run around the suburbs on her own to work on automatic.

With his situation flourishing, Manny had his friend Gerald send him some good weed to smoke. He kept a low profile and enjoyed the beauty of the snow every morning.

Then, one day as he was walking down Cicero Avenue toward his room from the store, he noticed a beautiful old Rolls Royce pass him by very slowly. It was green with gold-plated accents, and seemed to be going to the same place he was on his way to.

Manny didn't think much about it because there were numerous hotels all clustered up near the one he was staying in, as well as a TGI-Fridays that got a lot of traffic in the same lot. But he made a mental note to himself to put Chloe on notice about watching her step, because everything about that car indicated that there was a pimp in the area.

Teresa was due to be in that part of town later on that day as well, so he figured a general "heads up" couldn't hurt at all. But when he brought the news her way, Teresa responded with unexpected familiarity.

"Daddy, are you telling me that you don't know about the green and gold? That's an old pimp named Don Juan. Everybody's heard of him in this game, and if he's in the area, he must be lookin' for somebody. I doubt he's out here huntin' for hoes, though. He got a team that goes all over the world from what I've heard, but I'll be careful just in case," she said before they ended their call.

He saw the same car a lot more times over the course of the next few days, and on more than one occasion he saw the older gentleman inside looking at him. The man was timeless in a way that made it impossible to determine his age. Curiosity got the best of Manny one day and he sent Chloe to the store just to see what would happen, but she reported no harassment at all.

Finally, one day Manny was about to climb into a taxi cab to keep from walking in the snow when the Rolls Royce pulled to a stop next to him. The window slid down and the man he knew to be Don Juan was revealed up close.

"Hey, young pimpin'. Let that cab go find a hustle somewhere else while I take you where you need to be. People like me and you don't do taxi cabs. Come let me get at you right quick," the man said.

Manny hesitated. This was Chicago, and it was common knowledge that it was not wise to go hopping in strange cars if you wanted to remain among the living.

"No disrespect, big bruh, but I don't know you to be all in yo' car like that," Manny replied carefully.

"Look, lil brotha, I need you to think for a minute. Tell me when was the last time you heard about a murder, robbery or kidnap being put down out of a car this noticeable? I know by now you know exactly who I am, so don't be stupid. Get in the car, man."

Of course the guy was right about Manny knowing who he was. And he was definitely not dressed for any kind of rough stuff with his shimmering clothes and gigantic jewelry. So Manny got into the car, trying and failing to not show how impressed he was at the sight of the extreme luxury of the vehicle.

Don Juan saw Manny's eyes taking in everything around him, and he allowed the younger man to do this for a moment before he decided to speak.

I hope my ride meets your approval, young playa. Or should I address you as young pimpin'? I wasn't sure at first when I saw you doin' all your own footwork. But then you surprised me when you sent that pretty cornfed bitch outside the other day. That's when I knew you was confident and checkin' to see what I was up to. I gotta salute you for that move, man, 'cause it ain't a pimp anywhere else in America that would've did that if he knew I was down and around. But ya ho stayed in pocket, though, so I respected her management and gave her a pass.

"I recognize instincts in you that I ain't seen in a long time. Most of these new-wave niggas got this shit so fucked up, I don't even speak to them for free. But I know the truth when I see it. And you the truth. So what's ya name, young brotha?"

"I'm Manny Fresh, out that West Coast."

"Oh, OK! I think I been hearin' about you. Where you from out west? I'm guessin' the Bay Area or Seattle."

"I'm from the Bay. How you know that?"

"Man, when you been as many places as me, you recognize the kind of stamp every section of this country puts on the people that live there. And you far too serious about yo' program to not be from a place that breeds your kind of people. I don't see no real thuggish vibe in you, so I wouldn't consider you to be an ex-gangbanger. And out the West, that only leaves the Bay Area, because everywhere else got Bloods and Crips. Only reason I say Seattle is because those cats get a little bit crispier with it from dealing with all them snow bunnies," Don Juan said offhandedly. Then he looked more serious as he went on with the rest of his thoughts.

"It's good to finally meet you, young Manny. You been across the map from coast to coast, but don't nobody really know you. You keep to yourself and pimp on your hoes. But people in the Game do notice you enough to speak on you, though. That means you must be doin' some real pimpin'. With that bein' said, I still got a question for you."

"What's that, big bruh?"

"Why is it that I been askin' myself for a while now if this up and comin' pimp I been hearin' about was in some kind of love with that Mexican bitch you had?"

Manny was caught offguard by the question, but because he felt caught anyway, he gave an honest answer. When he was done telling Don Juan the whole story of Rosa, there was a brief silence in the car as the older man processed what he had been told. Then after pulling into the parking lot of the Clarion where Teresa was, he parked his beautiful car and got more comfortable.

Looking over at Manny, Don Juan slowly shook his head and said, "Young brotha, you gave the game a black eye and got spanked for it. But what I do respect is that you kept that bitch workin' instead of bein' on some cupcake-type shit. Your problem is that you was tryna dedicate or commit yourself to this Game when you married that bitch. But it sent mixed messages to the bitch, though, because now she think she made it to the finish line while you thinkin' y'all at the starting point of a real deal.

"The rules of this Game are in place for a reason, man, and now you know this for yourself.

"You or nobody else can ever come along and rewrite the book on what a real pimp supposed to do. Every new bitch you got made that ho think you was movin' away from the goal instead of toward the goal. So she thought if they was gone, y'all would get to where she thought y'all was already at, or supposed to be. You had the poor lil bitch confused, man!"

Manny was surprised to hear this, because he agreed with his words. He just had not reached this understanding on his own because he'd never shared his details with anyone to receive any accurate feedback. He told this to Don Juan who acknowledged what he said and continued on with his own perspective about how he saw Manny's situation.

"Little brotha, some people pursue this life as a result of a decision they made. But others don't have a choice, because this life pursues them. Everywhere you turn, you meet another ho or spot another trick. That's because it's in you, not on you, man! You gonna always see how to send a bitch, or where to send a bitch, or which bitch you can send, while the rest of the world is on some other shit. So sit back and hear me out so I can try to drop some jewels on you."

He locked the doors and turned the heat up a little so they could be comfortable in the car. This left Manny with no choice but to listen.

"The first thing I need to point out to you is that the blonde-haired vet you got up in that joint is a real go-getter from way back. I had a protege who used to have the bitch down and around this whole area and all through the south. She cut out on him about ten years ago and ain't got down for nobody else since then. My potna had a problem with his temper and ol' girl got a mouth on her when she starts drinkin', so that was a bad combo. My point is that she'll take all the pimpin' you ever put on her as long as it ain't gorilla pimpin'. So don't go soft on her, because as long as you keep ya hands to yourself, she'll be a goldmine for you.

"You should already know you catch more bees with honey than you do with vinegar anyway, man. And you should never have to beat on a good ho, so if she's a knucklehead, I suggest you shake the bitch and go find the right one. The problem is that so many people are in this shit who don't belong in it but are tryin' to do it anyway. And all they qualify for is dumb bitches or knuckleheads. So do good by the good ones and get the bad ones away from you."

He paused to let Manny digest this information. When no question came, he continued. "The next thing I want to tell you is to treat yourself at all times. You deserve it, because your life is gonna bring you more pain and frustration than any man on earth. I heard you got yourself a pretty lil Cadillac and a clean-ass Impala out there in Vegas. That's cool, but step yo' game up to the kind of shit that is above average.

"The kind of money I know you playin' with should have you pushin' the biggest and the best. I got an Italian boy who got a Mercedes he been tryna sell me with real low miles on it. It's a big body with the V-12 engine and all the options on it. You need that thang in yo' game, man. And you spend top dollar to get top dollar. The Benz is a few years old, so the price won't be no six-figure number, but you'll get the same kind of results.

"Be sure you expand your mind and recognize your possibility as a real cross-country pimp. The whole country is your ATM machine. But remember this: It don't all start and end with pimpin'. I know that's all you see, but you gotta know what you can do just as well with anything else you get into. Women come to us because we are more than they ever saw before. So don't get stranded on a steppin' stone, because that's all pimpin' should be for you, man."

Manny listened closely to every word Don Juan said to him. There wasn't much to say in response, but he was grateful that someone so well-known and highly respected would take the time out to make sure he knew everything he needed to know.

"Man, big bruh... I appreciate the guidance fa sho. I'ma take yo' advice to heart as soon as I step out this car and get on my bitch. But let me get the number for ya boy with the Benz for sale."

Don Juan scrolled through the contacts on his cell phone and let Manny copy the number into his own phone. Next, he made sure they had each other's phone number before he unlocked the door to let Manny out.

Holding out his hand, he said seriously, "Shake on this deal, young brotha. Promise me you gonna pick up that Benz, and don't ride a taxi cab never again. Next time I come check you out, I wanna see you whippin' and dippin' in that V-12."

Manny shook his head and declared, "I promise you I'm on it, bruh. Don't even trip. We got a deal, so come get wit' me and you gonna see."

With that said, they parted company with Manny feeling like his game was more complete than it had ever been in his life.

The Clarion Hotel had a bar and restaurant in the lobby, and that's where Manny found Teresa sipping on a Pepsi and munching on some fries at the bar near the entrance, so he ordered himself a beer and sat next to her.

Turning sideways on his bar stool he asked her conversationally, "Sup, T? I see you down here all sexy lookin' like a French fry lover. Enjoyin' your snack, or what?"

She leaned playfully into him with a twinkle in her big blue eyes. "Don't sit there and play me like you ain't just had an event. Only reason I'm havin' a snack is because I was on my way to grab some condoms and saw that green and gold parked out there. So here I am stalling until he left, and who do I see jump out of it but my very own Daddy-man. But why am I not surprised? And he driving you around, too? Did you already know him or something?"

"No, Ms. Nosey! I didn't know him from the man on the moon. But he say he heard about me and our program, so he pulled up to drop a few jewels on me. Cool old dude to be honest with you."

He instantly decided not to tell her what he'd been told about her. He'd just act according to what he knew. They talked a little more before Manny sent her to handle her business, while he checked on the Mercedes-Benz that was hopefully still for sale...

CHAPTER 22

PIMP SHIT

"It'll be greater later, but it'll get worse first."
– Old Pimp Proverb

A couple of weeks later, Manny met the sunrise as he did on most days. . . hard at work on the planning of his program. He rarely slept for hours on end unless he was somewhere off on his own, so in the company of his team, he took naps for the most part and was almost always awake before anyone else.

Don Juan's friend was as available as Don Juan's valuable encouragement was. And within a week, the short, stocky man named Antonio sold Manny an immaculate black S-Class sedan with a gigantic V-12 engine on 22-inch rims. The interior was black and gray with wood trim that was so polished, it shined like glass all across the dashboard, steering wheel and center console, with inserts in the door panels as well. The car was huge, with everything available at the touch of a button, and when he first got it, he took a quick road trip to Kentucky where he picked up Amanda whom he'd been in steady contact with since meeting her in Minnesota.

Now he was back in a suburb outside of Chicago after a busy night, watching the snow cover his Mercedes like a buried treasure.

"Let me guess what you're doing right now," Teresa said to him as she wrapped her arms around his waist from behind as he stared out of the window. "You're obsessing over your new car as if maybe it might magically disappear overnight. So you just had to look out of that window while it's sitting right where you left it. And unless I'm wrong, you better be thinkin' 'bout how you got yourself some damn good hoes. Am I on point, or what?"

Manny smiled and squeezed her arms affectionately before playfully correcting the last part of her guess. "See, bitch, you was almost right until you got to the part about some good hoes. What I was actually thinkin' was how lucky my hoes are to finally find a good pimp who improved their ho status in such a major way. Now y'all can be professional prostitutes and stand to show what an average ho is 'posed to be aiming for."

Never one to be shot down, though, Teresa took it in stride without missing a beat. "Oh, well, I was right, then. Your description just got more words to it than mine do. So when am I gonna get to drive that damn car?"

"When we get out of this damn snow so I ain't gotta worry 'bout nobody sliding on the ice and tearing shit up. Please believe you'll be helping me on the ride back home. Just let me finish breakin' this new bitch in and we'll be out of here. You commin' wit' me to buy breakfast for everybody?"

"Of course, I'm coming. Just let me take another shower while you go check yo' money from yo' children," she replied, mocking how he talks.

She liked to refer to the rest of Manny's team as "his children," and Manny humored her with this. Whatever it took to make her feel good about what she was doing, even if she needed to put herself above the rest in her own mind.

Chloe and Amanda had separate rooms with a connecting door between them, so that each one was in reach of a teammate if the need arose.

Manny used his key to enter Chloe's room to get the day started and see what they wanted from Denny's. He also wanted to collect whatever they'd made the night before. Climbing into the bed with Chloe, still wearing all of his clothes, he wrapped himself around her to provide a dose of the cuddling he knew she liked so much. He rubbed her huge breasts from behind and nibbled on her ear to wake her up.

She came around slowly, unwinding to stretch like a cat against him. "Hmmm... Is that you, Santa Clause?" she murmured like a baby still caught in a dream. "I left you some green cookies next to the T.V."

Manny pressed up against her softness and mumbled into her ear. "And were you a good little girl last, or a bad one?"

Chloe giggled and responded, "Oh, I was very, very bad, and my customers loved it. I think your new chick is in her own little competition with me. I'm gonna start saying I got a lot more than I really do just to see if that makes her get more. She's a ding-bat, but she tries hard as she handles her business. Why are your clothes still on, Daddy?"

"Because I need to be dressed and you need to be getting ready for work if you plan to catch that morning rush for me. What do you want from Denny's for breakfast?"

"I'll take whatever you bring me. Go get my next-door neighbor up and post our ad so we can get at it. I got this."

Manny hopped out of the bed with a final squeeze and a peck on the back of her neck. He grabbed the money from the dresser next to the T.V. and went next door through the connecting door.

There he found Amanda completely naked and snoring like a baby bear. He crept up to the side of the bed and looked down on her as he counted the money Chloe had just given him. Then he took a fifty-dollar bill and tickled Amanda's nose with it until she snuffled into consciousness. He spoke to get her on track.

"You smell that money, girl? Straight mullah, baby! It's time to rise and shine so we can get on our grind. How you doin'? Everything go OK for you last night?"

He knew to take her mind immediately to where he wanted it to be or she would drift into her perpetual goal of trying to seduce him.

She blinked and sat up. "Hey, baby – I mean, Daddy. I meant to say Daddy. No disrespect. Yeah, last night was a good one. I still can't believe how the money comes knocking on the door for us," she said as she crawled out of bed and pulled her money from a drawer. "Here you go!" she announced proudly. "I'm hungry this morning. Can we go get breakfast before the day starts, or are you gonna bring it?"

"Actually, I'm serving it up this morning, cutie. That's what I came to see, aside from how your money looks. What you want from Denny's?"

"Ooooh, can I get a Denver omelet and some sausage?" she chirped immediately, still thrilled at the idea of getting some good food.

234

"I got you on that fa sho. Now I need you to keep ya lil ass awake so I can get yo' phone back poppin' for you. I'll be back with yo' food in a minute, OK?"

She assured him she would do as he asked and he was on his way.

Sitting in his Mercedes, he texted Teresa to meet him there while he posted everyone's ad and heated up the car's interior. Another day was successfully started...

$$\$\$\$\$\$$

Manny Fresh liked Chicago and Chicago was good to him in every way. Even in the cold of the snow there was something about the place that made you want to go get out there in it. Every business seemed to prosper, and it was worthwhile to get dressed to go anywhere you might be on your way to, because you never knew who you would meet next.

It was alive, vibrant, and active. But the people still weren't caught up in pretense, or full of themselves in any way. It took all of your senses to truly experience, enjoy and survive Chicago, because what you saw with the naked eye was far from being all there was to see.

Springtime was pushing its way in past the winter season, but the cold was stubbornly holding on. The snow was melting slowly, and the beauty was changing from day to day into a dirty slush-filled substitute for what the scenery was like when Manny arrived a few weeks earlier.

It was time to go home for a little while and take a break to put his money up. He never wanted to, but he knew it was a must.

He'd shown his car to Don Juan and gotten the approval of everyone who laid eyes on it. The Game had given him his salute and he was overdue for a break, so he rounded up his team and made his way back to Las Vegas to relax, even though it felt like he was leaving an old friend behind. Chicago would truly be seeing him again many times over, but until then, Interstate 70 would be the road he travelled to get back to the Wild West...

$$$$$

Sometimes success can be a double-edged sword when you're dealing with other people's perspective on what a mission being accomplished actually looks like. Demands can develop that can create resentments if they remain unacknowledged. So when Manny noticed Amanda starting to show that display of a sour tinge to her normally bouncy personality, he knew to address it quickly.

Being in Las Vegas was a bit of a culture shock for Amanda because her online ad didn't draw the same kind of attention as it did in Chicago. So she had to put in a lot more footwork than the rest of the team, and her lack of any real sophistication made the street more profitable for her than the casinos.

"Daddy, why do I get all the grunt work while the rest of the team gets to work the glamorous life?" she asked one day when he opened the subject about how she was doing.

Manny knew that was more than likely the question that was coming. Folding the money she'd just given him, he explained. "That's a good question, actually. But I don't ask myself that question because I don't question why I want you in my world. I just accept you however you come, and consider you to be as precious as everybody else.

Each one of you have your own lane in this game. Those hoes don't rock the track the way you do, just like you don't do what they do well. Chloe got those titties so she do good online, and Teresa is that casino specialist because her experience carries her further with that level of clients. But none of that is more important to me than the other, because every machine has more than one part. Take out one of those parts and the machine is incomplete, so you count just as much as anybody else. And one thing fa sho is that you ain't workin' while they sit on their asses chillin', right?"

"No... I can't say you're fuckin me over like that. We all know you're not big on takin' breaks. It's just that what they do seems like it's so much more fun and classier compared to me. I wanna feel like a boss, too, sometimes, instead of the bottom of the totem pole!"

Manny regarded her closely, wondering if her complaint was the real issue, or if there was something else going on with her. Because work was work, so unless she just didn't want to work, it should be obvious that whatever paid the best is what she needed to do. So what was really going on?

"Talk to me, baby girl. What's the problem for real? I feel like you still ain't told me what's bothering you," he persisted insightfully.

Amanda looked nervously at him and bit her lip before blurting out, "Damn it, Manny, I just feel like a robot lately! All I know is I'm doin' a lot more than I ever done before to get you this money. I respect what you say about stackin' it all up and all. That's smart. But even if it's stupid to do it, I wanna blow some of this money just because we can afford to. Not on stuff to work in, either. Even if it's wrong, that's how I feel!"

She was crying as the admission poured out of her. The frustration was genuine, and Manny could tell that is was built up to a boiling point. He had to really get a grip on himself in order to keep from laughing out loud. He patiently allowed her to get her emotion out until the intensity of her sobs were under control.

Then he asked her, "How long have you been feelin' like this, Amanda?"

"A couple of weeks, I guess. I mean... I'm happy and all... but I'm just sayin'," she replied.

"Well, I know you tryin' to be the best bitch you can be. But a good bitch is honest, first and foremost. If you would've mentioned it sooner, we could have already taken care of it for you."

"I know... But I didn't wanna sound like the young dumb one in the bunch. I guess I am, though, since both of my wifeys are older than me and must be used to having money like this. I just wanna be able to enjoy it if I'm gonna be always out here gettin' it."

"Yeah, but I ain't even mad at you for that. The thing with me is, if you go weeks with somethin' on yo' mind that you keep to yourself, it's not fair to the team. Because first off, you keepin' secrets. But more importantly is that you not givin' me the chance to fix it for you. And that ain't cool at all."

Seeing her shrink from his rebuke made him want to pick up her spirits, so he switched directions with the rest of his response. "I'll tell you what. How about tomorrow me and you take an extended lunch break and go crazy at a few of these malls they got scattered all over this city? I'll bring a couple stacks and we can run around till it's all gone. But lunch is on you. Do we have a deal?"

"Oh, hell yeah, we got a deal! Thank you so much, Daddy! I wasn't sure how you was gonna react to me feelin' like that. Oh-my-God! Let me go do my job so you don't regret givin' me what I want!" she squealed with joy as she bounced out of the car after kissing him quickly.

Manny watched her wiggle her way across the street happily, and mentally congratulated himself for being on top of his game. Amanda didn't know it, but her reaction was enough to make sure he had no regret. Her happiness would count more in the future than whatever he was about to spend on her, because she would pay him many times that amount. So this was the least he could do, and he'd gladly do it to keep that crooked-toothed smile on her face.

He made a note to himself to do something big and expensive for her on her upcoming twenty-first birthday before going on about his business. And that next day, he took her to do exactly as he told he he was going to do...

$$$$$

A week later, after riding around with Teresa and Chloe in Manny's Impala while enjoying the booming sound system while smoking blunts behind the privacy of the tinted windows, Amanda got dropped off on Koval Avenue a couple of blocks away from the Las Vegas strip.

She hopped out of the car with her heart set on having as much money as possible when she met back up with her folks in a couple of hours. But little did she know, the multiple sets of eyes that saw her step onto the track were attached to a couple of separate agendas that had their goals set upon a certain outcome as well.

One of the watchers saw the Impala turn onto Koval as he turned off of Las Vegas Boulevard toward that same direction. Adrenaline flooded his system as he hurried toward the corner as fast as traffic allowed him to. Once he reached it, he followed the same way the Impala had gone just in time to see Amanda hop out of it, but the car went on through the stop light and turned at the far corner before he could catch up.

He cursed his luck with a surge of anxiety as he sat stuck as a red light. Then he turned his attention back to Amanda who was his only connection to the target that had just slipped away from him...

Fresh on the block, Amanda wanted to snatch up a date as fast as possible. Her ambition eroded her caution, and her enthusiasm increased her confidence, so she got right to work on trying to catch the eye of every guy who drove by in traffic. With winks, waves, and a seductive smile, she did all she could to attract the attention of potential customers.

Manny had schooled her to not do certain things in the streets, and his lessons kept her safe. But she made exceptions to certain rules based on her own personal judgements. So when a good possibility pulled up on her in a white Suburban, she ignored the risk. *Why not?* she thought to herself with the memory of how well she did dating Black guys in Chicago. She figured it was at least worth checking it out.

"Hey there, sweetie! First, I need to ask, are you a pimp?" she said immediately when she got into the truck.

"Naw, lil mama, I ain't no pimp. Just a dude in town lookin' for a good time, willin' to pay my way into makin' it happen," Petey Rock said in his best impression of a square.

"OK, well, if you wanna pay to play, it's all good. But my folks ain't goin' for no games, so this is strictly business," she declared for the sake of clarity.

When he agreed to her terms, she directed him to a nearby motel, but he said he felt safer at his own room in "North Town," so they made their way to the freeway.

Meanwhile, others saw the scenario unfold and their plans adjusted as the opportunity presented a possibility that could be very useful...

$$$$$

Once in the motel room to handle their business, Amanda's "client" seemed to have a different aim. Sex didn't seem to matter to him as much as talking about her personal business did.

"Look, honey, I'm just tryin' to get paid and be on my way. No disrespect to you, but I don't need no personal connection right now, so are you here to bust a nut or not?" she said brusquely after he'd gone so far as to ask if her man was somewhere watching while she worked.

"Bitch, you got me fucked up if you still think I'm tryna buy some pussy!" Petey Rock barked at her in furious frustration.

When Amanda rolled her eyes and went for the door, all efforts at intelligence were cast aside in exchange for the tactical use of brute force. Petey Rock grabbed her by the hair and slammed her viciously to the floor, placing himself between her and the door.

In the blink of an eye, Amanda produced a knife from her bra and bounced up to her feet. "Either I leave, or you bleed, sweetie. It's your choice," she said bravely as she flicked the blade out and advanced in his direction.

Petey Rock went for the weapon and she slashed clumsily at his hand, slicing a gash into his arm. Her seriousness both surprised and enraged him.

"Aaaaaagh! Bitch, you think this shit a game?" he growled angrily as he held onto her hand and overpowered the knife from her grip. "I should fuck you in the ass with this goddamn knife, bitch! You lucky I need your help or you'd be a done deal!"

He stood menacingly over her with the knife in his fist, gesturing wildly with rage. "You 'bout to tell me where that nigga Manny Fresh is at or I'ma cut yo' lil stupid-ass in pieces, ho!"

As soon as his unexpected words found meaning in Amanda's desperate mind, they were both surprised by what happened next...

$$$$$

The surveillance was sketchy because the target was a ghost who only ever stayed around town long enough to be heard about before disappearing again by the time snitches informed about him arriving.

Recently the information about him having a 90s Impala Super Sport became available. And as luck would have it, the vehicle was reported to be seen around the area. But that luck was limited so far, because only Manny's girls were ever in the car, never Manny himself.

So the detectives kept an eye on the car whenever it was within city limits, hoping it would lead them to the target of their current investigation. It wasn't hard to intercept once they pinpointed the particular areas it travelled in. The only problem was that it left Clark County every night, eluding their jurisdiction.

A decision was made to build a case on some of the girls and then turn them as State's evidence against the suspect on a human trafficking charge. And the girl that they'd just followed to the motel after engaging in open solicitation was in the act of committing the crime they would use against her to gain cooperation at that very moment...

$$$$$

BANG! BANG! BANG!
Open up! Las Vegas Police! We know you're in there!" Detective Nelson and his fellow officers demanded from the other side of the door.

Petey Rock's rage turned into panic as he looked back and forth between Amanda and the door. Ignoring the pain of his injured arm and barely-healed shoulder, he pounced onto Amanda and straddled her body to place his hand over her mouth. The look in his eyes was enough to communicate to her that he was demanding silence.

BANG! BANG! BANG!

"This is your last chance! We saw you enter this room! Open up or we'll force the door open ourselves!" Detective Nelson declared aggressively.

That's when Amanda's mind went to work. She bit one of the fingers that covered her mouth as hard as she could. Her thinking was that if the cops were right there, then Petey Rock couldn't do much harm to her.

However, her assumption was terribly incorrect.

As soon as he yanked his hand out of her mouth, Petey Rock raised the knife in his other hand to strike her. Amanda saw how big of a mistake she'd made and screamed at the top of her lungs. "HELLLP! He's got a knife!"

She bucked him off of her and scrambled onto her hands and knees. "Help me! He's gonna kill me! He kidnapped me and he's gonna kill me!" she managed to scream before he was on her again.

This time his aim was not to subdue her or keep her quiet. This time he was disconnected from any rational thought at all, and the only thing left in his existence was all the built-up anger and the pain behind that knife in his hand.

The last calls for help heard from Amanda as the police kicked in the door were very real ones. But sadly, her rescue was a few seconds too late. Her life was lost in a collision of jumbled plans, and Petey Rock was shot enough times to kill five people. When he lost his consciousness this time, there would be no waking up for him ever again.

Detective Nelson was furious that his case had just died before his eyes, and he blamed Manny more than ever for the death of this "innocent" girl who would still be alive if she wasn't "forced" into this situation by the "monster" of a man who "put her in harm's way."

$$$$$

Overdue vengeance and a bad decision had cost Amanda her life, but Manny and his team were unaware of this, thinking she'd run off until the news burned like wildfire all through the vast community of street walkers in the area.

Chloe had a regular client who was a metro cop that told her the details about what happened without ever guessing that he was updating her on the demise of a member of her "family."

A fellow soldier had fallen. She was a problem child to a mild degree because of her ignorance, but she was more deserving of pity than punishment. Chloe cried when she broke the news to the rest of the team, and each one of them mourned in their own way at the loss of a teammate.

Teresa advised Manny not to get involved with the situation since Nevada law could get tricky when the cops wanted to get something on a person. And the best move he ever could've made was to take her advice, because the last thing they needed was for any of them to get tied into Amanda's irreparable issue.

Manny thought back to the small apartment in Louisville, Kentucky where Amanda left her mom alone with a hillbilly boyfriend when she skipped town with him. He sent a money order to cover funeral costs to the address in hopes of soothing the sick feeling of sadness that had scorched the walls of his soul.

And just to be on the safe said, he left Nevada in his rearview as he drove toward the east coast with what remained of his team....

To be continued. ...

THE CELL BLOCK

BOOK SUMMARIES

MIKE ENEMIGO is the new prison/street art sensation who has written and published several books. He is inspired by emotion; hope; pain; dreams and nightmares. He physically lives somewhere in a California prison cell where he works relentlessly creating his next piece. His mind and soul are elsewhere; seeing, studying, learning, and drawing inspiration to tear down suppressive walls and inspire the culture by pushing artistic boundaries.

THE CELL BLOCK is an independent multimedia company with the objective of accurately conveying the prison/street experience with the credibility and honesty that only one who has lived it can deliver, through literature and other arts, and to entertain and enlighten while doing so. Everything published by The Cell Block has been created by a prisoner, while in a prison cell.

THE BEST RESOURCE DIRECTORY FOR PRISONERS, $17.95 & $5.00 S/H: This book has over 1,450 resources for prisoners! Includes: Pen-Pal Companies! Non-Nude Photo Sellers! Free Books and Other Publications! Legal Assistance! Prisoner Advocates! Prisoner Assistants! Correspondence Education! Money-Making Opportunities! Resources for Prison Writers, Poets, Artists! And much, much more! Anything you can think of doing from your prison cell, this book contains the resources to do it!

A GUIDE TO RELAPSE PREVENTION FOR PRISONERS, $15.00 & $5.00 S/H: This book provides the information and guidance that can make a real difference in the preparation of a comprehensive relapse prevention plan. Discover how to meet the parole board's expectation using these proven and practical principles. Included is a blank template and sample relapse prevention plan to assist in your preparation.

THEE ENEMY OF THE STATE (SPECIAL EDITION), $9.99 & $4.00 S/H: Experience the inspirational journey of a kid who was introduced to the art of rapping in 1993, struggled between his dream of becoming a professional rapper and the reality of the streets, and was finally offered a recording deal in 1999, only to be arrested minutes later and eventually sentenced to life in prison for murder... However, despite his harsh reality, he dedicated himself to hip-hop once again, and with resilience and determination, he sets out to prove he may just be one of the dopest rhyme writers/spitters ever .... At this point, it becomes deeper than rap .... Welcome to a preview of the greatest story you never heard.

LOST ANGELS: $15.00 & $5.00: David Rodrigo was a child who belonged to no world; rejected for his mixed heritage by most of his family and raised by an outcast uncle in the mean streets of East L.A. Chance cast him into a far darker and more devious pit of intrigue that stretched from the barest gutters to the halls of power in the great city. Now, to survive the clash of lethal forces arrayed about him, and to protect those he loves, he has only two allies; his quick wits, and the flashing blade that earned young David the street name, Viper.

LOYALTY AND BETRAYAL DELUXE EDITION, $19.99 & $7.00 S/H: Chunky was an associate of and soldier for the notorious Mexican Mafia – La Eme. That is, of course, until he was betrayed by those, he was most loyal to. Then he vowed to become their worst enemy. And though they've attempted to kill him numerous times, he still to this day is running around making a mockery of their organization .... This is the story of how it all began.

MONEY IZ THE MOTIVE: SPECIAL 2-IN-1 EDITION, $19.99 & $7.00 S/H: Like most kids growing up in the hood, Kano has a dream of going from rags to riches. But when his plan to get fast money by robbing the local "mom and pop" shop goes wrong, he quickly finds himself sentenced to serious prison time. Follow Kano as he is schooled to the ways of the game by some of the most respected OGs whoever did it; then is set free and given the resources to put his schooling into action and build the ultimate hood empire...

DEVILS & DEMONS: PART 1, $15.00 & $5.00 S/H: When Talton leaves the West Coast to set up shop in Florida he meets the female version of himself: A drug dealing murderess with psychological issues. A whirlwind of sex, money and murder inevitably ensues and Talton finds himself on the run from the law with nowhere to turn to. When his team from home finds out he's in trouble, they get on a plane heading south...

DEVILS & DEMONS: PART 2, $15.00 & $5.00 S/H: The Game is bitter-sweet for Talton, aka Gangsta. The same West Coast Clique who came to his aid ended up putting bullets into the chest of the woman he had fallen in love with. After leaving his ride or die in a puddle of her own blood, Talton finds himself on a flight back to Oak Park, the neighborhood where it all started...

DEVILS & DEMONS: PART 3, $15.00 & $5.00 S/H: Talton is on the road to retribution for the murder of the love of his life. Dante and his crew of killers are on a path of no return. This urban classic is based on real-life West Coast underworld politics. See what happens when a group of YG's find themselves in the midst of real underworld demons...

DEVILS & DEMONS: PART 4, $15.00 & $5.00 S/H: After waking up from a coma, Alize has locked herself away from the rest of the world. When her sister Brittany and their friend finally take her on a girl's night out, she meets Luck – a drug dealing womanizer.

FREAKY TALES, $15.00 & $5.00 S/H: *Freaky Tales* is the first book in a brand-new erotic series. King Guru, author of the *Devils & Demons* books, has put together a collection of sexy short stories and memoirs. In true TCB fashion, all of the erotic tales included in this book have been loosely based on true accounts told to, or experienced by the author.

THE ART & POWER OF LETTER WRITING FOR PRISONERS: DELUXE EDITION $19.99 & $7.00 S/H: When locked inside a prison cell, being able to write well is the most powerful skill you can have! Learn how to increase your power by writing high-quality personal and formal letters! Includes letter templates, pen-pal website strategies, punctuation guide and more!

THE PRISON MANUAL: $24.99 & $7.00 S/H: *The Prison Manual* is your all-in-one book on how to not only survive the rough terrain of the American prison system, but use it to your advantage so you can THRIVE from it! How to Use Your Prison Time to YOUR Advantage; How to Write Letters that Will Give You Maximum Effectiveness; Workout and Physical Health Secrets that Will Keep You as FIT as Possible; The Psychological impact of incarceration and How to Maintain Your MAXIMUM Level of Mental Health; Prison Art Techniques; Fulfilling Food Recipes; Parole Preparation Strategies and much, MUCH more!

GET OUT, STAY OUT!, $16.95 & $5.00 S/H: This book should be in the hands of everyone in a prison cell. It reveals a challenging but clear course for overcoming the obstacles that stand between prisoners and their freedom. For those behind bars, one goal outshines all others: GETTING OUT! After being released, that goal then shifts to STAYING OUT! This book will help prisoners do both. It has been masterfully constructed into five parts that will help prisoners maximize focus while they strive to accomplish whichever goal is at hand.

MOB$TAR MONEY, $12.00 & $4.00 S/H: After Trey's mother is sent to prison for 75 years to life, he and his little brother are moved from their home in Sacramento, California, to his grandmother's house in Stockton, California where he is forced to find his way in life and become a man on his own in the city's grimy streets. One day, on his way home from the local corner store, Trey has a rough encounter with the neighborhood bully. Luckily, that's when Tyson, a member of the MOBTAR, a local "get money" gang comes to his aid. The two kids quickly become friends, and it doesn't take long before Trey is embraced into the notorious MOB$TAR money gang, which opens the door to an adventure full of sex, money, murder and mayhem that will change his life forever... You will never guess how this story ends!

BLOCK MONEY, $12.00 & $4.00 S/H: Beast, a young thug from the grimy streets of central Stockton, California lives The Block; breathes The Block; and has committed himself to bleed The Block for all it's worth until his very last breath. Then, one day, he meets Nadia; a stripper at the local club who piques his curiosity with her beauty, quick-witted intellect and rider qualities. The problem? She has a man – Esco – a local kingpin with money and power. It doesn't take long, however, before a devious plot is hatched to pull off a heist worth an indeterminable amount of money. Following the acts of treachery, deception and betrayal are twists and turns and a bloody war that will leave you speechless!

HOW TO HUSTLE AND WIN: SEX, MONEY, MURDER EDITION $15.00 & $5.00 S/H: *How To Hu$tle and Win: Sex, Money, Murder Edition* is the grittiest, underground self-help manual for the 21st century street entrepreneur in print. Never has there been such a book written for today's gangsters, goons and go-getters. This self-help handbook is an absolute must-have for anyone who is actively connected to the streets.

RAW LAW: YOUR RIGHTS, & HOW TO SUE WHEN THEY ARE VIOLATED! $15.00 & $5.00 S/H: *Raw Law For Prisoners* is a clear and concise guide for prisoners and their advocates to understanding civil rights laws guaranteed to prisoners under the US Constitution, and how to successfully file a lawsuit when those rights have been violated! From initial complaint to trial, this book will take you through the entire process, step by step, in simple, easy-to-understand terms. Also included are several examples where prisoners have sued prison officials successfully, resulting in changes of unjust rules and regulations and recourse for rights violations, oftentimes resulting in rewards of thousands, even millions of dollars in damages! If you feel your rights have been violated, don't lash out at guards, which is usually ineffective and only makes matters worse. Instead, defend yourself successfully by using the legal system, and getting the power of the courts on your side!

HOW TO WRITE URBAN BOOKS FOR MONEY & FAME: $16.95 & $5.00 S/H: Inside this book you will learn the true story of how Mike Enemigo and King Guru have received money and fame from inside their prison cells by writing urban books; the secrets to writing hood classics so you, too, can be caked up and famous; proper punctuation using hood examples; and resources you can use to achieve your money motivated ambitions! If you're a prisoner who want to write urban novels for money and fame, this must-have manual will give you all the game!

PRETTY GIRLS LOVE BAD BOYS: AN INMATE'S GUIDE TO GETTING GIRLS: $15.00

& $5.00 S/H: Tired of the same, boring, cliché pen pal books that don't tell you what you really need to know? If so, this book is for you! Anything you need to know on the art of long and short distance seduction is included within these pages! Not only does it give you the science of attracting pen pals from websites, it also includes psychological profiles and instructions on how to seduce any woman you set your sights on! Includes interviews of women who have fallen in love with prisoners, bios for pen pal ads, pre-written love letters, romantic poems, love-song lyrics, jokes and much, much more! This book is the ultimate guide – a must-have for any prisoner who refuses to let prison walls affect their MAC'n.

THE LADIES WHO LOVE PRISONERS, $15.00 & $5.00 S/H: New Special Report reveals the secrets of real women who have fallen in love with prisoners, regardless of crime, sentence, or location. This info will give you a HUGE advantage in getting girls from prison.

THE MILLIONAIRE PRISONER: PART 1, $16.95 & $5.00 S/H

THE MILLIONAIRE PRISONER: PART 2, $16.95 & $5.00 S/H

THE MILLIONAIRE PRISONER: SPECIAL 2-IN-1 EDITION, $24.99 & $7.00 S/H: Why wait until you get out of prison to achieve your dreams? Here's a blueprint that you can use to become successful! *The Millionaire Prisoner* is your complete reference to overcoming any obstacle in prison. You won't be able to put it down! With this book you will discover the secrets to: Making money from your cell! Obtain FREE money for correspondence courses! Become an expert on any topic! Develop the habits of the rich! Network with celebrities! Set up your own website! Market your products, ideas and services! Successfully use prison pen pal websites! All of this and much, much more! This book has enabled thousands of prisoners to succeed and it will show you the way also!

THE MILLIONAIRE PRISONER 3: SUCCESS UNIVERSITY, $16.95 & $5 S/H: Why wait until you get out of prison to achieve your dreams? Here's a new-look blueprint that you can use to be successful! *The Millionaire Prisoner 3* contains advanced strategies to overcoming any obstacle in prison. You won't be able to put it down!

THE MILLIONAIRE PRISONER 4: PEN PAL MASTERY, $16.95 & $5 S/H: Tired of subpar results? Here's a master blueprint that you can use to get tons of pen pals! *TMP 4: Pen Pal Mastery* is your complete roadmap to finding your one true love. You won't be able to put it down! With this book you'll DISCOVER the SECRETS to: Get FREE pen pals & which sites are best to use; successful tactics female prisoners can win with; use astrology to find love, friendship & more, build a winning social media presence. All of this and much more!

GET OUT, GET RICH: HOW TO GET PAID LEGALLY WHEN YOU GET OUT OF PRISON!, $16.95 & $5.00 S/H: Many of you are incarcerated for a money-motivated crime. But w/ today's tech & opportunities, not only is the crime-for-money risk/reward ratio not strategically wise, it's not even necessary. You can earn much more money by partaking in any one of the easy, legal hustles explained in this book, regardless of your record. Help yourself earn an honest income so you can not only make a lot of money, but say good-bye to penitentiary chances and prison forever! (Note: Many things in this book can even he done from inside prison.) (ALSO PUBLISHED AS *HOOD MILLIONAIRE: HOW TO HUSTLE AND WIN LEGALLY!*)

THE CEO MANUAL: HOW TO START A BUSINESS WHEN YOU GET OUT OF PRISON, $16.95 & $5.00 S/H: $16.95 & $5 S/H: This new book will teach you the simplest way to start your own business when you get out of prison. Includes: Start-up Steps! The Secrets to Pulling Money from Investors! How to Manage People Effectively! How To Legally Protect Your Assets from "them"! Hundreds of resources to get you started, including a list of "loan friendly" banks! (ALSO PUBLISHED AS *CEO MANUAL: START A BUSINESS, BE A BOSS!*)

THE MONEY MANUAL: UNDERGROUND CASH SECRETS EXPOSED! 16.95 & $5.00 S/H: Becoming a millionaire is equal parts what you make, and what you don't spend – AKA save. All Millionaires and Billionaires have mastered the art of not only making money, but keeping the money they make (remember Donald Trump's tax maneuvers?), as well as establishing credit so that they are loaned money by banks and trusted with money from investors: AKA OPM – other people's money. And did you know there are millionaires and billionaires just waiting to GIVE money away? It's true! These are all very-little known secrets "they" don't want

YOU to know about, but that I'm exposing in my new book!

HOOD MILLIONAIRE; HOW TO HUSTLE & WIN LEGALLY, $16.95 & $5.00 S/H: Hustlin' is a way of life in the hood. We all have money motivated ambitions, not only because we gotta eat, but because status is oftentimes determined by one's own salary. To achieve what we consider financial success, we often invest our efforts into illicit activities – we take penitentiary chances. This leads to a life in and out of prison, sometimes death – both of which are counterproductive to gettin' money. But there's a solution to this, and I have it...

CEO MANUAL: START A BUSINESS BE A BOSS, $16.95 & $5.00 S/H: After the success of the urban-entrepreneur classic *Hood Millionaire: How To Hustle & Win Legally!*, self-made millionaires Mike Enemigo and Sav Hustle team back up to bring you the latest edition of the Hood Millionaire series – *CEO Manual: Start A Business, Be A Boss!* In this latest collection of game laying down the art of "hoodpreneurship", you will learn such things as: 5 Core Steps to Starting Your Own Business! 5 Common Launch Errors You Must Avoid! How To Write a Business Plan! How To Legally Protect Your Assets From "Them"! How To Make Your Business Fundable, Where to Get Money for Your Start-up Business, and even How to Start a Business With No Money! You will learn How to Drive Customers to Your Website, How to Maximize Marketing Dollars, Contract Secrets for the savvy boss, and much, much more! And as an added bonus, we have included over 200 Business Resources, from government agencies and small business development centers, to a secret list of small-business friendly banks that will help you get started!

PAID IN FULL: WELCOME TO DA GAME, $15.00 & $5.00 S/H. In 1983, the movie *Scarface* inspired many kids growing up in America's inner cities to turn their rags into riches by becoming cocaine kingpins. Harlem's Azie Faison was one of them. Faison would ultimately connect with Harlem's Rich Porter and Alpo Martinez, and the trio would go on to become certified street legends of the '80s and early '90s. Years later, Dame Dash and Roc-A-Fella Films would tell their story in the based-on-actual-events movie, *Paid in Full*.

But now, we are telling the story our way – The Cell Block way – where you will get a perspective of the story that the movie did not show, ultimately learning an outcome that you did not expect.

Book one of our series, *Paid in Full: Welcome to da Game*, will give you an inside look at a key player in this story, one that is not often talked about – Lulu, the Columbian cocaine kingpin with direct ties to Pablo Escobar, who plugged Azie in with an unlimited amount of top-tier cocaine at dirt-cheap prices that helped boost the trio to neighborhood superstars and certified kingpin status... until greed, betrayal, and murder destroyed everything....(ALSO PUBLISHED AS *CITY OF GODS*.)

OJ'S LIFE BEHIND BARS, $15.00 & $5 S/H: In 1994, Heisman Trophy winner and NFL superstar OJ Simpson was arrested for the brutal murder of his ex-wife Nicole Brown-Simpson and her friend Ron Goldman. In 1995, after the "trial of the century," he was acquitted of both murders, though most of the world believes he did it. In 2007 OJ was again arrested, but this time in Las Vegas, for armed robbery and kidnapping. On October 3, 2008 he was found guilty sentenced to 33 years and was sent to Lovelock Correctional Facility, in Lovelock, Nevada. There he met inmate-author Vernon Nelson. Vernon was granted a true, insider's perspective into the mind and life of one of the country's most notorious men; one that has never been provided…until now.

THE MOB, $16.99 & $5 S/H: PaperBoy is a Bay Area boss who has invested blood, sweat, and years into building The Mob – a network of Bay Area Street legends, block bleeders, and underground rappers who collaborate nationwide in the interest of pushing a multi-million-dollar criminal enterprise of sex, drugs, and murder.

Based on actual events, little has been known about PaperBoy, the mastermind behind The Mob, and intricate details of its operation, until now.

Follow this story to learn about some of the Bay Area underworld's most glamorous figures and famous events...

AOB, $15.00 & $5 S/H. Growing up in the Bay Area, Manny Fresh the Best had a front-row seat to some of the coldest players to ever do it. And you already know, A.O.B. is the name of the Game! So, When Manny Fresh slides through Stockton one day and sees Rosa, a stupid-bad Mexican chick with a whole lotta 'talent' behind her walking down the street tryna get some money, he knew immediately what he had to do: Put it In My Pocket!

AOB 2, $15.00 & $5 S/H.

AOB 3, $15.00 & $5 S/H.

PIMPOLOGY: THE 7 ISMS OF THE GAME, $15.00 & $5 S/H: It's been said that if you knew better, you'd do better. So, in the spirit of dropping jewels upon the rare few who truly want to know how to win, this collection of exclusive Game has been compiled. And though a lot of so-called players claim to know how the Pimp Game is supposed to go, none have revealed the real. . . Until now!

JAILHOUSE PUBLISHING FOR MONEY, POWER & FAME: $24.99 & $7 S/H: In 2010, after flirting with the idea for two years, Mike Enemigo started writing his first book. In 2014, he officially launched his publishing company, The Cell Block, with the release of five books. Of course, with no mentor(s), how-to guides, or any real resources, he was met with failure after failure as he tried to navigate the treacherous goal of publishing books from his prison cell. However, he was determined to make it. He was determined to figure it out and he refused to quit. In Mike's new book, *Jailhouse Publishing for Money, Power, and Fame*, he breaks down all his jailhouse publishing secrets and strategies, so you can do all he's done, but without the trials and tribulations he's had to go through...

KITTY KAT, ADULT ENTERTAINMENT RESOURCE BOOK, $24.99 & $7.00 S/H: This book is jam packed with hundreds of sexy non nude photos including photo spreads. The book contains the complete info on sexy photo sellers, hot magazines, page turning bookstore, sections on strip clubs, porn stars, alluring models, thought provoking stories and must-see movies.

PRISON LEGAL GUIDE, $24.99 & $7.00 S/H: The laws of the U.S. Judicial system are complex, complicated, and always growing and changing. Many prisoners spend days on end digging through its intricacies. Pile on top of the legal code the rules and regulations of a correctional facility, and you can see how high the deck is being stacked against you. Correct legal information is the key to your survival when you have run afoul of the system (or it is running afoul of you). Whether you are an accomplished jailhouse lawyer helping newbies learn the ropes, an old head fighting bare-knuckle for your rights in the courts, or a hustler just looking to beat the latest write-up – this book has something for you!

PRISON HEALTH HANDBOOK, $19.99 & $7.00 S/H: *The Prison Health Handbook* is your one-stop go-to source for information on how to maintain your best health while inside the American prison system. Filled with information, tips, and secrets from doctors, gurus, and other experts, this book will educate you on such things as proper workout and exercise regimens; yoga benefits for prisoners; how to meditate effectively; pain management tips; sensible dieting solutions; nutritional knowledge; an understanding of various cancers, diabetes, hepatitis, and other diseases all too common in prison; how to effectively deal with mental health issues such as stress, PTSD, anxiety, and depression; a list of things your doctors DON'T want YOU to know; and much, much more!

All books are available on thecellblock.net website.

You can also order by sending a money order or institutional check to:

The Cell Block; PO Box 1025; Rancho Cordova, CA 95741